"I'd rather be in a Pack."

Mother slapped the table and stood, a finger inches from his face. "Don't you ever say that, Kaehl, ever. The Packs are much worse than anything we have here. Much worse."

"Nothing is worse."

"You don't know." Her voice was hard. "They're much worse."

"The Packs are free, Mother. When you're in a Pack you have power, you're not trapped behind four walls, you can go where you want to. You and Selda won't be beaten."

"You don't know what you're talking about."

He pushed his bowl aside and looked up. "Do you?"

Mother picked up the bowl and walked to the cupboard. "Yes."

WELLTOWER

First Run

Lester Yocum

Dedicated to my wife, to whom I dedicate everything.
And to Angie for her inspiration
and Joanne and Ben for their help.

ISBN-13: 978-1479384273
ISBN-10: 14879384275

Originally published via CreateSpace October 2011.
Last revised May 2017.
Cover art and book design by Lester Yocum.

Explanation

This is definitely not your average science fiction shoot-'em-up; its purposes are to point out the state of today's societies and to propose solutions, which is an obligation I feel with all my work. Like our society at times, the story can be brutal; however, a strong spiritual quotient is woven throughout.

Books two and three continue and broaden these concepts.

Lester Yocum
April 2013

Above, below
inside, out,
Light is what
life's all about.
—Welltower government slogan,
2nd installation

Contents

Home

Kaehl stared into the light.

The young man gazed through a grate, pressed between dust-covered pipes, pea stones, cables, and cobwebs. Greasy black hair plastered his head; dirt clung to his clothes.

He had wormed his way through a narrow access tunnel, twisting and hauling himself around aging ducts and conduit as wide as his waist. Now he lay at the far end, his face pressed against the metal, unable to go farther.

He gazed through the bars at an immense shaft on the other side, a colossal gap that ran from the penthouses above to the foundations below, reaching so far beyond him that he couldn't see the ends. Light filled the chasm, bright and strong, intense enough to hide the opening's far side. Grates, pipes, ladders and hatches patterned the stupendous walls, curving away until they disappeared in the glare. Fitful winds howled through the structure and then died to a whisper only to rise again, carrying vapors that wrinkled his nose and stung his lungs.

Kaehl leaned back, his eyes half-closed, his breathing relaxed. He lay quietly, seemingly asleep, smiling at the coolness of the currents that bled into his access port, tracing noises that rose above the wind. Idly, he wondered what other people they had touched.

After a time, he stirred. Casually, he wrapped his fingers around the grate, his hands moving lazily. He tightened his grip. The pressure slowly increased. His knuckles paled and then turned white. His lips pressed back. He hissed air into his lungs and held it, his tongue pressed against his teeth.

Then all at once his body snapped and twisted, cracking against the walls, his muscles standing out under his pale skin. He yanked at the bars, rattling them until his veins stood out like cords. His mouth worked noiselessly. The fastenings popped and creaked. Sweat stood out on his brow, his face turned purple, and his eyes bulged as if to pop out of his head.

With a groan, he released his grip and collapsed onto the floor, gasping for breath, his fingers cramped into claws. He panted, his body curled like a newborn's. Tears threaded through his tightly-screwed eyelids, mingling with the sweat and dust caking his face. His whole body trembled.

Winds sifted in from the core again, stirring his hair. They cooled him where they caressed his skin, raising tiny goose bumps. He relaxed and slowed his breathing.

His eyelids parted. He wiped his face. His blurry gaze wandered, taking in the stony confines of the duct into which he had dragged himself, the dusty pipes, the hoses, the rough walls, and the unyielding grate.

He sighed.

Grabbing the grate again he bunched his muscles and clenched his teeth. With an explosive gasp, he yanked once more at the bars, his body contorting, sweat beading his forehead. Tears coursed from his eyes; his face smoked with heat. He strained against the metal, shaking and twisting it, his body whipping. He fought with the barrier a few moments more and then released it again, a cry breaking from his lips.

He shifted his position, braced his knees, took another breath and snapped forward, ramming his shoulder against the hatch. Blood appeared on his shirt. His toes dug into the walls of the port. Again and again he hit the grate. The metal did not move. At last he crumpled and sagged, his breath draining. He moaned, dropped his head, and sobbed.

After a time Kaehl fell silent, his eyelids drooping. He felt like an empty sack. One hand drifted to his face, fingering recent bruises. The ones on his cheeks still ached but the pain was fading. Something had matted on his scalp. He pulled a flake of it away, held it in front of his eyes, sniffed it and drew his tongue across it. Dried blood. He flicked it away.

Kaehl settled against the wall and closed his eyes. He remembered the first time he had come to this place, a tiny ventilation shaft with a grate at the end. It was years ago. Screaming, crying, pulling at the metal bars he had been terrified; frantic to get away. He had wanted to find a ladder or cable or opening on the other side and escape into the mighty gap beyond, but the bars had held. There was no place to go. He had been trapped.

He had gone quiet, then, waiting for what seemed like years, his heart hammering. For a long time he had breathed only lightly, terrified that his screams had given him away. What would happen if his father had looked in and found him there, he wondered. Would the man crawl in after him, spewing curses, his fingers clawing at Kaehl's feet? Or would he try to dislodge his son with a long pole, or by throwing rocks or something more sharp until he moved? Maybe he would wall up the pipe and leave Kaehl inside to die. The man was capable of anything.

But his father had never appeared.

At last Kaehl had relaxed. Even after so many years he remembered releasing his grip on the bars and the pain as he had stretched his knotted fingers. But he had still waited. Eventually he had fallen asleep, his head against the grate, tears drying on his cheeks. Later that evening he had returned to his family's apartment, tiptoeing into the sleeping room, terrified of what he might find but more afraid of being alone. With relief, he had seen that Father was asleep. Exhausted, young Kaehl had curled up in the jumble of blankets and slept—what little sleep he could get among his father's snores. The next morning, Father's hangover had distracted the man enough to keep him from bothering about his son. Returning from work that evening, mostly sober, Father had apparently forgotten everything.

Since that day this small shaft had served as Kaehl's daily resort, a place he could visit while everyone else slept, a sanctuary of escape, thought and peace. Each morning he awakened early, crawled off his mat, tiptoed out of the apartment, jogged through the quad and wedged his way into this covert. Before Two Clock each day he returned to his sleeping family. As far as he knew, no one ever suspected.

Now he spat through the bars. One day, he promised himself, he would be free.

For the present he relaxed, gazing into the vast void beyond the grate.

Nothing stirred but an occasional palm-sized insect. The intense light was everywhere, in some places softened by the mist. Water gurgled from cesspits and cooking pots. A stiff, hot breeze stirred against his forehead, carrying the scent of rot, sweat, and waste to his nose.

He smiled. It smelled like home. *I love this place,* he thought.

This place had become a home for him because it was not like home. The cramped confines of the vent gave him a sense of peace, lifting away the ache in his back and the throbbing in his head. Here he was alone and at peace. In the apartment, everything was dullness, boredom and limitation and moments of screaming, stupefying pain. There he was trapped by locked doors and hallways filled with terrifying gangs. Here he could rest and his mind, at least, could fly free.

Sometimes something would pass through the Shaft, a rock or a bag or some larger, unknown object, whistling through the thick air, sometimes banging off the walls. He never heard them land.

He shivered as they passed. The awesome distances in the shaft excited him, the raw immensity raising bumps on his arms.

But even as they thrilled him they also terrified him. They seemed to draw him outwards as if trying to pull him through the bars. He pressed his face into the grate until the bolts creaked then he backed away. The thin metal was a barrier but it was also an opportunity, a call for freedom. The wind that moaned through the tunnel seemed to call to him, begging him to open the barrier and climb to freedom. It was a spark that burned him while also chilling him, drawing him like a moth to the flame.

He wondered at times about the shaft. If he succeeded in slipping into it but fell, sailing through the light, his mouth an open square, would anyone notice? Would anyone miss him? Would he scream?

He thought of his neighbor's daughter and shivered. Mother once told him that she had wormed through a crack in her quad's grate and fallen into the Shaft. That image had tortured his dreams since. At times he thought he could hear her as she fell through the darkness, her scream high and shrill and ragged, fading floor after floor. Then he would wake, bathed in sweat, frantic to save her. But he was always in the sleeping room, surrounded by his family. "It's only the wind," he would repeat to himself as he lay back and shivered in his blankets. "Only the wind."

He picked at the rough wall of the shaft. At least she was free, he thought.

He rubbed his arms and examined the skin. Four new red marks blazed near one wrist, each as long as an adult finger. Gingerly he drew a hand to his face, wiped his mouth, and peered at his fingers. No blood, he noted. Nothing permanent. Good.

Kaehl had considered taking his life. He knew suicide was the ultimate rest. It was a cheap and easy way to freedom and sometimes it beckoned to him loudly but the way to it only opened on the other side of the grate. He could never take his life in his home, lying there in his blood for Father to stand over, laughing. He could end his life elsewhere, in the halls perhaps or possibly after a Sabbat meeting. That would show his father, maybe even hurt him in some small way. Maybe the parent would realize what he had done to his child.

But the boy didn't have it in him, the will to leave this life. He had a reason to live: his sister. She was as much a prisoner as he; more so, really. She needed him.

He smiled. Ah, but if he could escape into the Shaft and not fall to his death but instead climb to freedom and find someone to help him, then he could return to his home and rescue her. Then big men could escort them away, the sister and her brother, and maybe Mother as well, and Father could only stand aside and glare.

Sister. Living to save her was much better than dying and leaving her to their father's brutal care.

Anyway, it didn't matter. The barrier was too well built; it would not give way. It was not weak like his neighbor's. "Praise to the Framers," he said ruefully, nodding his head three times.

Once again he pulled at the bars, rattling them, straining to push them into the emptiness. They held. He spat again into the gap. One day they would burst open and he would be free, climbing into the void beyond, disappearing into the light until he could find help. He smiled at the idea. Then he could end the pointlessness and the pain and the hate. He shook his head and released the grate. But not today.

With practiced care Kaehl drew a stone out of one of his pockets and drew it to his chest. He examined it in the narrow confines, angling it in the light. It was half the size of his fist; flat, round at the edges and smooth. It had been a gift from his mother. There were plenty of stones in the halls but very few were this perfect. It would sail through the shaft nicely. She had been very proud when she had presented it to him.

He pulled a scrap of cloth out of another pocket and laid it under the rock. Time to write his message.

His mother had started teaching him to write shortly after birth. She had been taught how to do it at one of the factories. Being only 14 at the time, her pregnancy had not gone well. With no family or medical support, her growing belly had made her increasingly unable to meet production quotas, limiting her profit-making potential. One day the boss and a couple of guards had grabbed her by the arms and thrown her out. Weeks later she had survived the pregnancy, birthing a son and swearing to make life better for him.

So, in his infancy she had begun.

Now Kaehl was one of the few people in their community who knew how to write. People would come to him at Sabbat gatherings and ask him to write them something, perhaps their name or an inspiring word. They would bear away the result carefully, with unsure but shining eyes, somehow bettered by feeling that they were holding something significant. Some would shyly hand him messages for him to read. They would gather around with wide eyes and watch as he sounded out the words and pronounced them, one by one. Some words he didn't recognize—those he guessed at or made up. For the most part, though, he could read everything put before him, and the skill and the fame it brought, however small, made Kaehl extremely proud.

Today he pulled a bit of wire out of a crack in the wall and poised it over the stone, composing his thoughts. He licked his lips and bent the tool to the surface. Very carefully, he began to scratch.

Tongue out, brows tight, he stayed with the task for several minutes, small chips falling from the stone. At length he held it up, blowing away the dust and squinting at the result. "FIND ME," he read, and smiled. The letters didn't line up precisely and the last few characters crowded the edge but it was very readable. *Fine work,* he thought, and put the wire away.

With a few practiced twists he knotted the piece of cloth around the rock, pulled it tight, and braced himself against the wall. He cocked his arm, and tensed.

BOOM.

He jerked up, banging his head against a pipe and dropping the rock. Rubbing his skull he sagged against the vent, making faces. That was One Clock, the first of the morning wakeup calls, a warning that could be heard throughout the entire building. It was The Framers' way of keeping everyone on a schedule, something that had to be very hard to do in a world that was always filled with light.

He was running late.

As he reached for the rock a spider startled him, scuttling past his face and onto a nearby pipe. Its body was longer than his thumb. As it moved it dislodged dust and flakes of metal. He licked his lips. *Tasty,* he thought and made a grab at it. It leaped to one side and darted out of reach. His gaze followed it until he was forced to blink. *Marvelous creature,* he thought, rubbing his eyes, able to move so many parts so smoothly. All those legs and still so able.

The spider moved above his head and stumbled over a large patch of dirt. Pieces came loose and plopped onto Kaehl's chest, the dusty splash making him sneeze. The spider recovered its footing and continued along the wall. Kaehl watched it crawl into the Shaft and disappear. "Free," the young man sighed.

His gaze returned to the pipe. His eyes narrowed. The spider had uncovered the underlying pipe and revealed something beneath the dirt. Kaehl squinted. It was words of some sort.

Grunting, he edged a hand along his body and pulled it to his head. Rubbing his thumb along the pipe he dislodged more dirt, blinking away what fell into his eyes. The letters were strong and very sharp, impossibly regular. His eyes sparkled—the letters were breathtaking! How could anyone create letters so perfect, so beautiful, so powerful? They practically screamed importance.

His forehead furrowed as he sounded out the words, his lips moving: WARNING: EXTREMELY BRIGHT. DO NOT CUT.

Below, in smaller letters: RISK OF

The rest had corroded away.

Some of the words were unfamiliar to him; he certainly didn't know what "bright" meant (he pronounced it "brig-hu-tuh"). And he knew of nothing that would cut through anything as tough as that pipe.

Perhaps Mother would know. She knew a lot. Without question, she was the smartest person he had ever met. Father boasted that he knew a lot but his knowledge was mostly impractical—machines and gears and such and how to make them run. Kaehl had never seen a machine and dismissed the concept as ridiculous. Mother, on the other hand, knew how to cook and mend rat bites and recover Sister from her shaking fits and how to calm a mean drunk. She could read and write. Mother knew facts that mattered. Mother would know.

Maybe he could write the words down and show them to her. He could, if he dared tell her where he had found them. But if he told her about the words he would have to tell her where he had found them, and when. He could lie but she knew him too well, and he didn't want to give Father another opportunity to discipline him. If he told her the truth it would give away his sanctuary. He could never do that. She would almost certainly tell Father, and then Father could find Kaehl's retreat. Kaehl shuddered; he could never allow that.

Twisting, grunting at the pipes pressing into his back, he picked up the rock again, shifted it toward the narrow gap between the grate and the wall, angled it as far back as he could, and threw. He craned his neck, pushing against the mesh, straining to follow the fluttering stone as it arced across the Shaft. It disappeared into the haze and distance, swallowed by the light.

He closed his eyes. His mind flew with the rock, traveling to other levels, finding new places, discovering new secrets, passing other people, rushing to land with a glorious crack among the others he had thrown. Someone nearby would jump at the sound and rush to find it, holding it out with a shout and then stand, staring into the mist and vowing in a loud voice to find the one who had sent it. Maybe this person had found all Kaehl's stones. Kaehl imagined the person sorting them out, one by one, as they lay in a special collection in the man's room, pondering the words etched into them until at last he connected them into a message. Then he would run to other people, maybe the Tower's leaders, shouting out his discovery. And they would come to Kaehl's apartment and rescue him.

Or maybe Kaehl himself would find it, one day when he was grown and had become a scholar and an explorer and had scaled the heights and depths of the Tower, searching out all its secrets. He would find it among all the other stones littering the base of the Shaft. He would sift through the piles, looking for the telltale rags, his face triumphant when he found each message. Then he would show the stones to others. He would pick them out and display them to his followers and they would catch their breath and sigh. "Beautiful," they would say. And then they would turn to him and applaud and he would bow to each admirer, one by one, acknowledging their praise. One day he would find those stones, he vowed. They were his messages to the future, to the whole world, his passage away from home. One day he would find them all and the whole world would change.

A tear trickled down his face. *Welltower*, he thought. *I love this place.*

Something flew past his face. He looked up. A water pipe had vented. He gasped and snapped out of his dream. Grunting, he began worming out of the tunnel.

He hefted and pulled and grunted himself around bent conduit and rusted pipes, untangling his clothes when they caught against ragged metal. The hole widened as he reached the other side, giving him room to turn around. He scooted toward the large screen covering the end of the pipe and peered through, listening, searching the empty closet on the other side. He pulled the panel aside and levered himself out, carefully replacing the cover. He brushed the dirt from his clothes, swept aside the evidence, and padded quickly out the door into the quad.

Crossing a handful of rooms, he paused at the entrance to his family's sleeping area, listening for the rock-slide rumble of Father's snores and the chirrup of Selda's occasional cries and nothing the rise and fall of Mother's shoulders. Still asleep. He smiled. Lips tight, he tiptoed over the jumble of bodies, edged onto his mat and lay down, flicking his blanket over his face. He wiped sweat from his forehead.

BOOM.
BOOM.

Two Clock. Second Warning. Time to get up.

Kaehl stilled his breath. Father's rumbles grew shallower and then died. Selda's cries crumpled into rattling whimpers and choked away. Mother spun to one side and tried to become part of the wall, shrinking under the blankets.

Father groaned. He hacked, coughed, spat, and rolled off his mat. With a grunt, he put his hand on Kaehl's shoulder and levered himself into a sitting position, crushing Kaehl into the mat. Kaehl kept the blanket over his head and stayed still. Several things could happen, he knew. Normally, Father would survey the room with bleary eyes and scowl. If he noticed Kaehl at all and remembered last night's arguments there could be trouble. If the man's hangover was strong enough, however, and if he ignored his son and if he chose to leave Mother alone and if he overlooked Sister's cries then he would rub his stubble, stretch, and push himself to his feet. Then he would clump out of the room, scratching, and the rest of the family would be at peace.

There was some rustling and groaning and a few uneven footsteps and then there was silence. Kaehl lowered his blanket and peered out. *Ah,* he thought as he released his breath. *Gone.*

The lump that was his mother lost its tension. She rolled over in her blankets and stretched. Pushing herself to a sitting position she caught Kaehl's gaze and fluttered a smile. Then, slowly, with a hand on her back, she worked herself to her feet and limped out of the room.

Kaehl turned to look at his sister, still asleep in the jumbled blankets. One year younger than him but nearly his height, she was all angles and joints and bones. Her skin stretched across her face like a ragged drumhead. Her mouth was open; she had slobbered all over herself. Her hair was thick and greasy, clinging to her thin face. He sighed. Another bath today. She hated baths.

Gently, Kaehl tugged at her blankets. She didn't move. He smiled and tugged again. She startled and caught her breath, her eyes still closed. "Wake up, lazybones," he whispered, nudging her shoulder.

He lifted a strand of hair out of her face. "You're so beautiful," he sighed. She batted at his hand. "Silly girl," he smiled. She opened her enormous, dark eyes and turned them toward him, focusing. A smile beamed his way. "No," he breathed, "Angel."

"Kahh," she murmured.

"Sahh," he returned.

Kaehl turned toward the kitchen. "Selda's awake," he called to Mother. He heard an answering grunt. Awkwardly he rose and stretched, yawning, and then bent to straighten the blankets. He discovered a bundle of twisted rags and held it out to Selda, waggling it in front of her face. "Betsy," he said.

Selda's eyes opened wide. "Bahh!" she squealed, reaching for them.

"Doll," he said.

"Dahh," she repeated.

"Here," he said. "Practice first." Searching along the wall he pried out a small rock. Turning back to Selda he opened her hand and placed the stone in the center. He gently bounced the hand, flipping the stone in rhythm.

He held the doll in his other hand and waved it in front of her, moving his fingers in a simple pattern and chanting:

One a finger, two a finger, three a finger, four
Jump a stone 'till there ain't no more
If you raise it high then it drops so low
One a finger two 'till there ain't no more.

On the words "ain't no more" Kaehl pulled his hands behind his back, hiding the doll. Selda, who was bobbing to the rhythm, usually squealed with anxious delight and searched for the doll. This time she dropped the stone and looked away.

He brought his hand forward again showing her the doll. "Come on, say it. Go ahead."

He bobbed his hand, motioning for Selda to start.

"Bahh," she said.

"Not bahh, *'One a finger, two a finger...'*"

"Bahh," she repeated.

"You're not going to try today, are you?"

"Bahh!"

He sighed. "Well, thanks anyway." He handed her the doll.

She grabbed the bundle and hugged it to her cheek, rocking, her smile immense, her eyes closed.

"We'll try again later," Kaehl said sternly, smiling as he got to his feet. Selda stuck out her tongue. He gave the blankets a final tug and moved out of the room.

Father was finishing in the cesspit, Mother was making breakfast, and Sister was happy with Betsy. For the moment, Kaehl was free.

He left their apartment and moved into the common area, turning from the path that led to his hiding place. The commons was a circular room bordered by four apartments with a short corridor on one side leading to the hallways that ended at a heavy door. Four families had once shared these living areas, which Mother called a quad. The other apartments were just like his: a central living area with rooms to the side for cooking, storage, sleeping, and waste. Each apartment had been built to house four people—two parents, two children—with four apartments making one quad. The neighboring three apartments had been empty for years. When his parents were absent Kaehl had explored them in great detail. Their shelves were empty, their rooms bare. Only one had an access port leading to the Shaft.

He crossed into a neighboring apartment and used its waste room.

Kaehl heard his mother call. He returned to their apartment. Glancing into the sleeping room as he headed for the kitchen he saw Sister among the blankets, snoring, the doll in her arms.

Kaehl entered the kitchen. Father was finishing his bowl of spiced potato pancakes and tubers, quaffing potato beer. Father finished his beer and eyed him. Kaehl tried to appear casual, leaning against the door.

Father stood up, stretched, and belched. He brushed past Kaehl—*Wow, he really needs a bath,* Kaehl thought—hefted a ragged-looking rucksack and headed into the common area and down the corridor, stopping beside the hallway door. Kaehl followed him at a respectful distance and stopped opposite him at the door. They bent to the heavy wood, listening intently. Father set the parcel down and together they unfastened the door's straps.

After removing the last strap, they braced their hands against the door, holding it in place. Father bent and hissed at Kaehl. "You pay attention, boy. You're gonna be out there soon. You live or die by what you know." Kaehl nodded solemnly, trying hard not to wrinkle his nose. He had heard the same warning every morning for years.

Father's lips curled into a thick smile. He slid open the spy slit, listening. Kaehl put his ear to the door.

Something was moving in the hall. Kaehl focused intently. A muffled slapping arose down the hall, dim at first but growing louder. It paused at intervals then resumed, drawing near their door.

Father quickly covered the slit. The slapping continued, growing louder, and then it stopped. Whatever it was, it had stopped outside their door.

Kaehl and his father bent closer to the hatch, neither breathing. They concentrated on the space beyond the slit. Kaehl looked at his father, questioning. The slapping noise began again, continuing down the hall, pausing, resuming, growing dim and disappearing.

They straightened and sighed, still holding the door in place.

"What was that?" Kaehl whispered.

Father backhanded Kaehl to the floor.

Kaehl sprang up, his eyes wide, and returned to his place, a little farther from his father, his hands pressed against the door. Tears wet his cheeks. His face was red.

Father raised his fist again, shaking it under Kaehl's nose. Kaehl flinched. "You forgot, didn't you?" he hissed. "Don't you ever learn? Never talk at the door! Never let them know you're in here. Never wonder what's out there. Be glad you're at home, safe."

His gaze held Kaehl's eyes for a moment and then he turned away. "Prob'ly some sentry mixin' up the rules, keepin' us off balance." He bent to the door and slid aside the cover, listening again. "And don't cry. You're not a woman." Kaehl wiped his eyes with a sleeve. His eyes never left Father's.

Father glanced at Kaehl and nodded. Quietly they slid the lock out of its hole in the floor. Listening carefully, Father put his shoulder to the door and eased it open. Edging his head out, he looked left and right. Glancing back at Kaehl he eased his body through.

Kaehl picked up the rucksack and passed it to his father, who swung it over his shoulder. Kaehl stared at the light beyond the door. The hallway was filled with its usual impenetrable glare. They stood, their breathing shallow, listening. Kaehl could see his father's breath quicken, his chest rise and fall.

Father bent near. “Pay attention to the sounds. They’ll be coming soon. You have to be ready.” Far away, a deep rumble arose from the hall. Father’s eyes were wide, alert.

“They’re coming. Get ready, boy.”

BOOM.
BOOM.
BOOM.

They looked at each other and nodded. Three Clock. Time to go.

The rumble grew louder. Kaehl saw figures appear down the hall, barely visible in the glare. They were jogging in his direction.

The foremost runner saw Kaehl’s father and let out a challenging bellow. Father responded with his own roar then stepped into the center of the hall. He began jogging as the crowd neared, matching their speed. Then they rushed by in a wave, enveloping him and taking him with them. Kaehl heard his father’s triumphant shout as he moved away. Quickly, Kaehl pulled the door into place and shouldered it shut, fastening the straps and shooting the lock. He was done before the crowd passed.

As he secured the last strap a resounding BOOM shook the reinforced frame. Kaehl fell back but leaped to the door again and leaned hard against it. He heard footfalls and jeering laughter fade down the hall. He pulled open the spy cover, listened, and then closed it again.

Turning around, he saw Mother standing in the kitchen doorway, a pot in her hand, staring at the door. She was shivering, her face white. Catching his gaze, her eyes caught the new red mark on his face. She spun and returned to the kitchen.

Kaehl checked the fastenings once more and joined her. “Mother, are you okay?” he asked.

She continued her work.

"They're just testing the door, you know. Keeping us off balance."

"Yes," she said after a moment. "Just testing the door. For our good." Her voice was strained.

"They hit it pretty hard, didn't they?"

Mother nodded.

"Father says new rules, maybe. Do you think something's wrong?"

Mother didn't answer.

Mindless songs lifted from the sleeping room. Kaehl walked toward it passing his mother as she headed to the door. She had a bag under her arm and was wrapping a worn shawl over her shoulders. "I'm going shopping," she told him. She stopped at the door and waited. Kaehl turned and joined her.

"You got enough dolls, maybe?" he asked, looking at the bag.

"Enough. I hope we get some luck at the market. We could use something other than potatoes."

Kaehl nodded. "I'll give Sister a bath while you're gone," he said. His mother smiled and ran a hand along his cheek, stopping at the fresh bruises. Quickly, she pulled her hand back and looked away, her face hardening.

Kaehl smiled, then bent to the door and listened. With a nod to his mother he began unfastening the straps. "I wish you didn't have to do this," he whispered.

"I won't be gone long," she replied. "We have to get more food sometime."

"I know, but it's not safe."

"It's safe enough," she answered. "I like to get out. The Packs don't come out until evening."

"Usually," he reminded her.

"Usually."

"Can't I go? I'd like to get out, too. And I can protect you!"

"Of course you can't; your father would kill you! I'd be more worried about him than the packs."

"I'm old enough."

"He wants to teach you more, show you where to go, take you with him a few times."

"I know what to do."

"We've been through this. You wait. Your turn will come. I'll be all right."

"You can go but I can't."

She glared at him.

He kicked at the floor. "Don't you need a commuter crowd to get you there safe?"

She snorted. "Buncha stupid male hooey. Hopped up manchild fantasies. There are no Packs out at commute times. You know that. And even if there were, they wouldn't attack a pack of rabid men on the way to work. They'd wait till they were gone and then attack the homes. That's what they do; it's safer for them. Commuter Crowd!" she spat. "That's just men's excuse to become a Pack themselves."

"You seemed pretty tense when they tested the door this time."

Mother looked away. She pulled the shawl tight and motioned to the door.

Kaehl finished the straps and lifted the lock. He opened the door and peered out.

Mother peered around his shoulder. He shuffled aside and let her pass. She moved into the hall, her whole body alert.

After a few heartbeats she turned, waved, and started down the hall, puffing along at her best speed. She did not look back.

Kaehl re-seated the door and secured it. He listened intently for a time; one ear pressed against the slit, and then slid the hatch shut. He leaned against the door, sighed and slumped his shoulders. Scuffing at the floor again he turned and plodded toward the sleeping room.

Selda was still singing. She looked up as he entered holding out her doll. "Bahh," she informed him.

Kaehl nodded his head. "Yes, I know, this is Betsy." He stood over her holding his hands out. "Come on, it's time for your bath."

"NAHH!" she screamed, throwing herself into her covers and clutching her doll. "NAHH!"

"Yes, Sister, it's time. Let's not do this today, okay?" He reached down and tried to fish her from the blankets.

"NAHH! MAHH!" she screamed.

"Sister, will you settle down? Calling for Mother won't help. Stop!"

He wrenched an arm from under the blankets. She screamed and threw her doll at him. He dodged and watched it sail out of the room. "BAHH!" she screamed and began flailing her arms.

"Now, see there? You've thrown Betsy away. What is she going to do without you?" Kaehl stood back, hands on hips. Selda continued screaming. "Throwing a tantrum won't help," Kaehl said. Still screaming, Selda began crawling toward the door.

Kaehl moved past her and picked up the doll. Selda quieted and crawled to him. She stopped just out of reach and held out her hands. "Bahh!" she pleaded.

"Yes; 'Betsy.' Say 'Betsy'." He shook it firmly, just out of Selda's reach. "You can have her, but you have to say 'Betsy' first."

Selda shook her arms. "Bahh!" she said.

"Betsy. Say 'Betsy'."

"Bahh!"

"Betsy!"

"BAHH!" Tears glittered in the corners of her eyes.

Kaehl sighed and handed her the doll. Selda went very quiet, her eyes wide, crushing the bundle of rags to her chest.

"Come on, sweetie, let's take that bath."

"Yahh," she responded. She pushed herself to her feet and followed him out the door.

Selda sat in the hollow in the floor they used as a tub, splashing happily. Her doll watched from the safety of a nearby shelf.

"Here, use this," he said, handing her a rag. Selda grabbed the rag and buried it in the water, pulling it out and squeezing it over her head. She shook herself, gurgling happily. Water flew everywhere. "Don't splash!" he warned. "I'll make you clean it up!" Selda stuck out her tongue but calmed.

"Oh, Sister, what am I going to do?" he sighed, sitting across from her. "Stuck in this stupid house all day, making dolls. Every day! I get to leave for a few hours on Sabbat, that's all. Not like Father; he's always gone." He frowned and slapped the floor. Selda looked up.

"I'm going crazy, Selda, that what I'm doing. They don't trust me and it's driving me crazy! I can be trusted; I can run the chores. I'm old enough, I'm fast enough. Show me, tell me, give me some directions, I'll do it! Whatever, just let me out, let me do something, just once in a while." He kicked at a trail of ants trooping toward the waste hole. "I wish they'd trust me." The ants re-formed their line. Selda continued playing with the rag.

Kaehl flopped onto his belly and began doing push-ups. Selda watched him, fascinated. He huffed through several and turned over again.

"I wish there were some other families in our quad, or somebody nearby at least."

Kaehl pushed through several more then turned over, sweat beading his face, and began working through some sit-ups. Selda gurgled in the tub.

Kaehl finished and sat against the wall, breathing hard. "If only there was something useful to do." He looked at his sister, who had grown quiet. She sat in the hollow, eyes wide and fixed on him, her arms intertwined, tight against her body. She was shivering.

"Oh no," he gasped. "Sister!" He jumped to the faucet and cranked open the tap, pouring hot water into a pot. He emptied it into the hollow and shoveled warm water over her. Selda's eyes stayed on his. He continued covering her with warm water but couldn't bring himself to return her gaze. Eventually she settled into the basin, splashing the warmth over herself. Her shivering subsided.

Kaehl sat back, his shirt front soaked. "Cold, weren't you?" he said. "I'm so sorry. I got so wrapped up in my little problems. I'm so sorry." He grabbed another rag, soaped it up, and began lathering Selda's hair. She protested at first but eventually gave in, screwing her fists into her eyes as the water and soap cascaded over her. She began to sing loudly. Kaehl smiled and cuffed her shoulder. "Noisy!" he teased. She bobbed and continued to sing.

"Well, that's better," he said after emptying another bucket over her. He sat back and sighed. "They're doing this for my own good, aren't they, our parents? They don't want me to get hurt. 'Just a little while longer,' they say. 'It's much too dangerous.'"

Selda looked up. Kaehl held his hands out, warding off her glare. "I know, I know, me and my little problems. Don't worry, I won't forget about you again, I promise. I won't let you get cold." She returned to her splashing.

Kaehl stood up, rinsed her once more and handed her a towel. "Now don't drip water everywhere; you towel off right there. And don't drop the towel in the water!" He dried his hands. "Come on out when you're done," he called over his shoulder as he left the room.

Kaehl shuffled through a pile of clothes in the back of the sleeping room and pulled out an outfit for her. She shuffled into the room, wrapped in the towel.

"Here's your clothes, lady," he said, standing up. "Put them on. Mother should be back with breakfast in a bit." He walked back into the living room.

Kaehl rubbed his belly. He was hungry. He was always hungry. Not just casually interested in a snack but achingly, gnawingly, needfully empty.

Father wasn't. They all knew that Father needed to eat so he could build up his strength to run with the commutes and get through the day. After all, he was the father. Fathers had certain needs. He was the one who provided for his family, who handled all the dangerous tasks. His drunken nighttime stories were full of them.

However, his needs made some days very tough for the rest of his family. When there wasn't enough money for food they went without until Mother could barter something from the vendors. Sometimes her trips were very successful and sometimes they weren't. The family accepted that; they all accepted their roles. They were patient; if they waited long enough they always ended up with something to eat, even if it was a few rinds. They had seen others whose lives were much worse; very much worse.

Still, sometimes the waiting was tough.

Kaehl wondered if Father knew how hungry they were or if he cared. He hung his head and clenched his fists. Dangerous thoughts, he knew. That's how Mother had described them.

Kaehl straightened up the cleaning room and returned to the common area. Looking over his shoulder toward the sleeping room he sat down, cracked open the slit, and placed his ear against the door.

Nothing.

Selda came out of the sleeping room, swinging Betsy by the hair.

"Pay?" she asked.

"Ooh, good word, Sister. No, I'm not going to play, not now, anyway. Don't look at me like that; you get plenty. Later."

Selda stuck her tongue out and tramped into the kitchen.

"No snacks," he called. "We don't have enough as is. Tough it out." He leaned his ear against the door again.

"Tuft dout?" Selda peered around the corner, her eyes wide.

"Yes." Kaehl sat up and straightened his shirt. "Good words. Tough it out."

Selda stayed at the kitchen doorway, looking at him. Kaehl leaned back and closed his eyes. After several breaths he turned sideways. Then he turned to the wall. After a few moments he laid down. Finally he sat up again and turned toward her. She was still staring at him, her eyes moist.

He sighed and patted the floor beside him. "Come on, then." Selda squealed and ran to him, snuggling under his arm.

"I never could resist a beautiful girl," he purred. "Yes, I see Betsy. Yes, I know, she's beautiful, too. No, we can play the finger game later. Right now I just want to sit, okay? Quiet, please. Yes, Betsy too."

He put his ear against the door. Selda mimicked him. They stayed like that for several breaths.

He tensed. He thought he could detect motion, the scraping of a faint footfall. His eyes widened. There was something in the hall.

Selda looked up at him. "Oooo," she said.

Kaehl held a finger to his lips. Together they bent to the door again. The sound was coming nearer.

Now he could hear something swishing. His heart triphammered. The sounds stopped outside his door. His face blanched.

Tap-tap; tap, tap; tap.

He blinked in surprise. It was Mother's entry knock.

Kaehl threw open the spy slit. She stood outside the door, casting glances right and left. Selda crawled to one side while Kaehl tore open the straps and let Mother in. He shouldered the door shut behind her and latched it.

Her face was flushed; she was breathing harshly. A fine film of sweat sheened her skin. He took a bag from her and followed her into the kitchen. Selda stayed in the common area and began playing with Betsy.

"Back already?" He hoped the fear had faded from his face.

"Poor pickings," Mother grumbled, reaching for a swig of water. Motioning to Kaehl, she watched as he emptied the bag onto the table.

"Mrs. Haggins was there again," she said. "She insisted on taking the best of everything. After that rag-bag takes her pick, there's very little left for anyone else. Her and her mighty ways. What makes her so almighty great? No one dares say two words against her. Phah. Give me a chance." She spat and continued fuming as she piled the contents into the sink and began cleaning them.

"Old potatoes. Carrots. A few scrawny roots. Some salt. This is pitiful. Father will be furious."

"Did you get anything to drink?" Kaehl asked.

Mother put down a half-washed carrot and turned wide, watery eyes on him. She pulled a small jug out of another bag and set it on the table. "Potato beer," she stated.

"Just one?" Mother did not reply. They both stared at it solemnly for a moment and then Mother returned to the sink.

"I got some more clothing scraps," she commented, forcing brightness, motioning to another satchel still over her shoulder. "New ones. Some patterns, some bright colors. We should be able to make a good number of dolls today. I have a few ideas in mind."

Kaehl nodded, his face impassive. "Any rocks?"

"No," she said. "Not enough time. Sorry."

He nodded again, not very enthusiastically. He leafed through the pile, shrugged and hoisted a brief smile. They would go hungry again this morning. "I'll get the basket," he said.

Sorting

"Mother, what's it like on the Outside?"

Kaehl and his mother sat on the common room floor among small piles of multicolored rags and fibers. She had added this morning's market pickings and now sorted them into piles by color, style, pattern, and texture. Selda played in a corner with her doll and some throwaway scraps.

Mother looked at him blankly. "We've already talked about this. Don't you remember? You get out every Sabbat."

Kaehl said nothing but kept his eyes on hers.

"You think about the Outside too much, Kaehl." She sighed, picked up two scraps of cloth, and began twisting them together.

"Tell me about the Tower," he said.

She nodded. Kaehl smiled as the familiar stories began. Mother told him about Welltower, the cloud-scraping tower that stood above the burning landscape like a colossus, protected by guards and defensive systems and filters and massive walls, impenetrable, self-sustaining, immense. The structure had been built centuries before by a group known as the Framers, heroes who had defied society to save their planet. In the years before the Tower's birth, millions had been slaughtered in the wars, disasters, the poisoned atmospheres, and the creatures spawned by them. The Evil Days, they called them. Welltower was to be their shelter, their defense, their one hope for survival.

The Framers had begun the Tower on one of the few truly safe geologic formations left on Earth. Others had joined them, some providing money or labor or raw materials, others surrounding the site with troops to keep the uninvited at bay.

The structure had risen quickly and almost too late. Enemy nations had formed against them. Doubters had risen, corporations had balked, religions had proclaimed against it. Mobs had gathered, hoping for shelter, their numbers impossible, far too many to save. Unable to get in, they had launched waves of assaults against the site. The troops slaughtered many.

When the Framers finished the building, the soldiers broke The Chosen through the ring of Declined—the screaming mobs desperate to get in—and allowed them move into their residences. The troops followed, sealing the doors behind them. There was a massive roar as The Declined assaulted the building followed by a shrill hissing of gasses being released and an insanity of screaming. And then the sounds died away.

Many died at their doors that day. Many believe the area to still be unsafe. Even now, people who venture from the safety of the Tower into that blasted landscape, threading through the acres of bones, rarely return. Parents have frightened disobedient children for many generations with tales of the horrors outside. Kaehl's Mother had told Kaehl those stories many times. Some still drove like sharpened stakes through Kaehl's dreams.

Those who made it into The Tower survived. Food, power, air, security—the Framers had provided everything. Everyone owed them their all, even their lives. Because of them, they survived. And they were worshipped as a result. *Praise to the Framers,* Kaehl thought, listening intently, nodding his head three times.

Some people whispered that the Framers had been too generous, that their plan was flawed. The light inside the Tower was much too bright, for instance—you could barely see anything. Mother said it was for protection, to keep everyone safe. Still, dangerous things hid in the glare, things you didn't want to see or meet. More than just the physical problems of dead ends, unexpected outcroppings and sudden drops there were some things you didn't want to meet: Things that clicked or padded or dragged themselves along, unknowns you stumbled on that sent you screaming down the halls. Some made sucking or gasping sounds, invisible in the brightness. Some brushed against your legs, drawing their raspy tongues against your flesh, quietly licking their lips. Others simply oozed.

And then there were The Packs and the over-present light. In Sabbat gatherings to discuss these issues, some protested that the Tower needed more light. "More light?" his mother had spluttered, drawing her rags around her. "There's too much light already." Everyone knew they needed every drop of power they could save for the important things—the work centers, food production, and the exterior defense. There were many more needs, much more than they could afford. Energy couldn't be spent on controlling the light.

Kaehl agreed with her. Some things weren't right, he knew; he wasn't blind. He knew that some globes hung down or crackled ominously in the halls. There was never enough food ("But when did a teenager ever have enough food?" joked his mother). Some places were too hot, some too cold. The Packs were real; in the halls they seemed more brazen, louder, and dangerous than before. Couldn't the residents use the money to buy more protection?

But he'd never met any of those mysterious creatures or known anyone who had. Sometimes he thought that he never would, that it was all made up so he wouldn't worry his head about them. But then his father would tell him about some encounter with mysterious creatures in the halls and Kaehl would believe again.

The people were safe, weren't they? Overall? His mother said they were. And Doubting is Dangerous – how many times had he read that poster in the halls? Welltower kept The Outside at bay, and if they stayed in their homes and kept to their routines they would be fine. Mankind had survived many years like this, yes? That was enough for him, as it should be for all. Welltower was his home. Praise to the Framers (they both nodded their heads three times).

Mother looked up at him.

"What about outside our apartment?" he asked. "Is it just as dangerous out there? Is any place more safe?"

"You mean inside the Tower?" Mother asked, shooting him a glance. She picked up a square and folded it over a doll's head with a few practiced twists. "In the halls?"

"Yes."

"You know as much as I do. I told you all I know."

"I know what you've told me," he said, "and I know you've told it to me before, all the bad stuff: 'The halls are dangerous, too bright, empty, confusing. Meant for adults. I need to wait. I wouldn't want to go there.' But I want to know what it's really like."

She tore the square into smaller strips and added them to a pile.

"Mother, I want to work. Someplace…outside. Outside the apartment."

Mother's hands grew still and dropped into her lap. She stared at them, fingering a patched piece of threadbare fabric patterned with yellow flowers. The material came apart in her hands. She sighed and tossed the pieces to Selda. The girl gurgled and cooed.

Kaehl's eyes searched her face. "I'm old enough, Mother. You know I am."

"No!"

"Yes I am!"

"Wait," she said.

"Mother..."

"NO. Listen to me, son. We've talked about this. You're not old enough. It's dangerous, we won't let you. That's all there is. You'll just have to wait."

The set of his shoulders softened her expression. "It seems to last forever, doesn't it, being locked up in here. I know, it's been years for you. It was years for me, too, before meeting your father. But it will end soon enough. You'll have to go out sometime. We'll need you to. Father is teaching you, preparing you. Be patient, son, your time will come." She sighed and pushed back a pile of solids, reaching for another bundle. "And then you can risk your neck with everyone else who runs the halls."

"I know, Mother, but..."

"No."

Kaehl's hands brushed over a soft cloth. He folded it and set it aside. "It's Father, isn't it?"

Mother said nothing.

"It's not just that Father doesn't want me to go out there, is it? It's something else."

Mother balled up a rag and tossed it into a corner.

"He's afraid of me, isn't he?"

Mother laughed. She glanced up at her son.

Kaehl reddened. "Well, I think he is. He won't let me do anything. He keeps bullying me. He's afraid of something. I think he's afraid of me. Maybe he's afraid of my getting too big, taking over for him."

"Your father's not afraid of anything," she said, digging her hands into the pile. The fabric filtered through her fingers. "Sometimes I wish he was."

"I'm getting too big."

"You've got a way to go."

"I'm hungry, Mother."

Mother froze. Her hands made clutching motions in the air, reaching for fabric but not connecting. She straightened and brushed back her hair.

Kaehl thought he saw her hands tremble. “We all are, son,” she said at last, picking up a square.

“I can work. I can help you get more food.”

“I know you can.”

“The others at Sabbat are working already. Look at Kali, at Lenj. Philly’s been working for years.”

“I know.”

“I could start today.”

“Hah.”

“Well, if not today, then tomorrow. Talk to Father. I could do it. I could start tomorrow.”

“No.”

The room was very quiet. Selda twined several strips around her doll, smothering the toy in beautiful rags.

Kaehl glanced at her. “Is it Selda?”

Mother didn’t reply.

“You need me to take care of her while you two are gone.”

Mother started another doll.

“Well if it’s not that then it’s something else. I can’t spend my days in here taking care of her while you and Father go out for hours at a time. Mother, I’m bored, I’m tired of doing nothing, I’m going crazy, I’m starving. Sometimes I feel like I’ll bust if I don’t get out of here.”

“You’ve been listening at the door again, haven’t you?”

Kaehl faltered. He stared at her and cleared his throat. “Well, yeah. Of course; I’m supposed to. Whenever Selda’s asleep. Maybe a little. Just waiting for you.”

Mother flicked a frown at him. Kaehl’s face reddened again and he looked away.

“Been listening for the Packs?” she asked.

It was Kaehl’s turn to say nothing.

“Pretty exciting, aren’t they?”

"I don't know, Mother. I haven't been listening that much."

"We all did it at some time, Kaehl, back when we were younger. Still do, sometimes. I used to think they were the most exciting thing in the whole Tower, so much better than Sabbat or being home. I used to think they were the greatest." She returned to sorting. "Then I learned better. Nowadays I listen just to be sure they aren't coming for us."

"You're afraid of them, aren't you?"

She nodded.

"What are they like?"

"People."

"I know that."

"People just like you and me. People who are lost or looking for a home, people who have given up, people in trouble. People who are looking for a dream, or think they are."

Kaehl's eyes glowed.

"Some are crazy, some are criminal. Some only know hate. But they're looking in the wrong places. They're young people, mostly, boys and girls, teenagers and the like. Lawless, runaways. People who are trapped, I think; people who have been trapped by themselves, mostly."

"What do they do?"

"Violent, ugly things. Run from authority. Hurt people. Starve. Raid for food. Breed. Try to survive. Break into people's homes. Ugly stuff." She snorted. "Not a very good way to pursue a dream, is it?"

"Are they always on the run?"

"No. They hole up in abandoned apartments, try to hide. Come out at night or when decent folk aren't around. Try to live like other folks the rest of the time, I guess, in their own way. They have their own little world."

"Why are we afraid of them?"

"Because of their numbers. They kill, they break into our homes and steal our food. They raid our factories. They fight. They are the reason we bolt our doors, why we run in the halls, why you can't go out, why we fear.

They're the reason our Tower is breaking down." She sifted through a pile then set it aside. "Well, one of the reasons, anyway."

"Are you afraid of them?"

"Absolutely."

"Why hasn't anyone tried to stop them?"

"Many did, at first. The Tower didn't used to be such a fearful place. Our parent's parents used to leave their doors open or at least not latched—Praise to the Framers." She nodded three times and spat. "That's what they told me, anyway, before they died. Back when they were kids the Tower was better and people could go anywhere, do anything. But things fell apart. Things got older. People got hungry. People got sick. Many died. The Packs grew. Now they're out of control."

"Sounds like they run things in the halls."

"They're parasites, Kaehl, like those little angly worms we burned off Selda last year. They live off other people, dependent on them, stealing their food and clothes. Take away steady, hard-working folks like your father and I and they would die."

"How many are there?"

Mother sighed. She finished off the last bundle and began packing them up. "I don't know. Many; more than a few." Kaehl helped her carry them into the storage room. "They're no good, Kaehl. You don't know them so they seem fascinating, interesting, attractive but they are not for you. Not for any of us. They are no good. Stay away from them."

Kaehl stared at her solemnly.

"Now," she said, heading back to the living room. "Let's see about your studies. More writing for today, I think, while I start sewing these toys together."

Kaehl looked up from his pile of dolls. He had wound together 15 this afternoon after his writing lessons. Mother nodded her approval. The afternoon clock had sounded several minutes ago. Father would be home soon.

They piled their projects into the storage room and moved to the door. Kaehl listened as a crowd approached, then pulled aside latches at his father's coded knock. He held the door aside until Father rushed through then closed and latched it. Father leaned back against the wall, wheezing, his breath coming in shallow gasps. Sweat poured down his face. He sagged and bent forward, his hands on his knees.

Mother brought him a mug of beer. He looked up, grabbed it from her and sucked down the thin liquid. He handed the empty mug back to her and then shook as a heavy coughing fit gripped him. Mother and Kaehl helped him to a chair in the kitchen.

Father swung his rucksack from his shoulder and dropped it on the table next to him. Still shaken by coughs, he circled the bag with his arm and held it close.

Kaehl and his mother exchanged glances and waited. Eventually Father sat back in his chair.

"More," he croaked.

"Wouldn't you rather have water, dear?" Mother answered. "It's better for you..."

"MORE!" he roared. Mother scurried back to the kitchen. Kaehl stood behind him, frowning.

"Come over here, boy, where I can see you," Father ordered. Kaehl moved to the other side of the table, a little nearer his father. Mother returned, carrying another mug of beer.

"Here you are, dear. Be careful, there isn't much."

Father grabbed the mug from her and drained it in one long gulp. He raised it from his lips and crashed it onto the table, letting out a great sigh. "Better," he said. "More."

"Yes, dear," his wife said, picking up the mug. She hovered over him nervously. "How was your day?"

"Fine," he said. His brow furrowed. Then, without warning, he cracked his hand onto the table. Mother and Kaehl jumped. Selda whimpered.

Father grinned. "Very fine, in fact! Today a at work sideswipe from a crane laid Cutdirte in the dirt. My manager. Hah! What a fool. Wasn't watching what he was doing, of course. Blood everywhere. What a mess! Everyone came out to watch." He wiped his face.

"And, while they were busy with that," he added with a conspiratorial nod, leaning over his sack, "I snuck off and managed to pocket a few things. Right from under the quartermaster's nose. Look!"

Father upended his sack on the table. Out tumbled a trove of carrots, tomatoes, turnips, cabbages, and squash. Mother and Kaehl squealed. "No potatoes tonight, eh?" he roared. Mother crushed him in a huge hug, crying. Kaehl stood at the end of the table, his eyes blank, stunned. Father looked up at him and smiled ferociously. Kaehl blinked. Father winked at him. Kaehl, staring at the bounty, swallowed hard.

The meal was memorable. Kaehl and his mother prepared the food while Father finished off most of the beer. His spirits were good enough that he didn't seem to notice how Mother had thinned it with water.

Father finished off the last of the boiled squash and sat back in his chair. "Well, that was good," he said.

Mother beamed at him. Kaehl wiped Selda's mouth and folded his hands. Selda burbled happily, playing with her spoon.

Father surveyed the room, his eyes coming to rest on Kaehl. Kaehl looked away, suddenly feeling cold.

"You've been quiet tonight, boy. Problem?"

"No sir," Kaehl responded quickly, shaking his head. "No problem."

"Something wrong with the food?"

"No sir. Absolutely delicious!" He squirmed uncomfortably.

"Dear, tell me more about your day," Mother interjected. "What was it you said..."

"In a moment," Father ordered. He leaned across the small table.

"Problem, boy?" His face darkened. He lifted the mug again and drank. "Ughh," he spewed. "This tastes like dishwater." He flung the contents across the room and smacked the mug down. The room went silent.

Kaehl's eyes traced details of the floor very carefully. "I—I was wondering, Father..."

"About what?"

Kaehl wanted to crawl away.

"My boss. You wondering about Cutdirte?"

Kaehl nodded. The room seemed to grow very hot. "Just curious," he said, shrinking into his chair.

Father spat. "He lived. Carted him away, they did, but he was still breathing. I don't know what happened after that; I didn't follow up." His voice grew casual. "Why?"

Mother's voice cut in. "Oh, I'm sure he's just curious, like he said," she soothed.

"SHUT UP!" Father roared, his hand crashing onto the table. Selda whimpered. "Why, boy?"

"Just curious, Father."

"Curious. Always curious. Your curiosity is going to be the death of me, boy. You don't like what I did, do you?"

Kaehl shrugged, his eyes boring holes into the floor. "You run the crane, right?"

"Yeah." There was a long period of painful silence. "I didn't aim for him, if that's what you mean. I didn't plan for this to happen, he got in the way. What should I have done? Moved the crane away from him? Adjusted my timing? I saw him coming, of course; I could have moved the crane. But I didn't. I warned him. I was doing what I was supposed to do, to the letter. You can't do anything to hurt production, you know. If Cutdirte's timing was bad it wasn't my fault. What else could I have done?"

Kaehl kept his eyes fixed on the floor. "I don't know, sir."

Father rose from his chair and walked unsteadily around the table. Selda's whimpering grew louder as he approached. He cuffed her. She yowled and fell from the chair, quickly crawling out of the room. Father towered over Kaehl. The boy tried not to shrink away.

"Well?"

"I don't know. I was just asking, Father. The meal was very good..."

Father's face burned livid. "Yes it was, wasn't it?" he shouted, bending near. "You wouldn't have had any if I hadn't gotten it for you, would you? Those few vegetables you got from the market—you think that would have fed us? They wouldn't have lasted one meal. Then guess who would have been hungry tomorrow. Who?"

"We would have, Father. That's what I was saying..."

"That's why I brought them. You know why I did it, don't you? You know why I brought the food. I did it to feed you. I did it because you can't feed yourselves. Because you can't do it. Do you hear? Your stinking dolls aren't trading enough to support us. All this lousy food we've been eating; well, now we don't have to. You know why? DO YOU KNOW WHY? It's because I didn't move the crane. THAT'S WHY!"

He grabbed Kaehl by the shirt. "Cutdirte ran into it, yes he did. He wasn't expecting it to be there, had his mind on other things. Laid himself out good. No one saw me but I stopped the production line and ran to help him. Now I'm a hero! Do you know what they might do now, boy? They might promote me. Because he got hurt, they might pull me off the production line. They might give me his job. THEY MIGHT GIVE ME HIS JOB! Maybe we'll be able to get more to eat. Maybe we'll have better clothes. Maybe we won't have to scrabble any more. What would you have done, boy? WHAT WOULD YOU HAVE DONE?"

Mother moved beside her husband, tugging at his arm. "Dear..." she pleaded.

Father threw her off. His face was red, his eyes bulging. A coughing spell shook him again and drove him into the table. Kaehl stood and tried to steady him. Father shook him away. Mother refilled his mug with water, which he drank noisily and spat out. Together they moved toward the sleeping room.

"Stupid kid," he gasped between coughs. "No thanks, no gratitude, nothing! Who does he think he is?" She laid him on his mat. He could hear Mother trying to soothe him.

White-faced, shaking, Kaehl steadied himself against the table, fighting to hold back tears. His hands balled into white fists, his breath shallow and quick.

Kaehl felt a new emotion growing inside him: rage. It boiled in his chest, reckless, hot. Rage against this angry drunk, this man who was hurting his family, rage against the injustices he forced on them. Rage against the unfairness of it all. It pushed the fear away.

He had suppressed his anger before, buried it, covered it under layers of guilt. But even buried it had never disappeared. Somewhere inside him it had waited, simmering, poised to heat up again.

Now it boiled. It rose and turned him into a cauldron of hate, hate and a burning for revenge. His feelings steamed, seething inside him. His face crimsoned.

From another room Selda whimpered.

Kaehl gasped, staggered, took a step, and blinked several times. He screwed his hands into his eyes and sagged against the wall, the color draining from his face. His pulse slowed. He shivered and shook himself. Groggily he blinked again and surveyed the room.

Selda whimpered once more. He turned and stumped toward her voice.

He found her in the living room, huddled in a corner, rocking, her arms covering her head, humming a tuneless song. Her wide eyes stared at the floor. She looked up as he entered, her eyes red-rimmed and frightened. She covered her face and shrank into a fetal shape, sniffing.

His rage exploded, becoming incandescent, white hot, blinding.

Father. His sister. He had hurt her. Again. He smashed a fist into the wall, leaving blood.

He wheeled and centered on the sleeping room. Father and Mother were just visible above the blankets. His brow contracted, his eyes smoldering. He bunched his fists and strode toward them.

Selda whimpered again.

He stumbled and turned once more, listening. She was staring at him. He looked at his hands, turning them, flexing them.

She dropped her gaze and started singing again. After a moment he heard another voice join in. He recognized it—it was his voice. They were humming her "I'm not scared" song. Mother had taught it to them. They hummed it whenever Selda felt threatened, repeating it until she calmed.

She had been lucky today. She might have gotten a beating instead of just being swatted aside. She could be losing blood instead of just crying. Kaehl pushed that image away. She got lucky. He stared at his hands again.

No.

Ice water drenched his mind. His knees buckled. He staggered and sagged to the floor. Tears flooded his cheeks. He covered his eyes with his hands and pulled them away, shocked at the bloodied knuckles.

He had been here before. In his nightmares he had lived inside this moment. The mirror of his mind had shown him who he was, who he was becoming. He had seen himself and his actions and knew what he was planning to do, what he was like.

His belly tightened, his gorge rose. His hands grew clammy, his tongue dry. Confusion and fear and a desire for flight rushed through him, colliding, pushing against the rage. The emotions raced through his body, locked in battle.

"No," he moaned.

Horror gripped him, a horror of what he had thought of doing, of what his father had done to him, of what he was becoming. His skin crawled. He looked at his hands again.

They were his father's.

He balled them into fists and buried them under his arms. "No," he groaned. "I am not my father. I will not do this."

Covered with sweat, he crawled next to Selda. His head sank to his chest, one hand reaching up to stroke his sister's shoulder. She shrank away.

"Hey, Sister, it's me, it's me," he said. He reached for her again. She cried out and pushed him away.

"Sister, it's me."

She raised both hands to slap at him. He grabbed her wrists and shook her.

"Sister, it's me."

Selda opened her eyes. Through the blur of tears she recognized him. "Kahh," she cooed.

"I won't hurt you."

She curled into his arms. Stroking her hair, he let her sob, his emotions draining. Her cries faded. Eventually they fell asleep.

There was no beer the next morning to ease Father's headache. He took it out on the family. Kaehl and Selda stayed out of his way as much as they could. The crashes, shouts, and sobs from the next room made them cringe.

Kaehl rose quickly when Father bellowed. They met at the hallway door. He staggered and pushed Kaehl's hands away. Father threw open the door and stumbled into the hall, swaying. He belched.

The crowd came toward them. Almost overrun, Father picked up their pace and disappeared into the glare. As they moved off Kaehl wrestled the door into place. The last latch was nearly sealed when the door shivered under a crashing blow. Kaehl fell back but sprang forward again and leaned into the door. Someone laughed in the hall. The footsteps faded away.

He wiped his forehead and turned around. Mother sagged against the doorway, her head low, her hair disheveled. She swayed, holding onto the door post.

Kaehl hurried to her side, catching her as she began to fall. She raised her head to smile.

Kaehl gasped. One of her eyes was swollen shut, the other listless and dull. Her neck was red and raw. Her bottom lip was starting to swell.

Mother shuddered and moaned. Her good eye focused and suddenly widened, staring at Kaehl. She shook him off and grabbed the door frame, nearly falling over again. Swaying, she tottered to the sleeping room and fell into the blankets. Selda came up to Kaehl and stood in the circle of his arm. They listened to their mother sob herself to sleep.

There was no breakfast or lunch that day. They saved yesterday's leftovers for the evening meal. Mother limped around the apartment, moving through her chores in a silent daze, hiding her face. When the time neared for Father's return she put a pot of water on to boil.

Kaehl stationed himself near the door. His face was grim, his insides tight. His father had battered his family long enough. Someone had to do something. What that would be, he had no idea.

Kaehl held the door aside as Father rushed through. He closed the door and latched it shut. Kaehl automatically reached for the rucksack but was shoved aside.

"Woman! Drink!" he bellowed. Mother did not appear from the kitchen.

"Woman, where's my beer!" he shouted again.

"Bad day at work, Father?" Kaehl asked.

Father glared at him.

Mother slowly limped into the doorway. "I'm sorry, dear," she said hoarsely. "I didn't go out today."

Father surged to her side. Mother cringed against the wall. "What did you say?" he roared.

"I couldn't. I'm sorry. Dinner is ready." Her voice was weak, limp, trying to be disarming. She turned to enter the kitchen.

Father spun her around. "I want my drink!"

He raised his hand to strike. Kaehl grabbed his wrist. Father turned with an oath, flung his hand away and punched him into the wall. Kaehl slumped to the ground, groaning.

"Get off me, boy!" Father roared and turned again to Mother.

"No, Father," Kaehl pleaded, pulling himself to his feet, rubbing his head, his voice unfocused.

"What?" Father laughed, turning again. "No? You're telling me no?" He advanced on his son. "You who stay at home all day, too young, too weak to help your father. 'We're starving,' he moans, but all he does is stay home and play with dolls. What did you do to help today?" Father forced Kaehl back. Mother trailed them apprehensively.

"I want to work…" Kaehl protested unsteadily.

"Sure you do. Do you know what happened today? My managers told me. They told me."

Kaehl backed into the living room wall. Father crowded in on him. Kaehl shrank into a crouch. "Told you what?" he asked.

"Cutdirte survived. Did you know that? He was back at work today. His head was bandaged but he was okay. And he was telling lies. Now they blame me, or at least they suspect me. Did you know that? Do you know what that means? Everyone's staying away from me, keeping silent, staring, whispering. I didn't do anything—they can't prove I did. But everyone blames me. They say the crane wasn't where it was supposed to be, that I had moved it. They think I did it on purpose. Cutdirte walked into it and now I'm going to lose my job. All I ever did was protect my family, try to feed them, keep them safe. And they blame me! Me, the best worker on the line. My boss' accident was an accident. I was too busy, distracted. It wasn't my fault. IT WASN'T MY FAULT!"

Father struck the wall next to Kaehl's head. Kaehl saw blood on

Father's knuckles as he drew them away.

Father grabbed Kaehl's shirt and drew him up to his face. Father's breath was foul, his eyes wild, spittle flecking his lips. For a moment Kaehl didn't recognize him.

"And what do I get when I come home?" he continued. "Nothing, not even a drink. My family hadn't even left the house, didn't go shopping, not even for beer, not even for me. They didn't even try. You don't care about me, do you? You're just like my boss, you and your silent, judging ways. I hate you, do you know that? I hate my boss and I hate you. You're everything I was when I was your age, only worse. I HATE YOU!"

Father shook Kaehl like a doll. Kaehl was crying. Mother grabbed Father's shoulders but he shrugged her off. Selda crawled into the sleeping room and buried her head in a blanket, rocking.

"Father, please…" Kaehl pleaded.

"SHUT UP! SHUT UP! SHUT UP!" Father shouted. He smashed at Kaehl's face. Sparks lit up behind his eyes. He raised his hands to protect himself. Father pounded them away. There was a lot of noise. Then the world went white.

Kaehl awoke on his back in a stupor of pain. His face felt stiff; any movement of his lips produced the most pronounced hurt. He tried to roll over but gave up, gasping. His hands, his arms, his ribs—he ached everywhere.

With an effort he turned to one side and rolled into a sitting position. Waves of dizziness swept over him. For some reason, only one eye worked. It appeared to be glued shut. He reached up to touch it but drew away at the pain. Looking around he saw that he was alone in the sleeping room.

After some effort, Kaehl appeared in the living room doorway, swaying, leaning against the frame. Mother and Selda were separating rags on the floor. He tried to smile but could not.

Selda looked up and screamed. Mother looked up and gasped. She rose to her feet but remained rooted. Puzzled, Kaehl tried to speak. His voice came out in a harsh croak. He reached up to touch his face. For some reason it was covered with painful lumps. One of his ears was covered in a thick, itching scab. He limped to the kitchen and filled a bowl with water. Leaning over, he splashed some on his face.

Darkness popped in front of his eyes. The floor rose to meet him.

Kaehl awoke in the sleeping room feeling refreshed but famished. He pushed himself to his feet and limped to the door. His family was in the kitchen.

"Anything to eat?" he called.

He heard Selda squeal in the other room and was nearly bowled over by her ecstatic hug. "Easy, Selda, easy," he said, his ribs creaking. She looked into his face, squinted appraisingly, then hugged him again.

Mother came out, wiping her hands on a towel, a broad smile lighting her face. She hugged him joyfully.

"Not so tight, Mother," he groaned. She eased away. Kaehl rested one arm over her shoulders. He stroked Selda's hair.

Father appeared in the kitchen door and stood near the post, looking down, twisting a rag with his hands. Mother flashed a look at Kaehl then backed away.

"Hello, Father," Kaehl called. Father nodded. Kaehl's eyes clouded, wondering at Father's silence. Something about his look bothered him. It triggered a response, and then he remembered. He remembered the pain.

Kaehl reached up to probe his face. Father watched his son blanch. Without a word the man turned and stumbled back into the kitchen.

Kaehl reached out toward him. Mother stepped forward. "It's all right, Kaehl," she said quickly. "He's changed, he's a better man. Hasn't taken a drink in days."

"Days?"

"Yes. You've—you've been asleep for a while. We've been taking care of you. We were kind of worried."

They stood in the doorway, Kaehl's mind racing. Selda looked up.

"Well," Kaehl said at length, rubbing his sore belly. "Got anything to eat?"

With an ecstatic smile Mother helped him to the kitchen and eased him onto a chair. She scurried to spoon out some turnip mush for him. Father hung in the background, munching a carrot, the rag still twisting in his hands. Kaehl lifted a spoon to his mouth and winced. His lips were still sore.

Father flung the rag onto the table and headed for the hallway. Kaehl looked up.

"Is it morning, Mother?" he asked. She nodded. Kaehl tried to rise but his legs failed him. The table scraped over the floor as he fell against it. Father whirled toward him, his face anxious.

"You stay there, son," he said. "It'll be all right. Mother and I have worked things out."

"It's okay, Father, I'll be right there."

Mother brushed past his and patted his arm. "No, Kaehl, you stay. We'll be just a bit."

Kaehl sat back down and watched as they listened at the door. They began undoing latches. Before lifting the last one, Father turned around.

"You just rest today, Son," he called. Kaehl's eyes widened. That was a dangerously loud voice to use at the door.

They released the last latch. Father edged through and helped Mother wrestle the door back into place. She began replacing the latches. There was a brief rush in the hall and Father was gone.

Mother returned to the kitchen and poured Kaehl a mug of water. She sprinkled a spoonful of white powder into it and handed it to Kaehl.

"What's this?" he asked, stirring the mixture. It tasted sweet.

"Sugar."

"Sugar?" he repeated, his eyes widening. "We got sugar?"

Mother beamed. "Father got it. He's been bringing all sorts of things home, all sorts of food. He even brought home some good quality rags and decorations. We've done real good while you were asleep. Look."

She opened the door to their cooler. Kaehl's eyes bulged. The shelves overflowed with carrots, tomatoes, beans, and squash. Boxes and tins were stacked into corners, and radishes and pea pods peered out of bags.

"And do you know what we're having tonight, if you're feeling all right?" she asked.

"What?"

"Meat. Father brought some home last night."

Kaehl's spoon dropped into his bowl.

"Like I said," Mother continued, "he's been real good, lately. Except for going to work, he hasn't left your side since—well, since the next morning, after the..." Her face drooped. "He's been terribly sorry."

Kaehl stirred the mush. Mother brought over another spoonful of sugar. He raised his hand to stop her, but she ducked the spoon under his arm and emptied it into his bowl. She stood there for a moment, stirring it for him.

"Where did he get the food?" Kaehl asked, his eyes suspicious.

"I didn't ask." Mother put the spoon down, her eyes boring into his. "And don't you ask him. He's very sorry, Kaehl, like I said. He hasn't taken a drink since."

Kaehl spooned down several mouthfuls and sipped his water. "But what about you?" he asked, wiping his mouth. "How are you feeling? He wasn't exactly kind to you."

"I've never been better," she responded, sitting next to him, her eyes alight. "You don't know; he's been happy and helpful and very concerned. It's been wonderful!"

Kaehl remained solemn and probed his face. The lumps were fading. "I'm not so sure, Mother. It's only been a few days." His eyes darkened. "How long has it been—really?"

Mother picked up the empty bowl. "You wait, Kaehl, you'll see." She filled it and handed it back to him.

"Mother," he said, gripping her wrist. "If this happens again we'll have to go. We'll have to leave. We can't say here. He's going to kill someone."

Mother pulled her hand away. Her face darkened. "He won't, Kaehl. He's your father. He never would. You don't know him."

"I think I do, Mother. I think we both do."

She turned toward the cupboard.

"We can't stay here, Mother. It's not safe."

"There's nowhere else to go."

"Sure there is. There always is. There's got to be."

"No. There isn't."

"What about the Preacher? Does he know someone?"

Mother didn't reply.

"Mother?"

"Your father needs me."

"Maybe he does. But you don't need what he does to you."

She sat down.

"Mother, if he does this again, I'm leaving."

Mother's eyes widened then closed again. She patted his wrist and looked up. Her hands shook slightly. "No you won't. We need you. Who'll bathe Selda?"

He stirred his mush and avoided her eyes. "I'd rather be in a Pack."

Mother slapped the table and stood, a finger inches from his face. "Don't you ever say that, Kaehl, ever. The Packs are much worse than anything we have here. Much worse."

"Nothing is worse."

"You don't know." Her voice was hard. "They're much worse."

"The Packs are free, Mother. When you're in a Pack you have power, you're not trapped behind four walls, you can go where you want to. You and Selda won't be beaten."

"You don't know what you're talking about."

He pushed his bowl aside and looked up. "Do you?"

Mother picked up the bowl and walked to the cupboard. "Yes."

Kaehl watched her stand with her back toward him, her head on her chest. "Mother," he said, "If Father does that again, I'm leaving. If I... sometimes he makes me so mad. I want to strike out, strike back, hurt someone. Hurt him." His eyes grew haunted. "But that would be just like him, wouldn't it? Mother, I've never hurt anyone before. Could I become like him?"

Mother sighed. "All boys become like their fathers in some ways, sometimes good, sometimes bad. Life beats you down to it. It's a response. It's what you do."

Kaehl shook his head. "Not me. If I find myself becoming like him, anything like him, I'm going to leave. I would. I couldn't stand it. I won't stay. I won't do those things."

Mother turned. "Sounds like you've made up your mind to leave no matter what."

Kaehl looked into his bowl.

Mother knelt in front of him and gripped his hands. "It's better here, son, much better than anything out there. Trust me."

"It can't be."

"It is."

"How is it better?"

"Here we're a family. Here we have a chance. We can overcome anything if we work at it together."

"He almost killed you. How is that a family?"

"You don't run out. You keep trying." She stared into his eyes. "He won't kill me."

"He's beating you, Mother. He beats me. He beats Selda. What's next?"

Mother looked down.

"I'm not going to become like him, Mother. Staying here drives me crazy, makes me want to become more like him. It's happening every day."

"Nearly."

"Yes, nearly."

"I know; Kaehl, I know. That's why you should stay. You need us. We need you. Don't leave."

"We should all go, you especially. Find some safe place, any place. Work it out from a safe distance. Something. Anything but this."

"He needs us."

"He needs help."

"He's not a bad man, Kaehl. Not really. He does a lot of good for us."

Kaehl snorted. "What would you do if I became like Father and hurt him the next time he attacks you?"

Mother emptied the bowl. "You won't, Kaehl. You're too smart. There are better ways."

"You just said I won't. What if I did?"

"You won't. You'll be like him in some ways but you won't do the bad things he does. You won't."

"Mother..."

"Kaehl," she sighed, walking over and looking into his eyes again, "I appreciate your interest in defending us; it's very noble. But we can take care of ourselves. We've been doing it for a long time. We're used to each other. You can help but you won't change anything. You want to know what would happen if you went bad? If you truly became like him, if you became violent and maiming and started hurting others, you couldn't stay. One of you would have to leave. Otherwise one of you would kill the other. Or us. It's what men do." She shook her head. "They're not smart enough to fix things."

Kaehl's eyes widened.

"But you won't. Don't worry about it. You're our strength, our future, our safety. It won't happen, Kaehl, it can't."

Kaehl bowed his head. He took another swig of water. Looking up at her, he picked up the empty mug and held it out. “Any more?”

Sabbat

"Kaehl? Kaehl?"

Someone was shaking his shoulder. He brushed it off and rolled over onto his chest, burying himself deeper into his blankets.

"Kaehl?" More shaking.

"Hmmph?"

"I know you were up late last night but it's Sabbat. I wondered if you were going to go to church."

"Mmph." He turned over and opened an eye. Late night? He tried to focus. Oh, yeah—Father. It seemed like a dream. Father had sat next to him last night after dinner and opened up for hours. They had talked about many things, about Father's sorrows and concerns, his suspicions and fears, about the pressures at the factory and home and about the problems in providing for his family. Kaehl was dumbstruck and had spoken very little. Kaehl would have thought his father was drunk but there was no alcohol in the house.

Many tears had fallen. Father swore that he would never drink again or raise his hand against another person. He thanked Kaehl for bringing peace back into their home.

Kaehl was grateful but confused. Father had changed, all right. This sudden tumbling out of emotions had left Kaehl feeling exposed and vulnerable, very uncomfortable. Raw emotion was there, and he didn't know what to do with it. He certainly didn't trust it. But he had listened gratefully just the same.

There was something about Father's voice that had sharpened his hearing, a tremor almost, more like a trembling, something that felt to Kaehl like fear. Father's opening of his heart was very real but there were things he was not saying, things he feared deep inside. What they could be Kaehl could not imagine. What it all meant he did not know.

Neither Kaehl nor his father mentioned the accident with the crane and they said nothing about the beatings. Kaehl forgave his father, eventually, but he didn't trust him. The limp stayed with him for several days, making forgetting difficult.

"Is Father gone?" he mumbled, rubbing his eyes.

"Yes," Mother replied.

"What time is it?"

"Late, but we're fine. You feel like going?"

"Mmph." Kaehl shoved his blankets aside and headed to the cesspit.

Leaving their home was always a risk. Packs never traveled in the mornings, people said. His mother agreed. "Too many people in the halls," she said, "but you never know." She was skeptical by nature and, as Father said, a very "determined woman," so they risked it. Loaded down with bags and bundles, Kaehl and his mother locked the door and headed off, Selda on her leash trailing behind. They kept as silent as possible.

The halls were a uniform, unremarkable grey, made of smooth, cool stone arranged in concentric rings with spokes radiating from the central Shaft. There were very few working globes but the brightness was still intense, so intense that navigation was difficult and distances hard to predict. Location plaques and direction signs had been torn down years ago in an attempt to confuse the Packs. The marauders, however, had quickly adjusted, trashing the walls with graffiti and symbols, marking their territories. The only people who had gotten confused, it turned out, had been management.

Mother, however, led them quickly through the uneven light with practiced feet, Selda and Kaehl trailing behind. In the glare and sameness of the halls, even experienced people got lost. The only people who traveled freely were security teams and organized groups like the commuters. Others were on their own. There were no guarantees.

Sabbat religious services were held every week in each level's recreation center. Each level could each hold well over a thousand residents but with disease, consolidation, decay, and attacks from Packs the actual population numbers were always much lower. Some levels had combined to hold joint meetings. Traveling among the levels was much riskier than staying on one level, but as the communities grew more fractured the need for community and protection overrode caution.

Kaehl, Selda and their mother looked forward to attending Sabbat services. Kaehl enjoyed the brisk walk through the halls (he preferred running but Selda and Mother were unable to do more than a determined walk) but he enjoyed much more the opportunity to get out of the apartment, even if it was only the same short trip each week. They also enjoyed the chance to meet with others and hear what was happening in the Tower. It also gave him a chance to look for new rocks.

"Watch your feet," Mother hissed, leading them around a chunk of rock sticking out of the floor. Automatically they stepped around the familiar stone, a marker they moved around every Sabbat. Kaehl used it as a gauge of how far they had come. Almost there, he smiled to himself. He could almost smell the fried potato dough.

As they approached one intersection they slowed, a confusion of shouting where there should be silence. Mother motioned to them to stop. Cautiously they peered around a corner.

A few doors away a group of people had crowded in front of the remains of a quad entrance. The heavy hallway door had been smashed in and lay in several pieces on the floor. Clothing, bedding, and food containers were smashed and scattered over the splintered wood. A sack of potatoes had been ripped open, its contents crushed and scattered down the hall.

Mother motioned Kaehl and Selda forward. They approached the group, edging along the far wall to get around them. Kaehl heard a woman sobbing inside the quad, her voice rising over the murmur of the comforting voices. Still moving but trying to peer into the apartment he stumbled into his mother, who had stopped and was quietly talking with a tear-stained woman. After a moment Mother shook her head and gestured for them to move on.

"Mother?" Kaehl asked, his eyes wide.

Mother tugged at Selda's collar. "Come on," she said, her voice tight. "We'll miss the service."

They moved away again, pressing against the wall as a brace of grim-faced officials rushed past them, hurrying toward the home. Selda stared back at the crowd, her mouth open. Mother tugged at her collar again.

They slowed as they neared the recreation center. The halls grew crowded as families filtered in from nearby levels. Kaehl turned from the hallway tragedy as the smell of fried dough made him smile. Mother's mood lifted as she greeted friends, at once launching into deep conversations, her eyes troubled but shining. Kaehl smiled at her. She had once told him that church services were very important, but the time spent with her friends was essential.

Despite counsel from church leaders about respecting their holy day, the open area outside of the center became a market on the Sabbat. It was already crowded with vendors and performers, people hawking their wares and haggling and talking noisily together. Kaehl scanned the area, looking for new attractions. His eyes widened as he took in the toys and games and exotic foods and smells. A puppet show caught Selda's attention. Kaehl was drawn toward a juggler. Someone played a pipe a few booths away while someone else banged a drum. They watched for a few moments before an usher appeared from the center and invited everyone inside.

The center was noisy and crowded. It quickly grew warm and many people began fanning themselves. An organ blared in one corner, pumped by a dirty but very determined young boy, backing a choir of enthusiastic but mismatched voices. The rumble from the congregation rose to match the music. Friends arranged seating for Mother and Selda; Kaehl stood nearby. Selda began bobbing and singing with the organ but as the crowd noise grew more intense she sank into her seat and covered her ears, singing to herself.

A large woman in colorful, flowing robes appeared from a side room and moved behind a lectern. The number 321 was painted on the podium.

"Welcome, brothers and sisters, welcome!" she called. The noises continued.

"Welcome, brothers and sisters, welcome!" she called again. People quieted somewhat.

"WELCOME, BROTHERS AND SISTERS, WELCOME!" she shouted. The conversations died. The organ groaned softly behind her.

"My name is Sister Sorah. How are you doing today?" The crowd chorused a chaos of responses. "It's a glorious day in the kingdom of the Framers, isn't it?"

"Amen," answered the crowd. "Praise to the Framers!" replied some. A few heads nodded.

"Is it hot in here?" she asked.

The group acknowledged enthusiastically.

"It's always hot where the Spirit is. And we have the Spirit, don't we?" The organ swelled. Heads nodded. "Yes we do, yes we do. Now, before we welcome our preacher—the brother you've been waiting to hear—we have a few announcements. Brothers and sisters... are we listening?" The congregation quieted again.

"The neighboring levels have had break-ins." Everything silenced. Kaehl's ears pricked up. "There has been a terrible loss of life. Keep your apartments locked up tight, brothers and sisters, especially at night. We have noticed that some of your doors have not been secured very well. Please, if you value your safety, as long as the Devil allows these Packs to roam free, keep your houses safe. If you are having problems, if your door needs repair, if you are not well, please let us know. And check on your neighbors if they aren't here today, all right?"

"The northern sectors of levels 322 and 324 have lost power a few times over the last few days. The problem has been traced to the main router on level 320. We have contacted maintenance. People are working on it. If the power goes out, stay in your homes. If you must go out, travel in groups and only during church or commute times. People are working on it."

"We've been told that we have a new baby on this level." Happy murmurs arose. "The Sentas—are they here? No? Well, you can't blame them. They have their hands full, don't they?" Chuckles bubbled out of the crowd. "We ask you to keep them in your prayers."

"And lastly: Do not wander out of your homes in the evenings or at night. Yes, I know how nice it is to have one last chat or stroll, but with Packs roaming free, we all want to be safe. We have talked to the security force on level 320, and they have told us that they are working on it. We are grateful for their efforts, but until the problem is contained please observe the curfew. All right?" The crowd murmured their assent. "All right?" The crowd responded vigorously.

"All right. And now..." the organ began a rhythmic pulsing. The choir began to hum. "And now, we have been blessed to have the presence of our great preacher, a man the Framers have kept alive and healthy and strong, a man who has the Framers in the center of his heart, a man whom the

Spirit has blessed mightily—" The organ was braying now. The choir was near full voice. Some in the congregation began to sway. "Our preacher, the Honorable Brother Righteous!"

The woman moved aside as a large figure in billowing scarlet and gold robes swept out of the back of the hall. The choir was at full voice; the organ throbbing behind them. People in the crowd rose to their feet. The preacher jogged up the aisles, his hands outstretched, people touching him. The robe billowed against Selda's face as he blew past, startling her. She curled into a ball and smiled.

The preacher reached the front of the room and positioned himself behind the altar. He gripped it with both hands. The organ and choir made a final ascent before going silent.

"WELCOME, WELCOME, BROTHERS AND SISTERS!" he called, his voice deep and swelling. The crowd responded enthusiastically. "How are we today?" The crowd answered again.

"The Framers have called us together today to talk of his ways. And we are very glad he did. Isn't that right?"

"Are there any newcomers in the crowd, any brothers or sisters we haven't seen for a while? No newcomers? Brother Kullin, we've seen you before; put your hand down. All right. We are grateful for you, brothers and sisters, we are grateful for your faithfulness. Amen and amen."

"Are there any sick or injured among you? Are there? If there are, let them come unto me. No? Praise the Framers. If any come among you, you tell them of the joy they can feel here, of the healing the Framers can lend them, all right? All right!"

The organ began to groan quietly.

"Now brothers and sisters, the Holy Supplication—this marvelous verse we repeat every Sabbat—who can tell me where it came from? Anyone?"

Oh, no, thought Kaehl. *Not the Holy Supplication talk again. Things must be tight behind the altar.* He flushed at the heresy of his thought and quickly bowed his head three times.

"Little Reuben—look at him, brothers and sisters, so young, so full of a knowledge of the truth. Yes, Brother Reuben, where did the Supplication come from? Sister Sorah, can you help him out here? What?"

A voice burbled out of the background.

"Yes, that's right!" Brother Righteous said. "The Framers gave it to us, that holy trinity of inspired men who created all things, who under the hand of the Framers raised up this mighty tower, this powerful edifice, this glowing structure of light whose glory shall not be dimmed, whose power shall not diminish, whose power shall never die. Yes, these glorious beings who heard the voice of the Framers and raised up under his almighty hand a shelter, a mighty tower, a fortress against the powers of evil, a refuge from the storm, a bulwark against the wars and sicknesses and evils covering the earth. Amen."

"And where did this come from? It came from the Framers, brothers and sisters, that god from whom all blessing flow. They raised up this tower, our mighty Welltower, to keep us safe, to keep us happy, to give us joy. And it has, hasn't it?"

General assent rose from the background. Kaehl noticed a tightness at Mother's lips.

"Yes it has. It has kept us together, happy and safe, free from the powerful plagues and famines, raised us up to keep us free from the swirling death and the plaguing mobs that surround us. Praise to the Framers! Amen!"

Mighty assent from the crowd.

"And what do we do while we are safe in this tower, while the hand of the Framers punishes those who have brought such evil around us? Yes! We love one another. We look after each other. We lift the weakened hand, strengthen the feeble knee. We care for each other, think of each other, do for each other, sacrifice for each other. And we are glad to, are we not? Yes we are! We are glad to because of our wealth and our health and our happiness, which we are more than happy to share with our neighbors."

The organ swung low.

"Now brothers and sisters," he continued, "It took a lot of effort to raise this tower up, to raise it as an anthem to the Framers, to strengthen its mighty walls, didn't it? Yes it did. And it takes a lot to keep it going, doesn't it? Yes it does. It takes time and energy and sacrifice. Each of us must do our part, each of us must keep our house in order, each of us must be our brothers' keeper. Am I right? Yes! Yes I am! And you do so well! You do what needs to be done, don't you?"

"Yes, I know you do. But there are some of you who do not. Some of you who keep back. Some of you who would rather sleep than work, stay in your homes rather than celebrate the Holy Supplication, keep to yourselves than give to others. Is this good? No. Does this please the Framers? No. Does this make them happy? No. Does it make you happy? No!"

"So what should we do, brothers and sisters, what should we do? I'll tell you what we should do: We should give! We should work. We should sacrifice every moment, every effort, everything we have to the work of the Framers, every moment, right now. Yes! We should give. Even as these lovely sisters move throughout the audience..." a group of lades in long robes and incandescent smiles moved up the aisle, carrying small baskets. "...we should give, put in their baskets whatever we can, whatever we can sacrifice for the building up of our brothers and sisters, for the maintenance of our lives, for the keeping of our purity! Because we don't want to become like our unfortunate brothers outside, do we? No. We don't want to let this evil inside, do we? No. Do we want their sins to cover our faces, their sicknesses to afflict our bodies, their evils ways to take away our children? No we don't. We will never do it; we will never let it happen! We will fight and sweat and work to make good things happen, to keep the evil away. We will give, won't we, brothers and sisters? Yes! We will give and we will sacrifice. We will give!"

A sister with very alert eyes and a brilliant smile handed a basket to the first person in Kaehl's row. When it reached Kaehl he pulled a carrot out of his pocket, brushed it against his shirt, picked off a hair, and placed it in the basket. He looked around guiltily. It wasn't much, he knew, but it was all he had. Mother added a turnip. They helped Selda give another carrot.

The preacher roared on. "And as we give we bless the lives of others, because it is through your generosity that they are blessed. And as they are blessed they bless the lives of others, and on it goes, and so on, forever. Your one little drop in our huge ocean of giving will make ripples that will spread throughout eternity. Thank you, brothers and sisters, thank you."

"Are we done now?" He asked the women who were gathering the baskets at the front. "All done? Fine, good. Anyone else want to contribute to the poor? Thank you, brothers and sisters, thank you for this blessed bounty."

"And now, once again, brothers and sisters, I say again, are there sick or afflicted among you? If so, let them come unto me." He swirled his robes, indicating a position before the altar. "Anyone at all? Anyone? No? How about those who have chosen to accept the Framers, to give their lives to him, surrender their sins and gain their salvation. Anyone? Your chance for redemption, brothers and sisters. Anyone? No?" A cloud seemed to cross his face but it scudded past.

"And now, brothers and sisters," he cried, yawning his arms, "Framers willing, the time has come to recite the Holy Supplication!"

The organ swelled again, accompanied by applause and cheers as the crowd rose to its feet.

"Are we ready?" he shouted. "Are we ready, brothers and sisters? All right; say it with me!"

A discordant chaos rose from the crowd as Sister Sorah and Brother Righteous led them in chanting the verses, the choir backing loudly:

Holy Framers
Full of mercy, never changing Spirit.
Praise the Framers!

Thou hast chosen us to be Thy holy children
and separated us by these mighty walls from our brethren and sisters
and their false ways.
Thou hast elected to exalt us
to keep us from destruction
while all around us shall be cast down to Hell
because of their wicked traditions
which lead their hearts far from Thee.
We thank Thee again, Holy Framers, that we
are a chosen and a holy people.
Amen.

"All right! Well done! Amen! Are we warmed up? I think we are ready to give our Personal Supplication!"

Most of the congregation sat down but several of them walked to the front of the room, forming a line near the altar. Sister Sorah shepherded them into place and handed them a basket which they passed down the line, each adding a contribution.

The preacher struck a dramatic pose and repeated the Supplication, his voice rising and dropping dramatically. The organ followed along. After he finished, the congregation erupted in applause and shouts of praise.

The preacher turned to the line of believers. "Brother Harom!" he called, indicating the first person in line. "You are first! Come on over!" Brother Harom walked to the pulpit, stepped onto the footstool behind it and repeated the Supplication, looking for approval from the preacher.

"Yes! Amen! Well done! Perfect!" shouted Brother Righteous. The congregation echoed him. Brother Harom's eyes glowed. Sister Sorah ushered him back to the audience.

"Sister Wallich!" he said, indicating the next person in line. "Come on over!" Sister Wallich walked to the altar and repeated the prayer in a trembling voice. She smiled brightly when the preacher thanked her for her effort, having helped her with the words only twice.

The rest of the believers followed the same pattern, each person trying to say the same prayer, word for word. Kaehl turned to watch the rest of the congregation. Some were restless, some looked bored, but many of them were smiling or shouting encouragement. Some were straining to hear the words, mouthing the phrases to themselves and nodding their congratulations.

"All right!" said the preacher as the last person in line finished. "Is that it? Does anyone else want to add their voice in prayer? No? Okay, all right. We'll get a chance to try again next week."

"We will continue to keep the faith, brothers and sisters, and preach the word, as I'm sure you will, too. Let us not forget the Supplication that our fathers gave us, to keep us holy and set apart from the world. This is our world. They built this world, they built our homes, they made all this possible so that we could be here this morning and be safe from the evils outside. Praise be to the Framers!"

"Amen!" shouted the crowd. Many nodded three times.

"Be grateful for your homes, your families. Be grateful for being safe here while those around us are drowning in sin and oppression. Be grateful for the food you have, for the fellowship we enjoy here. Remember the poor and afflicted among you, and lift up their heads. Remember, they could be you; you could be them one day."

"Remember those outside these walls. Yes, remember even them. Although the Framers have exalted us and set us apart from them, we need to remember those poor, suffering souls with love. Their own traditions and wickedness have made them suffer in their poor dumb misery; pray that one day they will be converted and join us in our endless paradise here." Kaehl noticed a darkening to Mother's eyes.

"Pray for the day when we will all be joined together, when we will lift up our voices as one and praise the name of the Framers. Yes, one day we too will be able to lift our voices with our miserable brethren and sing praises to the Framers, if they will only repent and turn from their evil ways. Remember them, brothers and sisters, even as we enjoy the Framers' presence here. Bless you, brothers and sisters. Amen. Enjoy your Sabbat day, and may the Framers go with you!"

"Amen!" shouted the crowd.

The choir thundered a rousing hymn. Brother Righteous prayed long and loud, his voice swelling. Then the congregation rose to their feet and filed slowly out of the room, the choir roaring behind. Kaehl walked behind his mother, pulling Selda with him.

They joined the mob outside the recreation center, which was once again charged with conversation and activity. Mother attached herself to a group of chattering friends, found an open spot along the wall, and began setting up her dolls. Kaehl led Selda to the bulletin board. As usual there were no notices for him, just the usual crude notes scrawled on the slate listing items wanted or for sale or exchange. Some people, not being able to write, had pinned items to the board that they hoped people would understand, like half a broken pot—merchants would find the owner of the other half then haggle with them to sell replacements.

Kaehl sat Selda down in front of the puppet show and scanned the crowd. He caught sight of the juggler again, sitting in front of a crowd of small children, deftly twirling several balls. Kaehl edged closer, keeping Selda in sight. In the back, a thin-faced man scanned the crowd.

"Hi! What's your name?" the juggler asked as Kaehl came close.

"Kaehl," he returned.

"Hello, Kaehl, how are you?" he asked. The balls dropped. "Whoops! Oh, clumsy me. I'm so sorry! Well, goodbye, children, end of show for now. See you later!" The children clapped enthusiastically and moved away. "Bye bye, children," he said, waving theatrically. He shrugged and smiled.

"They'll come back," he said. "They always do. They love this stuff. How about you? Would you like to see me juggle?"

"Sure."

"Wonderful! I've been watching you with your mother and sister." Kaehl's brows knit together. "Just casually. I watch everyone, like we all do. That's your sister over there, isn't it, with the puppets? A lovely young lady, very sweet, yes?"

Kaehl nodded.

"I've been watching you for a long time, several Sabbats, really. No, don't look at me like that. Observing the crowds is how I get business. You have a wonderful little family, a pleasure to see you together."

He held up a ball. Another boy, his eyes curious, joined them. "Hello! Hi," the juggler said to the boy. "Private show, just for Kaehl, public show in a moment. All right?" Disappointed, the boy nodded and moved away.

The juggler turned back to Kaehl. "Look. See this? Yes, this is a ball. But you know that, don't you?" Kaehl smiled. "Yes! But wait—this is a very special one. See the silver stripes? I've been holding it especially for you." Kaehl frowned skeptically. "No, I really did—really! Watch! Can I write your name on it? Wonderful! What is your name?"

"Kaehl."

"Oh, a tough one, eh? Thanks! There. Can you read it?"

"Of course I can!" Kaehl said. In the background, the thin-faced man disappeared into the crowd.

"Sorry; of course, of course. Very sorry. Did I spell it right? Not many young men your age can read, you know. Well done. But then again, you're not a child, are you? Of course not." He bent over and picked up a few more balls.

"Now, I'm going to add your ball to these others and juggle them together." Kaehl nodded. The balls flew through the air, one at a time, until they were all circling in front of him. They whirled high and low, slow and fast. Kaehl was fascinated. Then the juggler appeared to stumble.

"Oops! I dropped one! Sorry about that. What a silly guy!" The juggler made a comical face. Kaehl laughed. "Oops! There goes another. Uh oh—now another! What's happening? Earthquake, earthquake, maybe a mighty wind? Phew, I hope not!" He waved theatrically at his backside. Kaehl continued laughing. "Now I have only one ball left. Hey, it's the one with your name on it! How about that!" He continued juggling the ball, tossing it up and down and around his back.

"Kaehl, what would happen if I dropped this ball?"

"You'd be out of balls."

"How right you are," the juggler laughed. "Amazing boy, such a bright boy! So I guess I'd better be careful, right? But what would happen to this ball if I dropped it?"

"It would fall, just like the others."

"Yes! Very good. Fall, a very important word. In what direction would it fall?"

"What direction?"

A few children had begun to gather nearby. Some adults were wandering close. The juggler's face tensed. He leaned closer. "Yes, Kaehl. In what direction would it fall?"

"The same direction as the others!"

"Yes! But what direction is that?"

"What direction?"

"Please be quieter," he hissed. "We don't want to attract attention." He stopped juggling. "Others are watching. A simple question: which direction?"

"You mean up, down, left, right?"

"Yes! Which direction?"

Kaehl looked to his right and left. He saw Brother Righteous moving through the crowd toward them, his robes flowing, followed by the thin-faced man. Kaehl ducked his head and moved aside. The small crowd parted.

"What is going on here?" the preacher demanded.

The juggler stepped back a few paces, his face drained of color.

"Nothing, nothing, noble preacher. Just doing some juggling," he said. He began picking up the balls. "Would you like a demonstration?"

The preacher slapped them out of his hands. The juggler averted his eyes.

"You are new here, are you not?"

"Just arrived a few weeks ago, Preacher."

"Did you go through our committee? Did they approve your application to entertain here? I didn't think so. We did not choose you. The Framers did not choose you. I've been told that you have been preaching evil doctrine. Is this so?" His voice was much louder than it needed to be.

"I am just a humble juggler, sir, about to move on. Here one day, gone the next. No harm—"

"You will not preach your alien doctrine here, antigod. Leave, do you hear me? Leave. Now!"

"Yes, Preacher, of course, instantly. Please, may I pick up my tools first?"

"Leave your toys for your master the Devil to retrieve. Leave before I call the guard!" The juggler hastily bowed and moved away.

The preacher watched until the juggler disappeared, then turned to the crowd. "That man is an Outsider, someone who comes into our churches and homes to lead you astray with false teachings. I have seen him before. He has caused much trouble in other places. I'm sorry we let him in. He came here to capture your hearts and force you to follow his evil ways, to turn you away from the Framers. His kind must be avoided. Stay away from them at all costs." The crowd moved restlessly, unsure of what to do.

The preacher turned. "You!" he commanded, pointing at Kaehl. The crowd scattered from him like water. "You were watching his show. What did he say to you?"

Kaehl glance around uneasily. "He asked if I wanted to see him juggle."

"And?"

"I said yes."

"And then he juggled?"

"Yes."

"Then what?"

"Then—then he wanted to know about the balls."

"Yes?"

"Yes. He wrote my name on one. He wanted to know how it would fall, what direction."

"And what did you say?"

"Nothing. I didn't understand."

"Didn't understand?"

"Yeah. I mean, it was a pretty dumb question."

"And how would it fall?"

"Down, of course."

"And what direction is down?"

Kaehl looked puzzled, then gestured toward the floor.

"Is that bad?" the preacher asked.

Kaehl's brows knitted. He shook his head, perplexed. "No?" he ventured.

The preacher's eyes narrowed. "Anything else?"

"No. Then you came. Honest."

The preacher considered Kaehl for a moment. "Pick up his tools and throw them into the cesspit, then come back to me. You must do penance for your sins." The thin-faced man whispered in the preacher's ear. "You!" the preacher said, pointing to the other boy. "You were there, too. Help him, then both of you come back and see me!"

The two boys looked at each other, their faces white. The crowd dispersed. The boys picked up the juggler's equipment and carried it to the waste room. Kaehl watched the ball with his name on it, the one with the silver stripes, disappear into the opening. "Praise to the Framers," murmured his companion. They sullenly nodded their heads. Then they turned and headed back toward the preacher.

Leaving

Weeks passed. The tongue-lashing he had gotten from the preacher still burned in his mind, although not as painfully as the bewildered look on his mother's face as she had stood beside her son, taking her own scolding. The preacher had blamed her for being a careless mother and harangued her about the evils of leaving your children alone. Kaehl had never been in trouble with the preacher before and he couldn't explain why he was now. He was grateful that the preacher had saved him from such an evil man but he still wasn't sure what evil the man had been trying to do. Mother had questioned Kaehl afterward but only shook her head. They both agreed not to tell Father.

Kaehl continued his morning trips to the shaft. He had decided that Mother knew about them. She was often awake before Kaehl arose. He could tell because her breathing changed. She stayed in bed, though, to avoid disturbing Father. Sometimes he could hear her sobbing, very softly.

Father, however, did not know about the shaft, and without discussing it Kaehl and his mother had agreed to keep it that way. Father would have disapproved. He may have changed, but years of pain kept the mother and son wary. Father was the one they feared, the one whose crashing right hand silenced arguments. Father was the law, the right, the power, the truth. You did not disturb The Father.

Kaehl feared him. But while he feared him he also loved him. He was his father and worked very hard to keep his family alive. Father went into the halls every day, laboring at the factory to feed them, even going without food, as he frequently told them, to give them the best. Kaehl appreciated all that he had done. He wanted to be like him some day—mostly. But for now he would stay out of the man's way.

Kaehl's leg eventually healed as did his ribs and arms. He continued to exercise while his father was at work, trying to keep himself busy. Secretly, he was proud of the way his muscles were developing.

Father continued to be happy and friendly, and the family had loosened their fears of him. He drank only boiled water and unfermented juices. It was a time of great peace.

A few months later there was a slight downturn in his mood, and Mother had confided to Kaehl that something had happened at work. There was some pressure building. Apparently something had gone wrong and some old anger had resurfaced, but she was confident they would go away. Father would be able to weather any change. He brimmed with confidence.

"I've been thinking of going back to my old job," he said one night.

Mother looked at him sharply.

Father cleared his throat. "Back then I was doing great work, important work. I did very well with it, too. Got promoted. Work has picked up and they need experienced hands, I hear. It was important stuff, what they were doing, crucial stuff. The Tower couldn't get by without it for even one day."

"You mean the factory?" asked Kaehl.

"Yes. The factory. They'll want me back; I'm sure of it."

Kaehl looked from Father to Mother, then back at the table. "Why did you quit?" he asked, eyeing a carrot.

"To find new opportunities, you know, to do new stuff. That's how I came to the Gardens. The pay was pretty good, too."

"Better food," said Mother, waving a hand toward the crop of vegetables on their table.

Kaehl crunched a carrot and spat. Part of it was black.

Father smiled. "Nothing like working in the Gardens," he said. "And they appreciated me more."

"So why go back?" asked Mother.

Father stirred a bowl of lentils. "I just think it's time to move on. You know. I've got a good job, but I'm getting bored."

"Bored?"

"You know, same stuff every day. Load this, unload that, fix this, oil that..."

"Do you think they'll have enough work?" Mother asked. "When you left..."

"I know, I know. Parts, shortages, breakdowns, foraging for replacements. Lack of trained labor. Laziness. Theft. Boredom. Incompetent managers. They wouldn't listen to me. All the bad stuff. No future in it. At least back then."

"That's what led to the accident," Mother said, nodding.

Father banged his bowl on the table. Selda jumped. "You're right, there. Only there wasn't just one accident, there were many, a lot. Dangerous place. Parts used to be easy to find, power reliable and good. But things fell apart."

"People only remember the big events," Mother sighed.

"Power problems. Couldn't see for days."

"You left right after that, right, Father?" asked Kaehl.

"Shortly after. Lots of people left. Not a very happy time. There was an investigation. Someone had stolen parts out of a transfer engine. It completely shut down. Blew out, if I remember. There was a noise and a flash and a lot of smoke. Some deaths. Blindness, too. Burned a hole right through the reinforced housing. Pretty bad."

"So you want to go back?"

Father nodded, mashing the lentils with his spoon. "I'm sure things are better there, now. If not, they'll need an experienced engineer."

"When are you leaving?" asked Mother.

"Soon," said Father. He pushed his bowl aside. "Maybe real soon."

Things changed several nights later. Father came home, his breath stinking, his clothes reeking, his walk unsteady.

Kaehl and his mother stood back, watching him compose himself against the wall, catching his breath. They exchanged glances. Kaehl could see the confusion and concern in his mother's face.

"Where's my drink?" Father gasped. Mother ran to the kitchen and returned with a mug of water. Father upended it into his mouth. He spat it out. "What is this junk?" he bellowed.

Mother's face was strained. "Dear, its water. Can I get you some juice? We haven't used alcohol for a while. Are you all right?"

"YES I'M ALL RIGHT!" he roared. "NOW GET ME SOMETHING TO DRINK!"

Mother hovered over him as he staggered to the kitchen. "You've been drinking. You promised you wouldn't do that anymore. What's gone wrong at work?"

"Nothing! Everything!" he shouted. He began tearing open cupboards. "None of your business! Ah!" He pulled a bottle from behind a vegetable crate. He broke open the lid and began draining it. Selda, who had been playing in a corner, slunk out of the room.

"We had been saving that," said Mother crossly, watching him guzzle the contents. Kaehl stared at her, his mouth open. Father put down the bottle and sighed. "Now," Mother said, her voice flat and cold. "Tell me what's wrong."

"Nothing. I'm just thirsty," he said, lifting the bottle again.

Kaehl could see the anger crackling in her eyes. She leaped forward and tried to pull the bottle away.

Father cuffed her. Off balance, she crashed into a counter top and fell to the floor. She held her head and drooped, beginning to cry.

Lowering the bottle, Father stood over her. "Never do that, woman," he growled. His breath was uneven and labored. Kaehl stooped down and pulled Mother to her feet. Father was still swaying next to the cupboard as they left the room.

Kaehl sat his mother on the floor in the cleaning room and examined her head. He found a large lump.

"There's no blood, Mother," he said, putting a wet rag to her head. "Why did you buy him that stuff? You should have thrown it out. It turns him into a monster!"

"He turns himself into a monster," she said, drying her tears. "He can get that stuff anywhere. I'd rather he got it at home, where I can watch him. But I thought it was hidden..."

Mother groaned and stood up. He watched her move to the kitchen.

"What are you going to do?" he asked.

"Help him," she answered, her teeth clenched. "He'll make himself sick like this."

There was a crash from the kitchen. The two of them rushed to the door. Father was on the ground, blood seeping from his forehead. Mother gasped and ran to his side.

"Help me lift him," she said, struggling against his weight.

Kaehl took a few steps toward them and stopped. "Why?" he asked. He watched her struggle to lift him.

"Something terrible must have happened at work," she answered. "Help me!"

He sighed and bent down. Together they wrestled him to his feet and helped him to the sleeping room.

Kaehl marveled at the concern in her voice. Selda sat in a corner, hugging a blanket, rocking on her haunches, staring wide-eyed at her father, humming a tuneless song. She caught Kaehl's glance and slunk out of the room.

Father slept noisily through dinner. After everyone was in bed he vomited himself awake. Selda scurried out of the room like a rat was at her heels. Kaehl replaced the blankets while Mother helped Father to the cleaning room. She fixed him some leftovers for dinner then stayed with him as he sucked down the last of the alcohol.

Kaehl joined Selda in the quad's common room. She rocked quietly in his arms as they waited, listening to the uneven voices in the kitchen. She hummed tunelessly to herself. Father's voice rose, followed by the sound of smashing crockery. Mother sounded like she was trying to keep him calm. Kaehl seethed.

"What can I do, Selda," he asked, "What can I do?"

Kaehl's eyes squeezed shut, trying to hold back the tears. He ached for peace, to be able to keep Father from hurting his mother, from hurting his family. If only he could stop this terrible disease from ripping their family apart. If only he could stop his father...

Eventually Father went back to bed. He snored so loudly that no one else could sleep. Mother helped Kaehl and Selda move their mats into another apartment then returned to her husband's side. Selda eventually fell asleep. Kaehl stayed awake long into the night, his anger hot.

The next morning, three-clock sounded before anyone stirred.

"Framers, we're late!" Mother cried, snapping awake, savaging his shoulder. "Wake up, dear, wake up! You're going to be late!" Father remained in a deep sleep. She savaged his shoulder. Kaehl appeared in the doorway and helped her sit him up.

"We have to get him going," she said, trying to pull him to his feet.

"He is in trouble at work again, something about poor performance and his boss. If he doesn't show up on time, he may get fired. Come on, help me get him up."

Kaehl heaved against his father's slack shoulders, levering the inert man to his feet. They moved him into the kitchen where Mother sloshed hot water into a mug and threw lentil powder into it. The liquid burned his lips. Father spat and shattered the mug.

"What are you trying to do, kill me?" he grated.

Kaehl's eyes narrowed. He picked up the broken pieces. "Ouch," he muttered. He watched blood ooze down one of his fingers, a sliver from the cup sticking out.

"Okay, okay!" Father grunted. "I'm going!" He hauled himself to his feet and swayed unsteadily.

Mother supported him out of the kitchen as Kaehl moved to the door and began undoing straps.

"Come on, dear," she said, stuffing carrots and potatoes into his pockets. "We've got to get you to work."

"Just a minute," he grumbled. "I've got to go to the cesspit." He broke from Mother's grip and tottered to the waste area. Kaehl and his mother looked at each other.

A thunderous crash and a roar erupted from the pit. Selda darted through the doorway and ran to Kaehl, huddling behind his legs. Kaehl bent down to see what was the matter. She trembled violently.

Father appeared in the door, holding his head. "SELDA!" he shouted, spotting her. He lurched forward.

"What happened, dear?" Mother asked, putting herself between them. Father stopped, his face like a furnace.

"That idiot daughter of yours got under my feet. Knocked me to the ground, just about killed me. Move aside. I'm going to teach her to watch where she's going."

Selda whimpered.

Father tried to push Mother aside. "No!" Mother cried, her voice frantic but firm. "You've got to get to work. Remember the problems with your boss!"

"I'll take care of him later. MOVE!" He grabbed her by the shoulders and threw her against the wall. He advanced on Selda.

Kaehl, who was holding the unlatched door shut, pushed him away with one hand. "Father, don't," he said. "Don't do it again, don't go back. Don't hurt us, please! Mother, I can't..."

"Shut up, boy," Father snarled. He shoved Kaehl aside, sending him stumbling into the wall. The door teetered open against the lock.

Selda was screaming now, trying to get away from her father. Mother threw herself onto Father's shoulders, tearing at his arm. Father roared in blind, drunken fury. He threw Mother off again.

Kaehl rose like a mountain and stood behind him. "Father, stop," he said. His voice was calm and deadly cold, his body taut as a whip.

Father turned and swung at Kaehl, missed, then turned back to Selda, who was scrambling to keep out of his reach. Mother sobbed, yelling for him to stop, holding him by the knees.

Deliberately, his face white, his steps steady, Kaehl moved into the kitchen. He returned with a stool and positioned himself directly behind his father.

"Father. Stop." His words were a cold command.

Father ignored him and picked his daughter up in one hand. Selda screamed. He raised a fist. Kaehl lifted the stool over his head. "Father," he called. Father whirled around. Kaehl brought the stool down, crashing it against the man's skull. His father dropped like a sack.

Selda crawled into a corner and hunkered down, rocking, humming to herself. Mother pulled herself away, trying to compose herself, wiping at her tears. Her eyes were wide, swiveling between Kaehl and her husband. Father groaned, stirred, and slowly turned onto his side. He retched.

Breathing heavily, his eyes hot, brandishing the stool, Kaehl watched his father. His fists flexed, the knuckles were white.

Father dragged a hand over his scalp and brought away blood. He looked up at Kaehl, his eyes unbelieving. Tears crawled down his cheeks.

"Son..." he croaked.

Kaehl's anger dropped out of him like a stone. Something acid dripped into his belly, crawling along the insides of his gut. His veins ran with frost. He trembled.

Fear. He knew what he was feeling. Fear of what he had done, fear of what he was becoming, of what he had become. He stared at his father and then at his hands. An icy feeling of horror spread into his spine. He shivered violently. The stool dropped to the floor.

Mother darted to her husband's side and knelt, pillowing his head in her lap. She looked fearfully at Kaehl, her eyes pleading.

"Father, Mother, what… I can't…"

Kaehl looked away. He felt weak. Using the wall for support he turned and made his way to the door. The whiteness in the hallway beckoned to him, absorbing, blinding, freeing.

"Mother. Father, I can't..." he said again. He held out his hand, staggering against the doorstep. Behind him Sister continued her "scared" song. Family sounds, the sounds of his life. "Mother, come with me," he pleaded, his hands reaching.

Father groaned, put his head in his hands, and began to cry. Mother looked up at Kaehl, her eyes venomous.

Kaehl stepped into the light and was gone.

Hall

Kaehl ran through the blazing halls like fire, his eyes streaming, his hands stretched in front of him, feeling his way through the glare. He felt like he'd been running for years. Long ago his dazed fear of what he had done to his father had been replaced by fear of what he was doing now. He was running in the halls, alone. The openness, the exposure, the blindness, the horror of running the halls unprotected pressed into him, squeezing his chest, trip-hammering his heart. He was an outcast adrift in a place where he could not see, where everyone could be an enemy, where packs of bloodthirsty savages and creeping monsters stalked the halls, waiting for him, hunting him, competing for his blood, licking their lips at his approach.

He ran until he felt his heart would burst.

Kaehl eventually slowed and collapsed against a wall, gasping, holding his sides, rubbing the tears from his face. How far had he come? He shook his head. More importantly, where was he going? He looked around groggily, his knees shaking.

The halls looked the same as the others he has seen on his Sabbat trips: the same lack of signs, the same drab walls and reinforced doors, the same occasional broken lamps. The graffiti differed in places but not by much.

He walked into a neighboring hallway and examined it. Same appearance. He tried another hall, then another. They all looked the same.

He was lost.

His heart quickened. He started running again; turned a corner and hit a wall, landing on his back. He bounded to his feet and hit another, staggering sideways and rubbing his forehead. He started again, running more slowly.

Something clicked down the hall ahead of him. Kaehl skidded to a halt. There was a dragging sound and then a slam.

His skin frosted. Barely breathing, he straightened and began edging forward, shooting glances right and left. His eyes were wide, his mouth open, his ears straining. There were no more sounds. To his fevered mind every comer hid a Pack, every hall held several doorways to evil, any of which could spring open at any moment to snatch him inside.

Turning a corner, he stumbled over something and hit the floor. Rubbing his shin, biting his lips to silence the pain, he squeezed his eyes shut and cursed under his breath. After a moment he opened his eyes and searched the floor. He focused. There was something there—a stone. His heart leaped. He knew that stone! He had seen it every week on the way to Sabbat. Standing, he centered himself and cantered toward the Center, sure of his direction, one hand on the wall, his hopes high. He passed the quad that had been attacked, now standing vacant, the door missing. He turned one corner, then another darting past many doors, his feet silent.

He rounded a corner and stopped. A dead end. An empty, featureless barrier, completely blocking the hall. Confused, he felt around the blockage, looking for an opening. Finding none he turned and walked back the way he had come, searching for a different path.

Kaehl jogged down another corridor. It ended at a locked door. Several locked doors. Dozens. They were all locked. He backed out and tried again, moving down an alley, his pace quicker. He was sure the Center was here someplace. He stumbled into some construction gear, picked himself up, and pushed forward again, running.

He stopped at the end of another hall, his sides heaving. Nothing. He was lost. Doors and alcoves and halls and ramps confronted him, all featureless, all empty, all the same. Hall turned into alley which turned into junction which turned into hall, all lined with barred doors, all of them closed, all of them identical, all of them unknown.

He started jogging again, aimlessly. Many of the globes were broken, many feeble and dim. Some had been torn out of the walls, their wires stripped. Some were still dark, patterning the walls and floors with crazy shadows. Kaehl kept away from them.

"Mother..." His small voice was loud in the silence. A lump in his throat made breathing difficult.

Kaehl thought about his family. He couldn't go back, even if he could find the way. He knew that. He had deserted his family, running from them like a coward, leaving them to Father and his abuse. He should have stayed to face his punishment so that he could recover and be there for Mother and Selda. But he had been too afraid. In all the ways he had feared and hated, he had become like his father and the results had blackened and shriveled him inside. Whatever had been waiting to comfort him at home was now erased beyond repair. All ties were cut.

He grimaced. Even if he knew the way home his father would beat him senseless or throw him into prison or the pit. Kaehl was alone, more than he had ever been. That solitude that he had so prized in his hiding place was now constantly around him. It was his greatest enemy. There was no going back.

Sounds echoed in the distance, footfalls, people jogging. His breath froze in his throat. The sounds came toward him. His heart hammered.

After a moment's thought he turned and sped away from it.

He rounded a corner and crashed into another wall. Staggering, he turned and darted away again. Dodging another distant set of footsteps he sprinted up a set of ramps and around a corner only to smash into a group of men, knocking them to the ground. He fled like a startled rat, sounds of angry pursuit fading quickly.

He took another set of ramps and found one exit blocked, heavy machinery pounding on the other side. Circling another set of halls he found another ramp and plunged down it, emerging only to crush back into a doorway as voices filled an adjoining hall. He fled again.

Confusion led to fear and fear to terror. His imagination kicked in. In his mind he saw his father pounding down the halls after him, his fists clenched, his mouth a square of screaming, murderous rage. He imagined packs of young teens picking up his trail, bludgeons and picks raised, tracking him like a rat, closing in on him when he stopped, screaming for his blood. He imagined a blood-eyed monster on his heels, tongue licking hungrily.

And then he heard a woman's voice. He stopped and listened, tracing it to a door a few steps back. She was crying. It sounded like his mother. He leaned against the door and pressed his mouth to it. "Mother?" he ventured. Had he stumbled back home?

"Mother!" he screamed. The voice behind the door went silent. "Mother!" he screamed again, pounding on the door. Someone pounded back. "Go away!" said a voice not his father's. "We're armed!"

"Mother!" he cried again.

The security slit snapped open. Fearful, angry eyes scanned him. "Go away!" shrilled a woman's voice. It was not his mother. This was not his home.

More footsteps approached. With an agonized cry he fled.

Every sound was magnified tenfold, every corner held a trap. He ran until cramps seized his legs and his sides and his thirst became a living thing. His breath seared his throat.

Kaehl sagged to the ground, bathed in sweat, his heart pounding in his ears. Shivers took him. Tears rivered his cheeks.

His breath froze again. Someone, some group, was coming down the hall at a slow jog, a regular pace, unhurried, not near but approaching.

Kaehl dragged himself to his feet. The sounds came closer. He staggered, fell, and rose again. Voices called. With an effort, he vanished down the hall.

Out of breath, he skidded around a corner and stopped. The runners were closer now, somehow. He must have mistaken their direction. He turned again and lurched away. His breath became labored, his sides burning with pain. *Rest, rest, rest,* he thought, his mind like mud. He needed a place to hide, food, water. He needed rest.

Gasping, choking, his chest heaving, Kaehl found a niche in a wall. Desperately clawing air into his lungs, trying to quiet himself, he hunkered into the hole, making himself very small.

Something appeared in the distance.

Kaehl held his breath, willing his heart silent. The sounds were clear, now: two pair of feet loping casually toward him. They passed him without pausing. Watching them disappear into the distance, Kaehl let out his breath like an explosion.

More sounds came, the sound of running feet following the first, their rhythm more casual and random. More people; a group. He crushed deeper into the wall and silenced himself again.

The crowd drew near. They made no noise, no sounds that a body might make other than the slap of their feet against the floor, the quiet swish of their clothing, and their regular breathing. They were all young, not much older than him, and whip thin. He counted perhaps 25 runners, their footfalls sounding within steps of his hold. He remained invisible.

They disappeared down the hall, a relaxed knot of figures jogging by. Their footsteps faded. *A Pack,* Kaehl thought, his eyes wide. Too relaxed to be commuters. He let his breath out again and started to rise.

Two more figures jogged toward him, following the others. Kaehl crushed into the crevasse once more, straining to throttle his thundering heart. As they neared his hold they slowed. They hadn't seen him but they suspected. Some sense had tipped them off. They were looking for him.

They stopped, their heads turning this way and that, searching. He could see their eyes. They knew he was here.

More Pack members? he thought. A rear guard? Should he get up and ask them for help? No. Think of what Mother and the Preacher had said. Think of the stories. Think.

Time froze. The hall stayed deathly silent. He crouched in his hold, alone, afraid. His thighs burned, his chest pounded, his pulse threatened to burst his heart. The figures remained still, listening warily. He could feel panic slowly rise in his throat, bile burning his tongue. The animal in him was coming to the fore. He fought down a desperate, clawing desire to break out and flee. What if the Preacher was right? What if they really wanted to kill him? Would they want to? Could he get away? He wouldn't make it; they would be on him like rats. He wouldn't stand a chance. He looked away, hoping they wouldn't sense his eyes burning into them. He fought his instincts and willed himself to become part of the wall.

The figures rustled quietly and disappeared. Their footfalls padded into the distance.

Kaehl held himself as long as he could, trembling, not daring to move, his eyes fixed on the floor. At last his heart could take it no longer. His breath exploded and he collapsed, panting, scrabbling at the ground like a wounded cockroach.

At length his breath returned. The trembling subsided. He hauled himself to his feet, stiff and sore. He was alone. He was cold and hungry, constantly looking over his shoulder in mortal fear. He needed shelter. He needed food. He needed water. He needed to go home. But home was out of the question. He shuffled his feet, casting for signs, trying to decide which way to go. All ways held the unknown except one, and that way held people. Brushing back his hair, his eyes stinging, he turned and limped after the Pack.

He had lost them. He knew it. They were familiar with the halls; he was not. They drifted like smoke through the passageways; he dragged his feet and groped in pain like a dying man.

The light, less brilliant in places, allowed him glimpses of the rough character of the hall he was moving along. It seemed older, less cared for, more abused. Corridors yawned at right angles to the main halls, some broken or blocked, some snaking dozens of steps before ending without warning. Most doors were closed and locked, their spacing uneven. Those few that were open looked broken or smashed in. All looked like they hadn't been used in a very long time.

Kaehl's thirst gnawed at his throat.

He moved into one of the side corridors. It ran for a few dozen paces before opening into another circling hallway, very much the same as the one he had just left. He continued across the hall, down another access way, and into another circling hall. He turned and trotted down that. The halls were apparently endless. The monotony was maddening. His trot turned into a run.

It was morning, just before the family was to arise. Kaehl rolled over and stretched. Mother was making a huge breakfast today, just for him. She had rolled turnips, potatoes, squash and peas into a blanket of fried potato dough and set them before him, with two huge pitchers of vegetable juice. Selda would squeal to see him and hide her doll in the blankets, just so he would have to dig to find it. Father would smile as he left for work, waving as he faded down the hall. "One day, Kaehl," he would say. "One day soon." Kaehl's eyes watered.

The apartment was cold this morning. Where were his blankets?

Maybe he had rolled out of them in his sleep. More likely, Sister had stolen them. He certainly didn't want to disturb her by trying to get them back. Maybe he could share Mother's. He reached out, feeling for her sleeping mat. Nothing. He felt only cold stone. His eyes snapped open. No one was there.

"Mother?"

There was no reply. "Mother!"

His scream echoed, crashing in waves against his ears. The noise died and he bolted up. He stared wildly about him, his eyes bulging.

Where was everyone?

He rubbed his eyes. He had been laying in an empty alcove somewhere, some place far removed from his home. There was no family, there was no food. There were no friends, there was no water. He pulled in his legs, bowed his head and rocked, hugging his knees, trying to remember. Where was he? What had happened?

And then he remembered. He had left his home, deserted his family. He was traitor, nearly a murderer. It might have been a day since he had left his apartment, or maybe two. Three? A year? Was it morning now? Where were the clock warnings? Where was he? He must have collapsed into some empty hole. He was alone.

A flicker caught his eye. In the blaring light he could make out something, a twist of motion, a squirm against the light.

There. Near the wall. A rat stood silently, its nose twitching, its pink eyes glittering in the light, its white skin a beacon. It was watching him.

Slowly, Kaehl drew his legs beneath him and turned toward the rat, drawing strength.

He sprang. Before his feet left the ground the rat had disappeared. He hit the wall and crumpled onto the floor, not moving. Pain thudded from somewhere new. His stomach cramped, gnawing at his insides. Tears flowed again. He curled in to a ball and sobbed. He sobbed until nothing was left and his breath was gone. After a few minutes he caught his breath, wiped his face, rose, and stumbled toward the hall.

Kaehl's thoughts were no longer focused. He had been running—jogging, mostly walking—forever. The hunger in his body had deadened, deafened by the shouting of his thirst. Thoughts of home floated around him like a cloud. He thought of going back, finding his way back home again. He laughed, his voice hysterical. He had gone up several ramps, down several more, and through endless halls. He was more lost than ever.

Standing, swaying in the endlessly circling hallways, his eyes focused enough to notice a bit of darkness against the light, a crack along the edge of one door. An opening! Dim though it was, it pulled him like a noose. Tears stood out from his caked eyes. His pace quickened. His throat tightened as emotions welled within him. His knees sagged.

The doorway cut open for an instant and a figure darted out. It looked like a man, a father—maybe his father! Words formed on Kaehl's lips, struggling over the sound of his stumbling feet. The furtive figure turned toward the boy and froze. He shouted and gestured.

"Father!" Kaehl rasped. The word choked in his throat. The scene blurred, the figure dancing through waves of tears. The boy broke into a limping run.

The figure snarled at him, turned, and heaved the doorway into place. Turning back to Kaehl the man shouted and waved his fists. Kaehl stopped. The man backed down the hallway. Behind him Kaehl could hear the faraway thunder of an approaching crowd. Commuters? He wiped his eyes and squinted at the man. It was not his father. His knees began to shake. The man turned and ran down the hall. Kaehl sagged against the door and fell. His eyes closed. All was light.

Kaehl wandered aimlessly now, no longer running. Time had died. In the brightness of the hallway there was no day or night, no time at all. He ran his tongue over his cracked lips. The hunger in his belly was a dull ache.

How he had escaped being trampled by the last crowd he didn't know. He didn't care. His whole being was focused on finding food, water, and shelter in the endless, circling maze of hallways and shuttered, unyielding doors.

Kaehl knocked on some, kicked and beat against others, pleading, raging against their silence. They remained unyielding, cold. There were no openings, no life. The boy was alone.

Kaehl sagged to his knees. His strength was gone. He gave up. There were no tears left. Senseless, he slumped against the wall.

Kaehl awoke again. He rubbed his face, stretched, and sat up. He leaned against the wall, his head bowed, his eyes half closed, his arms draped over his knees.

A noise touched his ears. It was the sound of feet, a quiet slapping against the floor. They drew close, almost on top of him then falling away, one after another. Something brushed against him and stumbled. There was a muffled curse, then more running. The sounds seemed far away, as if from another hall. Dimly, the sounds pressed against his ears.

He snapped awake. People! Water! Food! Staggering to his feet he lurched, heaving himself along the wall, crying out in a cracked voice. He followed the sounds. They faded and disappeared. He pressed on. His feet dragged as he traveled a few feet, then a hundred more. There was no sound now save his own harsh breathing. Mumbling incoherently, crying dry tears, Kaehl moved doggedly forward.

"All is lost, all is lost, all is lost," he thought over and over. He became insensate, a stumbling figure of failing mechanics, one foot lifting and dragging against the other. The hallways sparkled with iridescent colors. His vision blurred.

He rounded a corner and turned down another hall. Through unfocused eyes he thought he saw a group of figures gathered in a doorway, seated young figures that rose in alarm at his presence. His vision died and he fell. Once again, all was light.

Pack

Peace. Quiet. Kaehl wandered through a landscape of fog and rolling black mist. He was alone but he was at peace. The jarring, blinding light was gone. There was no sound, no movement.

His pain was gone, his thirst and hunger forgotten. He flexed his muscles and felt newly strong, robust, newborn, like he could leap from the earth and fly.

The fog parted and green spaces appeared before him, opening onto a dazzling landscape he had never seen, clear and beautiful and broad. He wandered among lush hills, feeling the breeze against his face, running, leaping, dashing against the wind. His hands brushed greenery that reached to his waist, waving brown, tasseled crowns. Verdant growths rustled above him, laughing in the bustling breeze. A broad river wound through the hills beneath him, sparkling and serene, dotted with elegant winged creatures that took flight or landed with raucous, joyous noise. The air was clean and cool and alive.

Kaehl sat against the bole of one of the large growths, chewing one of the tasseled stems. Something flew by his ear. He batted at it absently, its low thrum murmuring in the background. The noise grew stronger, becoming discordant. He batted at it again. The colors grew dim, faded, thinning as if run through a sieve. The brightness began to crowd in on him again. Fog banks reappeared, covering the sunlit fields. He felt his sense of wonder turn to ache and heaviness. He lifted his hands to the hills that retreated before him, his fingers grasping, empty. The murmuring buzz grew harsh, intense.

The brightness deepened; his heartbeat tripled. His eyes screwed against the white—where did the greens go? The whiteness beat into his brain. He raised his arms to cover his eyes and cried out.

The noises died away. He lowered his arms and opened his eyes. The greenness was gone. He was in a room, a space that a moment before had been dark but abruptly filled with light, as if a light globe had switched on or off. There were figures around him, young figures, moving, agitated. Their voices grated against his ears.

A shadow passed over his face. He looked up. A very thin, dirty girl bent over him. She watched him closely, peering through greasy strands hanging over her face. She caught Kaehl's glance, rose and left the room.

Kaehl lifted his head and looked around. He was in a small alcove in an apartment, lying on a mat on the floor. Others in the room glanced at him as they walked by, their eyes hard. An older youth, lean and rangy, entered and knelt next to him.

They observed each other for a moment.

"Hungry?" the youth asked. His voice sounded measured and sure.

Kaehl nodded.

Food and a bag of water was pressed into his hand. He gulped greedily at the warm liquid, gagged, coughed, and drank again.

"We have to go. This area has been hunted out. Get up."

Kaehl stood and leaned against the wall, his knees shaking. The youth motioned to a nearby boy. The boy grabbed Kaehl's shoulder and steadied him. The older youth walked off.

"Walk. Eat," the new boy said. They left the alcove, the boy half-carrying Kaehl, and entered a common room. The apartments were very much like his home except the rooms were bigger and dirtier. Twenty young people, male and female, were crowded in it. Some were shouldering backpacks, others stretching their legs. A few glanced at him. They seemed nervous.

Kaehl stood on his wobbly legs, holding onto the wall, pain lancing his muscles. People glanced up quickly then looked away.

Two large youth stood near the hallway entrance. Kaehl squinted. Something was wrong with the door. The leather stays were stretched; the metal spikes had been jerked from the wall. A shudder gripped him. The door had been smashed, broken down. These were raiders. This house had once been lived in, maybe recently. He shivered again. He had found a Pack. His eyes darted to the guards as they watched him with cool detachment.

The older boy, who appeared to be their leader, knelt in his alcove and then walked to the hallway door. At a gesture from him everyone went silent. The guards slid the door aside and two tall males slipped into the brightness of the hallway and disappeared. Kaehl stopped eating.

One of the guards slipped back in and nodded to the older boy, who nodded in return. He slipped out again. Quickly the group moved into the hallway and began to jog after him. Kaehl and his escort fell in at the rear, taking up a slow trot. Tired though he was, Kaehl fell into the rhythm of the group. His limbs warmed up, working out the stiffness and pain. In near silence they glided like ghosts through the hall.

Kaehl awoke with a start. He was lying on a mat in another apartment. A ragged girl was bathing his forehead. He started to get up but fell backward, darkness exploding behind his eyes. He felt like a wall had collapsed on him. The girl arose and left. Alone, Kaehl tried to remember where he was. He remembered something about an endless run.

The leader came in and squatted next to him. The two stared at each other for a moment, then the young man placed a thin finger against Kaehl's chest.

"Dead man," he said.

Kaehl tensed, his skin growing clammy. He watched the wiry, muscular figure sit back on his heels. The face was unreadable. Sweat trickled down Kaehl's forehead.

The figure continued watching Kaehl in silence. Kaehl did not breathe. After a dozen heartbeats the youth stood and passed silently out of the room.

Slowly Kaehl let out his breath. Dizziness overcame him and he faded back into the light.

Kaehl awoke as rough hands seized him, jerking him to his feet. Potato cakes and carrots were stuffed into his hands and a water bottle slung over his neck. Gnawing at the food, Kaehl looked around him. The leader stood nearby, watching. Kaehl gulped from the water skin. As the youth stepped near, Kaehl backed against the wall.

"Now," the hard voice whispered. "No sound, no noise. Come. Now." The youth melted into the next room. The others who had outfitted him were already gone. Kaehl stumbled after them.

Two taller youths stood by the open door of a larger room, peering into the hallway. The rest crowded into the room, watching the leader, not moving. One of the youths who was listening intently at the door turned to the leader and nodded. The leader raised his arm and let it drop. Like shadows they flitted out of the room. Kaehl stumbled and groaned as something hit him in the back. He turned around. One of the bigger boys was jogging behind him, holding a short staff, smiling grimly. Kaehl fell in behind the others.

Kaehl was winded and gasping for breath as the group filed into another apartment. He felt like they had run dozens of miles. His muscles popped and knotted as he wheezed and sagged against a wall. The rear guard entered and closed the door. One of them advanced on Kaehl, brandishing his staff. He grabbed Kaehl by the neck and flung him into the center of the room, where other members of the group were walking. The guard walked away. Dazed, dizzy, Kaehl hung his head and joined the others. The guards, too, began slowly walking back and forth. Kaehl realized that they were stretching their legs.

All attention focused onto the center of the room. The leader had appeared from the back rooms of the apartment. He raised one hand, fist clenched tightly, then opened it. The crowd relaxed. People began to file off, staking out sleeping spaces, settling against the walls. Low conversations arose. Kaehl found a slot along a wall and slumped to the ground.

The leader came near and squatted in front of him.

"Why you here, boy?"

Kaehl shrank against the wall.

"You alive?"

Kaehl nodded his head.

"You don't talk much. Good. Almost lost you on your first run. Would've, if I'd seen you fall. Would've left you. Thought you was a dead man. But you lucky; Damen pick you up and bring you. Now you here. Know why?"

Kaehl shook his head.

"We need you. Lost two good bruds in a fracas a while ago. Been looking for someone to fill in. You stumbled into our camp; you'll do. You'll be a carrier." He looked over Kaehl's ragged clothes.

"Know where your home is, boy?"

Kaehl stammered, his eyes wide, his head shaking miserably.

"Good. Home's here now. We'll be in this stayover a few days, maybe longer. Rest up." The leader rose and spat. "Welcome home, carrier." He spun on his heels and left. Kaehl watched him go, tears stinging his eyes.

A young girl came in and knelt in front of him. She passed him cold roots and vegetables and a pitcher of water. He gulped the meal down while the girl waited. He handed the pitcher back to her and looked up into her eyes. "I want to go home," he said. Tears trickled over his cheeks. She stood silently and left. He drew his knees up and sat for a long time, rocking, ignored by the crowd. The tears itched where they had dried against his face. Eventually he lay down, curled his knees under his chin, and drifted to sleep.

Someone knelt beside him. Kaehl turned away, averting his eyes. He looked at the walls, the floor, anywhere but at the person. The figure beside him remained silent. At last Kaehl turned and looked up.

It was another girl. Deep, wide eyes peered out through long, greasy strands of thick, black hair. Her willowy neck rose from a ragged set of threadbare clothes hanging from her thin shoulders. Her feet were bare. Her face was starvation thin. She carried a dish of cold vegetables.

Silently she offered him a carrot. Kaehl hesitated, but his hunger pleaded. It tasted delicious. She offered him a drink.

"You are to eat," she said quietly. "We may leave at any time. Everyone have been told that the next time you faint by the road you are to be left. We cannot risk staying in the open too long. Eat. You will need strength."

Kaehl stared at his food. He wiped his mouth and resumed eating as the girl watched him silently.

Kaehl finished his meal and drank again. The girl motioned to him and they rose.

"I will show you the Pack," she said. The slender girl turned and left the room. Kaehl rose and followed. The girl led him from room to room, speaking in low tones to the people they found there. Kaehl was mostly ignored. A few acknowledged him with a glance and a grunt. No one exchanged names.

Everyone in the Pack was young, in their late to early teens. The leader may have been older. There was a mix of males and females, mostly males. All were thin and solemn. They looked worn but tough.

Kaehl edged closer to the girl. "How long have you been a member of the Pack?" he whispered.

"I have grown a span since being welcomed," she responded. "Most come here young. We have no old."

"Where were you before?"

"Before, I was elsewhere. Today I am here. Tomorrow we move on." The girl turned to him, her green eyes catching his for a moment. "It is suggested that one not ask too many questions. We do not speak much. You will learn the discipline of the Pack. In the light, in the hall, all is silent. That is law."

Kaehl nodded and looked at his feet.

The girl led him into a room piled with supplies, motioning him to a pile of backpacks and bags. "This is yours," she said, picking up a backpack. "You are soft and weak now, but you will learn." The boy flushed again. She continued: "Soon you will carry supplies such as you see here. To be a carrier is important. You will learn to be very strong." She turned to him and did not smile. "Or you will die."

She flipped the empty pack to him. It was built around a light framework. She helped him put it on, extending it over his head and tightening it around his shoulders. She tightened the belly band.

"The pack is light but will hold much weight. Its strength comes from being carefully loaded. Your strength will come from balancing it properly."

She adjusted the straps, testing them for tightness and give. Then she removed the pack and set it on the ground. "We will practice loading." The boy watched as she placed items from the pile into the pack, snugging them close. Adroitly she arranged the boxes and bags of vegetables and dried seeds and flour and meat. Meat! She added containers filled with flint and burners and cords and sundries that would help a moving Pack. Then she wound it together with ratgut and tied it tight. When finished, the pack was completely full, all spaces used.

"Now," she said, "put it on."

Kaehl looked at the pack dubiously and walked to it. Bending down he grasped it by the straps and tried to lift it. The pack slid across the floor but did not rise. He tried again. Sweat popped from his brow. He released the straps and backed away.

The girl frowned. "Learn quickly," she snapped. He watched as she strode to the pack and, in one swift motion, knelt before it, slipped her arms through the shoulder straps, fitted the brow strap over her forehead and leaned forward. As the weight of the pack shifted to her back she leaned forward more. She shifted her weight, took one step forward, and rose. She flashed him a triumphant smile and jogged around the room. With a flourish she backed to a wall, slid the pack down it until it rested on the ground and then slipped from the straps and stood up. She seemed to tower over the boy.

"Now," she said evenly, "Practice."

Kaehl quickly learned how to load and unload his pack. Carrying the weight was another matter. The girl was stronger than her thin frame looked. He spent his time at this stayover practicing lifting, carrying, and jogging. The girl surveyed his efforts silently. Sometimes he imagined a flicker of approval on her face.

During the next move, Kaehl ran at the rear of the Pack. The weight he carried was heavy, but with proper balance it handled well. One strap chafed him about the shoulder so he adjusted it. The cramps that had crawled through his legs and back as he started out melted as he stretched his legs in the group's moderate gait.

The Pack ran silently, smoothly. Kaehl had no idea where they were headed; his whole focus was in staying near the figure in front of him. The light swallowed figures whole if they moved too far away.

Kaehl stumbled and nearly fell as he turned a sharp corner and the floor sloped upward. He quickly adjusted his steps. The hallway narrowed then opened again. Kaehl fell and skinned one knee as the slope suddenly ended. He picked himself up and hurried after the unhesitating Pack.

Kaehl halted abruptly, almost ramming a male who had stopped in front of him. The big youth turned and slammed him against the wall, clapping a dirty hand over his mouth. The rear guard rushed past.

The youth wagged a cautioning finger at the boy and released him, slowly moving ahead. No sound could be heard save the muffled breathing of the Pack.

Edging near, Kaehl saw a tight knot of figures kneeling near a poorly maintained door. One stood up. It was the leader. Silently the other boys rose about him. The two runners split up, one brushing by Kaehl. They stopped beyond the edges of the Pack, taking up sentinel positions.

An area was cleared about the leader. Four guards moved in front of him. They listened intently at the door. One of the guards looked up. They tensed. The leader nodded, and all four rammed their shoulders against the door. The heavy wood shuddered and heaved. They surged against it again, sending it crashing inward. Stumbling over the wreckage, they poured into the apartment. Other members of the Pack quickly followed.

Kaehl hesitated. Sounds of scuffling and smashing could be heard. Someone screamed. The runners shoved Kaehl inside.

The apartment was a chaos. Pack members dashed across the rooms, ransacking bins and pots, emptying cupboards. Sounds of struggle could be heard in the other rooms. The runners heaved the broken door back into place. Kaehl turned to help them. They propped the door up and tried to secure it but the leather fastenings were useless; the metal anchors had been pulled right out of the wall. They jury-rigged the door and stood against it.

The Pack members gathered in the common area. Food and supplies raided from the cupboards were piled in the middle of the room. "A good haul," someone whispered. The leader walked in from an anteroom and surveyed them. His face was bloody, his eyes shining. He smiled. Two guards emerged behind him. Through the agitated mass of Pack members Kaehl could see them carrying a limp, elderly figure. The electric tension in the crowd increased. The leader raised one hand above his head, palm forward. The Pack members raised their arms in token. Many of them made fists and dropped their arms.

The leader counted the remaining hands and smiled grimly. He nodded at the guards. They carried the old man to the door and waited while the runners pried it open. Then they slipped through. The door closed again.

Another guard appeared, dragging a crying, white-faced boy. A cheer went up from the crowd, which was quickly silenced. The leader moved toward him, peering into his eyes, feeling his ribs, squeezing his arm until the boy cried out. The leader nodded again and the boy was thrust into the Pack.

The guard returned to the anteroom. Further sounds of scuffling could be heard, followed by a despairing, sobbing scream that was suddenly cut short. The crowd roared again.

The guards appeared at the doorway carrying a limp figure between them. It was a thin, bedraggled girl, perhaps fifteen years old. A dirty rag had been tied over her mouth; her hands were bound behind her back. They dumped the semi-conscious girl in front of the pile of loot and backed away. A struggling line of males circled her, trying to keep the females of the Pack away. The girl shook her head and looked about, her eyes fogged and dull. Suddenly she snapped awake and backed into the pile of goods. Tears streamed down her face. She coughed and gagged, apparently trying to scream.

The leader moved through the ring of males and bent down to her. Kaehl could not hear his words but the girl shrank back even farther. He leaned forward to touch her face. She moved as if to slap at him. The leader stood up, smiled, and raised his arms. The men stood aside and the circle collapsed over the girl.

Kaehl felt weak. He leaned against the door, his knees trembling. He looked at the struggling mass of youth. Someone was screaming. The new boy was frantically pounded at a smiling guard.

Kaehl turned and saw the leader standing apart, looking at him. The elder boy smiled, his eyes dark. Kaehl heaved himself upright and moved into another room.

Nights were painful. Packed in among the other youth, Kaehl slept very little. He feared sleep. He feared his dreams. Over and over he would dream of his father on the floor, crying, his mother staring at her son with hate-filled eyes. Then Kaehl would see Selda, wrapped in her blanket, playing with her doll, cooing. Father would advance on her, again and again, his eyes red, his fists clenched. Kaehl could see the fear in her eyes as she glanced up. She would scream for Kaehl over and over. He was not there for her.

Kaehl would then awake, bathed in sweat. He would look around frantically, ready to fight, searching for his father, his mother, his sister. But they were not there. There was only the jumbled mass of the sleeping Pack.

Then he would sigh and lean against the wall, running a hand over his face. How many nights had he dreamed this? Sometimes he imagined his mother pleading with him, warning him to not join the Packs. "They kill, they break into our homes and steal our food. They raid our factories. They fight. They are the reason we bolt our doors, why we run in the halls, why you can't go out, why we fear." Then the scene would change. "We need you. Who'll bathe Selda?" He pictured Selda in her bath, shivering, her arms wrapped around her thin chest, her eyes accusing. He longed to go back to his family to help them, to keep them safe. But once again he would see his father on the floor, crying. Kaehl could see the truth, rising like its own nightmare: He was his father. He couldn't return. He could never return.

Night after night Kaehl sat against the wall, his eyelids drooping, his head low. Eventually he would drift to sleep. Some nights, if he was lucky, the dreams would not return.

Over time, Kaehl grew to be accepted by the Pack. He watched runners go out each day accompanied by four or five guards. They returned with foods the boy had never seen before and which no one could name. He longed to go out with them and leave the smelly confines of the crowded apartments. He watched them come and go, trying to learn their routines. He spent his free time exercising, building his stamina and strength.

Kaehl also learned more about his status in the Pack. He had started out as a newcomer, or "newt." All newts were given the hardest and most dangerous tasks. Their job was to carry the Pack's supplies. The goods they carried, if lost, could mean days of hunger for everyone. Ideally, on a run, they would be able to keep up, but if they slowed the Pack down they would be left behind. Sometimes in emergencies the older boys grabbed backpacks from the carriers and fled. Carriers were expendable.

The guards were prized for their strength and slow wit. They had charge of the attacks, breaking down the doors and subduing the residents. They also had the highest number of casualties. On runs, they formed the rear guard.

Other than the leaders, the most envied people in the Pack were the runners. They took the point position during runs and were most effective as scouts and spies. They were totally trusted and heavily relied upon. During stayovers the runners would range throughout the halls, testing doors, plotting routes, watching for rival groups, security teams, and vengeful residents. They were the eyes and ears of the Pack. They had their own spaces and were given unchallenged pick of the spoils. Most boys envied these youth and dreamed of joining them.

The Pack stayed in an apartment until driven out by hunger or force. They then began a Run, heading to the safest location the runners had identified. As soon as they entered their new home they repaired or replaced the door if possible, guards were stationed, and all would rest. If the Pack was short on food and none was found in the apartment, runners would immediately set out again, looking for other unprotected locations.

They would travel in pairs and return to inform the Pack, who would then set out to move in or assault the place. If they found sufficient food, the Pack would stay and raid from that location. Normally little sound carried between dwellings, but the noise of a raid could sometimes be terrific. They tried to raid far away from their stayover but occasionally that was not possible. Too much harassment would lead to reprisal and attacks upon the Pack itself. Long before that occurred, the Pack would be gone.

Rarely was the Pack called to defend itself during a run, but if they were attacked while in the halls, everyone would flee. They tried to stay together and follow the Runners but individual survival trumped loyalty. The strong survived. Pursuit usually didn't last long—no one knew the halls better than the Packs—but falling into the hands of vengeful locals was terrible.

At the moment there were five females in this Pack. All were thin and athletic. Girls were full members and given tasks based on merit. Physical attractiveness was unimportant. They joined the Pack by either being stolen or chanced upon. Most couldn't adjust to Pack life or didn't want to. These were abandoned or simply died. Those who adjusted were valued. Girls were adept at foraging, strategy, patience, and settling disputes. They were especially valued by the older boys, although Kaehl didn't know why.

The newest girls were terrified of being in the pack but were equally terrified of being deserted in the halls. The girls who had survived the pack the longest resented it the most, but they learned to live with it and in some ways rule it. They had a powerful hold over the male leaders, and their counsel was usually accepted. When fights broke out or when they welcomed newcomers they could be bitterly cruel. At these times, the males kept their distance.

Muscle and charisma made rule, and the strongest, most forceful boy was the leader. The whole Pack was his. The older girls formed a council through which he planned strategies, but the arm for carrying out and defending his policies was his own. Four big males extended his reach and were given special treatment to maintain their loyalty. Rivalry was crushed. Kaehl quickly learned which side to stay on.

The females kept to the back rooms when they weren't running some duty. Except for one or two, the leaders kept a strict separation between men and women. When the girls mixed with the general crowd, Kaehl noticed a definite change in attitudes. The boys became distracted, much more tense and competitive. Some became downright loopy but they were immediately disciplined.

One of Kaehl's assignments led him past the girls' area. He glanced into one of their cleaning rooms as he passed their door. On the other side of the door he stopped, backed up, and stared.

The girl they had claimed in the last raid sat on the floor next to the drain hole, clad in what used to be a white shift, a dish held loosely in one hand. A scraper lay on the floor next to the other hand. Her face was turned toward him but her gaze was on the ground. She did not move or look up.

Kaehl stared at her for several moments. Her face was deadly white, her eyes staring, empty, vacant. Her mouth bobbed slowly, mechanically, as if pulled by a string. Her hair was tangled and greasy; her body swaying slightly. She had lost much weight.

Kaehl debated about checking on her. Sickness was a terrifying thing in the Tower, but even more so in the Packs. With no medical services and very uneven food, a simple cold could kill. Someone should be told.

He opened his mouth to call to her.

"What do you want?" someone behind him demanded.

Kaehl whirled around. The leader's girl, her face very red, stood behind him, her hands on her hips.

Kaehl pointed. "That girl. She's sick."

The elder girl glanced at her over his shoulder, then glared at Kaehl again. "Get out," she said.

"But..."

"Get out!" she screamed. She thrust her fingers into his hair and jerked him away. Kaehl cried out, turned and fled. He did not look back.

He dropped to the floor next to the newest boy, who was hunched against the wall, his head down. Kaehl held out a bowl of roots. The boy looked up, startled. His eyes flashed to the bowl then turned away.

"Wow; that hurt," he said, rubbing his head. "Don't mess with the girls."

The boy drew into a ball.

"Hey, it's okay," Kaehl whispered. "I just wanted to say hi." The boy pressed into the wall and covered his head. A few eyes turned his way.

Kaehl bent near, trying not to attract attention. "You're new, I know. My name's Kaehl." The eyes drifted away.

"I just. . ." The boy jumped up and ran into a back room. Kaehl remained on his haunches. He picked up a few roots and chewed them thoughtfully.

The next morning Kaehl was assigned cesspit duty. "I want to see my face on that floor," smirked the senior girl, handing him a bucket and a long-handled scraper. The guard standing next to her guffawed. Kaehl forced a smile and turned to go, nearly knocking a figure behind him to the floor. It was the new boy.

"You're late, smiley," said the girl, handing him a bucket. "You're with him."

The new boy glanced at Kaehl and then lowered his gaze. Kaehl started toward the cesspit. The boy hugged the bucket to his chest and turned to follow. The guard aimed a kick in his direction, sending him sprawling after Kaehl. Laughter followed them to the cesspit.

"Smiley?" asked Kaehl, setting his bucket on the cesspit's floor. The boy's face burned. He set his bucket down and wrapped his arms around his chest. He closed his eyes.

"Here," Kaehl said. "Take this. Start scraping toward the hole." Kaehl shoved the scraper into the boy's hand. The boy took it and began pushing muck toward the drain hole. The smell was unbelievable.

Kaehl wrinkled his nose. "Ugh. These people are such slobs. Why is there so much blood?" Kaehl set his bucket under the tap and opened the valve. "I'd like to see her face on this floor all right. Well, at least in this stayover we have water."

The boy scraped muck into the hole while the bucket filled. Kaehl splashed water over the floor, directing the stream toward the drain. The boy danced away and waited for the water to disappear.

"One more time," Kaehl advised. "We gotta get rid of the brown stuff." The boy started scraping again. Kaehl sat the bucket down.

"You got a name?" Kaehl asked. The boy kept scraping.

"Smiley then. You okay? You look like you lost weight since the welcome. You eating?" Smiley said nothing. "You gotta eat. Mother ain't around no more."

Smiley's head dropped. His hands slacked. Kaehl heard a sob and saw tears splash onto the floor.

"Hey, guy, it's okay, it's okay," Kaehl said, putting a hand on his shoulder. The boy whirled way and faced him, brandished his scraper.

"NO IT'S NOT! IT'S NOT OKAY," he shouted. "WHERE'S MY GRANDFATHER?"

Kaehl backed away, his hands up. "Hey, I don't know. I saw them take him away. I don't know what happened to him."

"Why can't I talk to my sister? She doesn't look well. What's wrong with her?"

Kaehl's look was guarded. "She's part of the Pack now, Smiley. Newts like us don't talk to girls."

"She's not a girl she's my sister and DON'T CALL ME SMILEY!" He swung the scraper. Kaehl caught it easily and jerked it away from him. Pulled off his feet, Smiley crashed on the damp floor and started writhing slowly, clutching his head.

"Where's your mother?" Kaehl asked. "She live here?"

"Noooo," he moaned. "She's dead."

"How about your father?"

The boy brought his fists to his head, grabbed his hair, and screamed.

Kaehl knelt beside him. Guards appeared at the door. "He fell," Kaehl said, standing. "He's okay." They hauled Smiley to his feet, looked into his eyes, gave each other a knowing look, and began hauling him away. His legs dragged in the muck.

As they passed Kaehl the boy lifted his head. "Benz," he said. "My name is Benz."

"Kaehl. I'm Kaehl."

The trio left the room. "Please be easy on him," Kaehl called. He turned back toward the drain and lifted the scraper. "He's not well."

Many days later a guard approached Kaehl. The big youth swaggered up to him and jerked a thumb his way.

"Boy. Newt. Yeah, you," he said. "Come on. We need a carrier today." Kaehl felt his chest tighten. He nodded and ran for his backpack.

"Move yourself, Newt. Lots to haul." Kaehl fell in behind six other boys as they filed out the door and started down the hall.

They jogged smoothly through the heavy light, up one incline and another, then along another hall, then up several more. They pulled up at one end of a branching corridor. The leader pulled them into an alley. A regular mechanical thumping sounded in the distance.

"Tuerk, you lead," he said, pointing to the second guard. "You three will follow him. Grab and snatch, but keep it quiet. Hide anywhere. We'll go until the sacks are full. There is a door opposite our entrance. If discovered, head for that. We won't wait for stragglers. Remember how we came here." Kaehl wondered how anyone could remember the way without landmarks. "We three will hold the sacks. We'll spot for you and help you unload. Get ready."

The raiders distributed their sacks. The head guard lifted a hand, held it for a moment, then let it fall. The raiders moved down the hall toward the noise. They pulled off at a broken-down area, picked their way through fallen rock and emerged behind a stack of packing crates in a cavernous room that throbbed with wheezing machinery. Keeping low, the leader motioned to the left and right. Four raiders slunk off. The remaining three took up positions behind some crates.

Cautiously, his blood pulsing in his temples, Kaehl peered out from behind a box. He gasped explosively. The room was twice as high as any apartment he had seen and wider than a hundred sleeping rooms together. Baskets, cartons, crates and barrels littered the floor, all overhung with purplish, glowing boxes standing over long rows of trays.

The Pack's raiders moved among the trays, indiscriminately plucking items from them and stuffing them into sacks. Kaehl looked intently to see they were stealing. His eyes widened. Food! Vegetables! The room was crammed with them! Plants fingered up through soil packed in neat rows of in boxes lined by water troughs. Thousands hung from the ceiling, water trickling down long tendrils. The boxes were filled with their fruit.

One of the group slipped back up an aisle and exchanged sacks with the head guard. "No troops anywhere," he whispered, grinning. "I told you this would be easy!" He headed back down the aisle. Kaehl thought of the bounty each meal would be from now on. Another youth returned, then another. Kaehl turned to the leader.

"Are there places like this everywhere the Pack stops?" he whispered.

"No!" he replied. "We've only found three so far. There may be others. Now keep quiet!" Kaehl settled down again to watch. The air was so heavy with moisture that the plants dripped. Another raider moved up the aisle, carrying an overloaded sack of vegetables, smiling broadly. A tomato fell from the top of his sack. He stooped to grab it, straightened up and turned into the swinging end of a very large mace.

He never felt it hit.

Long before the blow had landed, the place was empty of raiders. A few screams sounded as Kaehl pounded down the hall, following two fleeing guards. Then all was silence, silence and pounding feet.

Much later the trio stopped in a broken alcove. Kaehl felt a wave of nausea snap up in him. He crashed to the ground, listening to his heart triphammer against his chest, his breath ripping out of his lungs. A pool of sweat widened beneath him. His legs trembled violently, his arms sagging uselessly over his chest.

How long Kaehl and the guards lay there he could not tell. Once they stiffened as a growling, cawing crowd rushed by, inches from their shelter. Then they relaxed again. As Kaehl leaned back against the wall his hand brushed against something yielding. He picked it up in astonishment. A sack! It was one of the sacks given to him in the garden. It was brimming with fresh vegetables. The others had left their sacks behind. Kaehl held it up to the others and beamed.

"Yeah, Hegwald. Two lost. Kip died right there, and Jurg says he lost Rapf. Ain't seen him since. Everybody else made it."

Surk stood before Hegwald, gritting out the story. Two sacks had been salvaged out of eight, only Kaehl's being full. Hegwald's eyes smoldered. Surk dipped his head and backed away.

"Newt," he barked. Eyes down, sweat dotting his palms, Kaehl stood before Hegwald. *Finally,* he thought, *I learned the leader's name.* Hegwald surveyed him critically.

"You've been with us three runs, a good carrier in one. You kept your head in that raid and held onto your sack. You run as well as the leads, some say better." The guards shifted nervously. Kaehl studied details of the floor.

"Rapf was a runner, the best one," Hegwald continued. "You'll run for us. Learn from Rec. He's the best, now."

Kaehl gaped. A runner? A runner! He smiled triumphantly and returned to the crowd, his head held high. Hegwald motioned to his guards and they moved away.

Kaehl felt a tap on his shoulder. He turned to see Rec staring at him sadly. Rec motioned for Kaehl to follow him.

Together they walked into the common room and sat against a wall. There was a long time of silence between them.

"You miss Rapf?" Kaehl eventually asked.

"Yeah," Rec replied, his shoulders sagging. "Been buds a long time."

Kaehl put a hand on Rec's shoulder. Rec shrugged it off. He sighed and got to his feet. "You gonna run?" he asked, looking at Kaehl.

Kaehl beamed eagerly and jumped up. "You bet!"

"Come on, then. Gotta scout new territory." He turned to go out the door but stopped and looked back. "One more: you ain't a newt no more. Got a name?"

Kaehl held his breath, momentarily dazed. It seemed years since he had used it. "Yeah," he mumbled at last. Then he grinned. "Yeah; Kaehl. My name is Kaehl."

Kaehl ran every day with Rec, heaving his legs before him, leaving a trail of perspiration. After returning to the stayover he would collapse into his new quarters, a room reserved just for runners, lungs aching. In the halls Kaehl learned of the circular arrangement of the Tower, with floors built around the gigantic central shaft. He learned the division of the Tower into general tiers, of which this Pack inhabited the lower middle. He learned where the hydroponics gardens were and where the power station and air circulation plants were. He also learned of the distribution of families around the Shaft. Five concentric hallways encircled the Shaft at each level, with some additional hallways along the furthest hall.

"You are living in the tallest building in the world," Rec announced as they shared a meal of roots and meat, delicacies reserved for the leaders. "Each floor was built to hold 1,800 people. But the population grew faster than the Framers had planned. People started having more children, many more, maybe twice as many as planned. And they all grew up and had children of their own. So they just added on."

"Where'd you learn that?" Kaehl asked.

"I've been around. My dad used to do maintenance on the breather systems, up and down, fix this, broken that… I used to think his job was the best, something I wanted to do. But then the stories got old. And Dad got old. After a while his stories drove me crazy."

"What happened?"

Rec's gaze dropped. He dug at the floor with his heels. "We split."

Kaehl watched a spider skitter across the floor. It stopped to investigate a dead worm. Unimpressed, it moved on.

"Anyway," Rec gestured down the hall with his chin. "Most of the time we try not to raid families. We try to live in empty quads, raiding farms, factories and storehouses far from our apartment. The gardens are usually too heavily guarded. If we're going to hit families, the best ones are those farthest from the core. They're the wealthiest, and they have the biggest places. Seems like they think that the farther from the Shaft they are, the better. The families in them think they've hit the big time, made it to the top, that they're all right. But really they're just dumb. Fat and dumb, careless, feeling too secure, just ripe for raids. Once we hit them they surrender quickly. Or they do until after the first raid. Then their neighbors know we're in the area. Then they fight back." He rubbed his head. "That's why we avoid them. They can be mean."

Rec had met two other Packs in the Tower. They circled each other around the core, not seeking attacks, not wanting war. Blood feuds, however, had been known to erupt, especially when food was scarce. Locals looking for revenge didn't care which Pack they hit or which had caused the problems. Kaehl learned the limitations and boundaries that kept the Packs in balance.

One morning, Rec roused Kaehl out of a sound sleep. Leaner and stronger now than he had ever been at home, Kaehl awoke easily, instantly alert.

"Gotta do a check-run today. Got some probs with the locals."

Kaehl nodded and stood. Padding about his morning business he pondered Rec's meaning. Evidently Rec and Hegwald had been in conference. Someone sensed danger from the locals.

Filling a small sack with vegetables and nuts, topping off his water skin, Rec and Kaehl walked to the guards, who pulled back the door. They slipped into the hallway and padded away.

Morning runs invigorated the flesh and moved the blood. Kaehl loped easily beside Rec, their feet thumping quietly against the floor. In the weeks that he had been working with Rec his muscles had hardened and lengthened. He had learned to stretch them carefully before and after each run.

The two had been running only a short distance when they pulled up at an alcove adjoining several dwellings. Rec motioned Kaehl to silence.

A few minutes passed. Kaehl could hear water running through a main somewhere near and occasional angry shouts from inside an apartment. Then, quietly, he could hear wood and leather scrape against stone. He recognized the sound—hallway doors were being opened. The pair pulled themselves deeper into the alcove.

Figures stepped into the bright hallway. Doors eased shut and latches were secured.

They could hear voices, sounding relaxed and familiar. They chatted quietly, conversationally, passing time. *Sloppy security,* Kaehl thought. Down the hall they could hear the boiling chaos of an approaching crowd. Kaehl looked in astonishment at Rec, suddenly fearful. Kaehl and Rec sat like statues. The crowd pulled up in front of the alcove and went silent. Rec shook his head at Kaehl. Together they became part of the wall.

Someone addressed the crowd. The voice was muffled in the crowded hallway but they could hear snatches.

"...Hit two in the garden... maybe... yeah, it's a Pack, all right. We'll get 'em, though!... Still working... discuss later..." the conversation was cut by babbles and rages from the crowd. More roaring erupted and the crowd moved off.

"How did you know they'd gather here?" Kaehl whispered after the crowd left.

"Experience," Rec responded gloomily.

"Were they talking about us?"

Rec returned a withering glare.

The two runners remained motionless a few moments more and then Rec arose.

"We gotta get back," he whispered. "They're out for blood, may come tonight, after work. They never attack during work hours. We'll have to decamp today."

Kaehl stood up, eyes troubled. "Already?" Rec nodded. The two trotted off. "Where will we go?"

"We got a place. Been scouted already. Always scout two ahead."

The Pack took the news stolidly and prepared to go. Kaehl and Rec rounded up the raiding party and then rested as their few belongings were packed and given to the carriers. Kaehl caught sight of Benz, the boy that had been snatched from the last raid. He was thin and pale and red-eyed from crying. Obviously, his adjustment to the Pack wasn't going well. The memory of his own introduction flooded back to him. With difficulty he pushed it aside.

So much food had been gathered that another carrier was pulled into service to haul it all. The Pack formed up inside the apartment, silent and tense. Kaehl and Rec slipped out the door, surveyed the hall for danger, and led off.

Kaehl followed close behind Rec, not knowing their destination. It felt good to be a leader, trotting easily at the head of the Pack. The lifestyle was abrupt and violent but here was respect and freedom. He had made a name for himself. People depended on him. He had arrived.

The Pack moved without incident through the halls. They ascended four floors and crossed to another side of the shaft, stopping outside the third hallway. Pressed into an empty storage room, they rested momentarily.

Rec and Kaehl advanced on a signal from Hegwald. Cautiously they approached a door. Kaehl saw nothing unusual about it. Rec looked back and motioned for the four guards to follow. They approached and took up positions, examining the door, listening.

All at once three of them stepped back and bulled forward. With a thunderous crack the door fell inward, smashing onto the floor. Screams erupted from the interior. The rest of the Pack quickly boiled in. Kaehl and Rec took up positions in the hall, anxiously watching for signs of Locals. Three Pack members struggled to refit the door back into its frame. Kaehl and Rec slipped inside just before it closed.

By the time they got inside, the interior of the house was chaos. Someone lay beside the door in a pool of blood.

Kaehl pulled Rec aside. "This is stupid!" he said. "We shouldn't raid a place with locals hunting us. We should have waited, gone to an empty quad or something. This is crazy!"

Rec shook him off and joined the Pack.

Residents had fled into the back rooms. Screams and scuffling could be heard in back. Pack members ransacked closets and containers for any goods they could find. Clothing, boxes, and dishes were strewn across the floor. Youth rushed back and forth, yelling, exulting over their finds. Kaehl and a guard stood near the door, watching, listening for noise from outside.

The sounds of conflict died. The pile on the floor grew. Pack members gathered around, talking excitedly. A cheer went up as the leader appeared, smiling broadly. He held up a hand, fist closed, and opened it. The people cheered again, and crowded close.

Kaehl watched in growing unease as two older figures were herded out of a room, their hands tied behind their backs, sacks over their head. Jeering, the crowd spat and slapped at them. They were herded out the door and away. The door closed.

A guard stepped forward, a young teenage boy by his side. The boy's face was pale but his head upright. He voluntarily walked into the Pack.

The crowd grew restless. From the smile on Hegwald's face they knew what was coming. They began to whistle and stamp their feet. The girls struggled to get inside the restraining ring of boys. Kaehl's eyes searched for Benz' sister. He didn't see her.

A guard stepped out of a back room, his face split by an ugly smile of triumph. A girl emerged behind him, blood oozing from her nose, trying to hold together her ripped tunic. The two stepped into the noisy celebration of the Pack. Then another guard emerged from behind the first, pulling with him another girl. Her head was erect, her eyes full of fire. The crowd went wild. The jostling became shoving, and bodies pressed forward. The first girl was thrust into their outstretched hands. The screaming began.

Kaehl noticed Benz at the back of the Pack, slumped on the floor, sobbing. Kaehl looked at the mob, then at Rec, then at the mob again. He turned slightly and put his shoulder to the door. It budged.

"C'mon, Rec, let's go. Let's find the next stayover."

Rec stared at him, astonished. "Hey, what about the welcome? They're just getting started! The run can wait."

Tears clouded Kaehl's eyes. He shoved against the door, wedged his body through, and disappeared. Rec grabbed at him but missed. "Kaehl!" he shouted, then cursed and pulled a confused guard to the door. "Close it!" he shouted, then squeezed out.

Rec found Kaehl jogging aimlessly, tears streaming down his face. "Idiot! What're you doing? You left the door open, coulda killed us all. And leaving during a Welcome... You rot, you know it?"

Kaehl said nothing, continuing to move down the hall. Confused, Rec took up a pace beside him.

"So why'd you leave?" Rec asked at last.

Kaehl turned to him and stopped. "Those families—this is evil! Our pack is killing people! The noise, the celebration—we're a mob, and we just shouted it to the whole neighborhood! And those girls—what are they doing to those girls? Those girls are scared to death—terrified! Whatever you're doing, they hate it. Bad!"

Rec motioned violently. "Keep your voice down! We're in the halls!" He shrugged. "I don't know; it's what we've always done. The girls hate it the first time but after that those who are still alive don't mind joining in. They protest a little but eventually they really go wild for it. Everyone knows that."

"No they don't." Kaehl whispered. "Wild? They were wild, all right. They'd kill you if they could. Did you see the girls in our Pack, that look in their eyes? They looked like they were going to kill those girls. It wasn't fun, for sure. Later on—I don't know, maybe that's all they've been told to do. Maybe they get used to it. I've only known my own sister. But it doesn't make sense. I would hate it and fight against it with everything I had. I would never do anything that made anyone as scared and angry and hurt as that! And killing someone…! Anything that hurts someone that much must be evil! Can't you feel it? Doesn't it hurt you? Wouldn't you be angry?"

"Well, I don't know, Kaehl," Rec mumbled. "I'd never thought about it. At least, I haven't thought about it much. It's just what we do. You get used to it, I guess."

"Used to it?" Kaehl choked, his voice rising. "And where did they take the older people, the ones they carried out? What happened to them? Do you know?"

"They're gone, Kaehl, gone. Too old to do anyone any good." His fists clenched. "They're the ones that hurt us. Get rid of them and we're safe. They're gone and I'm glad. Serves them right."

"Serves them right? What are you talking about, Rec? Those are living people. They're probably those girls' father and mother; they could have been your father and mother. Don't you care about that?"

"Ain't had a father or mother for years. Father was a drunk, mother a witch. I was glad to be gone. Glad, glad, glad I tell ya." Rec turned away. "It's what we do. It's what we're supposed to do."

They moved down the hall again, jogging in silence. Then Kaehl blurted out, "Where are we going?"

Rec started and recovered, grimacing. "Hah! I have no idea. This is your little trip, remember?" He turned a corner abruptly. "We're out here looking for the next stayover instead of being back at the Welcome, that's where we're going." He picked up the pace and they moved together down the hall.

After a few miles, Kaehl began to feel foolish about leaving the Welcome. Still, the screams of those girls—they echoed. He felt like he would hear them forever. He shuddered.

Rec led Kaehl up five levels of the Tower. The neighborhood grew poorer. They continued to jog.

Rec suddenly stopped and motioned Kaehl to silence. They moved into a more brightly lit alcove. Rec spoke in whispers.

"Back there, four doors. Unsealed. You see it?" Kaehl stared solemnly at him. "Daydreaming, huh? Well wake up. Unsealed door means easy pickings, or a safe, deserted shelter. The place may be empty or maybe there's people and they're sick or something. Maybe just careless. We'll go back and check."

Staying close to the wall, the two moved toward the unsecured door. Kaehl searched it with his eyes but could see nothing out of place. Rec pointed to two strips of leather jammed into the door, barely showing over the wood. Cautiously he and Kaehl bent to the door and listened. Silence.

"We'll come back later with a raiding party, see what's going on. Maybe it's being used as a storeroom." The two continued jogging.

Suddenly Rec halted, staring down the hall. Kaehl followed his eyes and gasped. A thin edge of darkness showed along one side of the doorway. An apartment door was open! Rec turned to Kaehl and whispered, "Easy picking here. We'd better bring a raid back here soon." He stared back down the hall. "Come on. The Welcome's probably over. I'm hungry."

Kaehl hesitated for a moment, watching Rec disappear down the hall. Then he stumped after him.

Kaehl and Rec slowed as they neared the stayover. Something was happening ahead of them; the hall was filled with sound. Not the sound of a family arguing behind closed doors, not rats fighting in the pipes, not even the thunderous roar of an oncoming crowd. Chaotic noise, random, violent. People fighting.

Kaehl felt his heart hammer against his chest. Unconsciously the runners picked up speed and raced forward.

Kaehl rounded a corner and tripped, falling on his face. He turned to see what he had hit.

It was a body. A teenaged male lay sprawled on the floor, blood seeping from under him. Kaehl recognized him as one of the guards from the Pack. Horrified, Kaehl pushed himself up and moved forward more cautiously.

Kaehl could hear sounds of combat. Angry shouts, people smashing into each other, the sound of wreckage. He slowed again, inching forward.

He peered around a corner. A knot of angry men stood at the entrance to their stayover, swinging makeshift clubs. The door was gone. *The locals must have smashed it in,* he thought. Men were moving in and out. Three or four teenagers lay on the ground. Kaehl stayed back, afraid, unsure of what to do.

"The locals must have followed the Pack from our last stayover," he whispered. "Bloodthirsty lot. Or maybe the new neighborhood had a long memory. This looks like revenge, very bloody revenge. I told them this was a stupid idea. Somebody heard us! I..."

With a howl, someone rushed past him toward the door, nearly knocking Kaehl to the floor. It was Rec. He picked up a fallen club and lashed out, bringing down two of the men at the door. The others gave way, astonished. Rec swept into the stayover.

The noise inside the apartment rose to a frenzy. Screams and howls erupted, followed by heavier sounds of combat. The figures outside the door shifted uneasily, looking at each other.

Rec burst out the door, crowded close by other Pack members. One of the men in the hall half raised his club, backing away. He went down heavily.

Howling, the remnants of the Pack streamed toward Kaehl. Rec rushed past. Kaehl backed up, stumbled, then turned and sped after him, the battle-crazed Pack at his heels. The locals were quickly left behind.

Rec led the Pack down the hallways, up ramps and through connecting corridors. At last, exhausted, he slowed to a stop. The Pack gathered around, breathing heavily.

Kaehl looked carefully at the remnants of the group. Ten members, all male. No leader, two guards, a few others. All wounded and very grim.

Rec spoke. "This it? No one else?" Heads nodded. He sighed. "Salvage anything?" No comments. "Okay, let's go."

Slowly, limping, the devastated Pack followed Rec along the corridors, down the ramps to the next stayover.

The door to their target hadn't changed since they had left it. There were no preliminaries. After listening briefly, three of their biggest members pushed at the open door. It fell inward.

Kaehl stood in the hallway, slumped against the wall, head hanging. He prayed that no one was inside that apartment; the Pack meant business today.

A scream erupted from inside. Kaehl's blood froze. There was another scream, and another. Kaehl leaped into the room.

The males were gathered in the center of the room. An emaciated girl leaned on her arms on the floor in front of them, her head hanging down. The boys were surging, angry. The ceremonies would be brief today. Kaehl looked around the room, his heartbeat quickening. Then he focused on the girl. A sob rose in his throat. Tears sprang to his eyes.

One of the guards bent over the writhing figure, trying to look at her face. The girl screamed again. Kaehl snarled and crashed through the Pack, knocking the guard to the floor. Kaehl reached the girl and knelt in front of her. He brushed back her hair and lifted her chin. She flailed her arms and bit at him and tried to pull away but he held her firm. Her face, miry with tears, was almost unrecognizable. But he knew her.

The Pack was rabid, angry, confused. They closed about the two, hovering. The girl looked up and screamed again.

"What are you doing, Kaehl?" asked Rec.

"Sister!" Kaehl shouted, turning toward them, his arms over her head. "She's my sister!"

The Pack backed away. The teenagers looked at each other, unsure.

"Did you find anyone else?" Kaehl shouted, his voice frantic. "Anyone else back there?"

Heads shook. "Empty," one said. "Except for her."

"No bodies?"

"No."

"Then leave her alone. Don't touch her. You can't do this," Kaehl said.

"Yes we can!" someone shouted. He surged toward them. Others followed. "The locals gotta pay!" someone shouted.

Kaehl felt his hands torn free and was lifted bodily over the crowd. He smashed against a wall and rolled to the floor, groaning.

The crowd noise grew louder. Selda's voice was a constant, ragged shriek. Kaehl leaped into the Pack, tearing at their backs. Members turned on him and beat him away.

"Stop! My sister!" he screamed. They ignored him.

In a frenzy, he scanned the apartment. Spying a chunk of wood from the shattered door he dived at it, picked it up and smashed it loudly onto the floor.

"Stop it! Rec, stop them!" he shouted. The crowd ignored him.

With an animal roar he laid into them, knocking members into the walls. Two males were on top of Selda, one gripping her throat. Kaehl connected with one's skull and heard something crack. The other rolled away, cradling his arm.

Someone grabbed Kaehl's waist. Kaehl kicked, sending him flying. He picked up his sister and backed against a wall, holding her behind him with one arm. He brandished his club at the Pack.

"Sister!" he shouted, gasping for breath, his eyes wild. "My sister. You can't!"

Rec stood in front of the mob, facing Kaehl. "Move aside, Newt," he said. His voice was low, threatening.

"You can't have my sister."

"We can," someone behind him said, a hand on his bleeding forehead. "We will. Give her up."

"No." Kaehl raised his club.

"Kaehl, you're outnumbered," said Rec. "You can't win. We fought for this. This is the wrong day to go against the Pack."

"It's the best day. Sister—leave her alone. Promise."

There was a movement. Something flew toward his head. He ducked. It shattered against the wall behind him. Selda sobbed.

“Let us go,” Kaehl said.

“Go?” said Rec. “Leave? You? You’re just a newt. You’d get lost as soon as you were out of sight.”

“Move,” Kaehl said. He stepped forward. The crowed tightened. Voices grew in the back, angry, impatient.

“Rec, please.”

Rec raised a fist, keeping it closed. The Pack growled but hesitated.

“Sister!” Kaehl repeated. The Pack was silent. Kaehl stood for a few breaths then dragged his sister along the wall toward the door. Rec splayed his fingers and the crowd parted. Panting, Kaehl and Selda stepped into the hall.

Rec followed them, his hand still up. The others crowded around him. Sister stumbled and fell, pulling Kaehl down after her.

“Where are you going?” asked Rec.

“Anywhere. We’re leaving.”

“Leaving? To go where?”

“Away from here. This is wrong. I can’t stay. I can’t do this.” He tightened his grip around his sister. “We can’t do this.”

Rec stepped forward and stretched out his hands. “Kaehl, we need you.” He gestured at the Pack. “We need you bad.” He lowered his hand. Slowly, the Pack moved toward Kaehl, blocking the hall.

Kaehl followed them with his eyes. “To do what? Hurt more old, sick people? Steal from workers? Scrabble like rats for food? Play tag with the locals? Murder children?” He brandished his club again. The Pack hesitated and then continued to surround him. “This is suicide, Rec. This is evil.”

“There’s worse. We’re alive.”

“Yeah, but for how long? You’re going to bring the entire Tower down on your necks.”

“Maybe. Let them try.”

“They just did.”

Rec motioned to Selda. “What about her? Think!”

"She's my sister."

"Sister," Rec mocked. "She's sick, weak. She shouldn't be alive. Don't do this, Kaehl. Let her go."

Kaehl looked up, hot, hostile. His mind whirled. "Weak? Alive? Yes, she's alive. She's my sister, she's all I have. There won't be any killing here, no Welcome for her." Kaehl jerked the rope belt from his pants and wrapped it around her neck. He stood up, gently tugging at her. She stood and took a few steps, swaying. He glowered back at the Pack. "We're leaving."

Rec stood in the light of the door. The others surrounded Kaehl, glaring, fists clenched. "Kaehl, you're crazy. You're a runner. We need you, especially now. Where will you go? You have no family, no friends. Leave your sister and stay with us. She's a cripple. We can't provide for her. No one can. Let the hallways take her."

Kaehl stared at him levelly, his eyes smoking.

Rec smirked. "The only ones who could fix someone like that are those who live at the top. The Money, the Bags; they can take care of her. They have doctors up there, in the penthouses. There's no chance for her here." His eyes flicked over her. "She's almost dead."

Kaehl's eyes lit up. "The top? They have doctors there?"

"Sure, from what I hear. And money, and power. They can fix anything. What did you think? You've never been there?"

"No."

"Well, me neither. But I know people who have. The rich could take care of her, if they cared to."

"Then I'll go there." Kaehl stood where he was for a moment, staring at the Pack. "How do I get there?"

"Fly, idiot," said a voice from the back of the group.

"Jump into the Shaft!"

"Try diving into a cesspit."

"Don't go, Kaehl," Rec said. "It was a joke! You'll never get there.

Even if you do they'll shut you out, or you'll get arrested and thrown in a pit. They don't mix with our kind."

"Our kind?"

"Yes, whatever isn't their kind. Dirty folks like us."

Kaehl's eyes focused on the ground, his hands twisting and untwisting on Selda's rope. His eyes flicked to Rec's.

"Will you go with me?" he asked.

Rec laughed. "No," he said, gesturing at the group. "I'm needed here."

"All of you then. Together. We could do it as a group. Maybe start a new kind of Pack."

Rec shook his head. Someone spat.

"Please?"

Someone laughed.

"Then I'll go without you. I'll find a job, find a place to live, find someone who can care for her."

Rec's voice gentled. "Kaehl, look at her. She's almost dead."

Kaehl's eyes widened. "No she's not! Stop saying that! She'll come around. I'll fix her. She's my sister. I'm not leaving her."

Defiant, Kaehl studied the faces staring at him, angry faces, flushed, surprised and frustrated. "Who's going with me?" he said.

The faces laughed. Kaehl lowered his head. "Then I'm going. Alone."

He waded into the Pack, they closed ranks around him. Kaehl glowered at them and raised his club, measuring their angry stares. He moved forward again, edging them aside. They pushed back. Kaehl shoved into them. The Pack began moving, restless. Their simmering anger began to boil. Something hit Kaehl from behind, making him stumble. The club fell from his hand. "Newt!" someone said.

The shoving turned violent. Voices rose. Someone tugged at Sister's leash. She cried out. Angry, Kaehl covered her with his arm and pulled her away, warding off blows. The voices started shouting.

Kaehl rammed through the crowd and ran toward a ramp, half carrying

Selda. Sounds of rage and frustration followed him. He heard Rec call a command. The shouting died away. Kaehl turned a corner, casting a glance over his shoulder. Burned into his mind for the rest of his life was the image of Rec standing in the middle of the shrunken Pack, his eyes questioning, one fist raised above his head, fingers outstretched. Kaehl turned and left.

Hall Again

Kaehl led his sister up the ramps at a jog, urging distance between themselves and the Pack. At first they simply spiraled toward the penthouses, ears alert for pursuit. After a few floors, however, Selda began to drag. Her bare feet plodded, stumbling over the bare floor. Twice she fell and had to be helped to her feet. Eventually Kaehl picked her up and carried her in his arms. When he could no longer carry her he set her on her feet and urged her forward again with the leash. After two more floors she collapsed in the middle of the ramp, a gasping mound of rags and bones. Kaehl, exasperated, stopped.

He paced the ramp, fists taut, head swiveling, eyes alert. He and his sister were targets here but she couldn't go on and he certainly couldn't carry her to the top without a break. As much as she needed medical help, they needed shelter and food first, some water and maybe some rest.

But where to go? They couldn't stay in the open, here in this ramp—what if the Pack changed their mind? Should he brave the halls, ask someone for help? No chance of that. Maybe try to find an empty apartment or a storage room?

Kaehl leaned his back against a wall and rubbed his eyes. He felt lightheaded. *Too much excitement for too long,* he thought. He glanced at Selda, who hadn't moved. He slid to the floor beside her. Just finding her had been excitement enough. Maybe a moment's rest and then a few more floors toward the top. How far did he have to go? He had no idea.

His mind began to drift. He fought it. He didn't want the nightmares to return. In the back of his mind, where he had worked hard to mask his guilt, he felt the swirl of the regret building, the familiar pain threatening to return.

He stood up again, bunched his shoulders and swung his arms. He boxed the air, jogged in place, did push-ups. He wanted to do something, anything, keep moving, keep active, move up the ramps, keep the thoughts away, anything but listen to his thoughts. But the leash held him back.

He didn't want to remember what he had found in his home: the squalid conditions, the emptiness, the missing people. He didn't want to dwell on Sister's emaciated body or on what the Pack didn't find in the back rooms, what Kaehl had been unable to verify. He fought to keep away thoughts of who was not there and where they had gone. He elbowed away any consideration of what might have happened to those who were missing, or how different things would be if he had stayed. He hid from any hints about whose fault it was.

Gradually, in spite of his efforts, weariness took over and the pain seeped in. He began to feel a creeping horror of himself and what he had become. Guilt grew inside him, seeping into his heart until it scorched him like fire. He saw himself as a different person now, the one he had feared, the one he had run from his whole life. No matter how hard he had fought it, he had become his father. He had turned brutal and angry, even murderous. He had carefully and calmly felled one of his parents, perhaps injuring him permanently, leaving Mother and Selda without support. Without him, without Father, where would Mother and Sister be? That one stroke, that one brutal blow may have murdered his whole family. He had left, maybe to protect his family, maybe to protect himself. If he had stayed, who else would he have injured? It didn't matter where he went or what happened to him now. Mother and Father were gone, maybe dead. Sister was dying. He was a murderer and he deserved whatever came.

Over and over he replayed Mother's searing stare, her furious gaze as she curled over her husband, protecting him from her son. She had lived with the man for many years, nourishing him, helping him in spite of his weaknesses, encouraging him to overcome, living on what he provided. Perhaps at one time she had actually loved him. Kaehl had judged him. His father had ended up on the floor, bleeding, sobbing in pain. Mother's withering stare of hate and fear burned holes through his heart.

At last, accumulated hurt and tension wore him down. His energy drained. His knees sagged and he fell like one of his mother's rag dolls. Tears streamed down his face.

What had happened to his parents? They had either deserted the apartment or been taken from it, that was sure. If not, the Pack would have found them. But why? How? How long had they been gone? The squalid apartment made it seem like they had been gone a long time. Where did they go? Why did they desert Selda? Or did they? Were they dead?

Why hadn't he been there for them?

He rocked his head back and forth. "That was the past," he mumbled. Time to move on, push forward, shove those thoughts aside. The past didn't matter; Selda needed him now. Focus on the now. Selda needed healing. She needed him here.

And yet it did matter. It was all his fault. He had deserted his home and left his parent to be murdered, his sister to starve and to be attacked by the Packs. She was dying. He had murdered them. He had murdered them all.

He shivered, wracked by exquisite guilt. It burned his mind and choked his throat, driving his fists into the wall. He cried great, heaving, body-shaking sobs. He cried for the lost opportunities, the broken promises, the empty words and the failures. He cried because he had let them down, because he had left them to die. He cried because he was a failure, because he had failed. He cried for the unknowns. He cried until he had wrung out his heart and was left exhausted on the floor, asleep.

He awoke bathed in sweat, his eyes glued with dried tears, his head and fists aching. His tongue felt thick. *Ugh, the dreams,* he thought. The nightmares left him groggy.

He raised his head and blinked. Where was he? Why was he lying in the hall? Why was he so thirsty? What had happened? Stiffly he turned over and pushed himself to his feet. A wave of horror washed over him. He had fallen asleep, in the open, exposed on one of the ramps. He took a step toward the hallway door and stopped. A rope was tied to his wrist. It held him back. Dully, he followed the rope with his eyes. It led to a lump of rags a few steps behind him. It didn't move. He prodded the rags with his toes. There was a groan.

Sister. It came to him through a fog: He had rescued his sister. He remembered.

She lay where she had fallen. Dully, he tugged at the line. She didn't move. He jerked it. Her eyes opened, glazed and dull. She moved to rise but collapsed on her face, unmoving. Kaehl turned to her and bent down. For the first time since the rescue he lifted her face to his.

He gagged. "Sister!" Her gaunt figure was now even thinner, a tissue of chalk-white skin stretching tightly over her bones. Her clothes stunk of sweat and saliva and waste. Her ribs stood starkly out of their emaciated frame, showing in places through her ragged clothes. The face leered at him beneath crusted dirt and mire like a death mask.

He was awake now. With infinite tenderness he bent down and hugged her. Tears again flowed down his cheeks. He rocked her gently, crying, sobbing until his emptiness could sob no more. Sister; he had forgotten his sister. He stared down the hall. "Help!" he croaked, his voice barely leaving his throat. He turned the other way. "Help," he cried. The halls were empty, deserted, secured, locking him and his sister out. He looked down at her, thin tears splashing her face. Her eyes fluttered but remained closed.

Help. The doctors. The Top.

Carefully, he lifted the feather-light weight into his arms and stood. Once again he put one foot in front of the other and moved up the ramps. Love and fear burned power into his muscles. He would not fail his family again. He would not let his sister die.

An hour later he sagged against a hallway entrance and lowered her to the ground. Sister had roused into a semi-conscious state of disjointed murmurs and pleas. Tenderly he caressed her grimy forehead and kissed her cheek. He scanned the halls, trying to peer through the glare. He spied a change in the light. Quickly, he untied the leash and jogged toward the emptiness. He slowed, recognizing a door lying against the wall, off its hinges, pieces of it scattered in the hall. He peered into the opening. It was an empty quad. The floor was littered with trash and broken furniture. It looked like it had been empty for a long time, raided by some Pack and never rebuilt. Jogging back to Selda he picked her up and carried her inside.

Kaehl sat his sister in a corner of one of the back rooms, as far from the door as possible. He searched the entire quad. There was no food. Water still trickled from the taps, however. He ransacked the cupboards. Finding an old bowl he filled it and bathed her face, trickling drops into her cracked lips. Sister gasped and surged upward, gulping greedily. She spasmed as a coughing fit shook her then sank down again and lay still.

The boy sat beside her, watching, thinking. Unbidden, his thoughts returned to the past.

Their mother and father had apparently been gone for a while. They were dead. But how could he know? He should have searched for their bodies. No. The Pack would have found them if they were there. They would have said something. But Mother never would have left Selda. Something must have happened to them. They were gone. They must be dead.

He pushed the idea aside. He'd worry about that later. His thoughts centered: Right now Sister lived and needed his help; that was most important. His eyes roved over her sleeping form. She looked like she had gone without food or water for many days. Kaehl could probably feed her for a while from the skills he had picked up in the Pack but he needed help.

Kaehl rose and stretched his legs. He picked up a large basin and filled it from the tap in the cesspit. Carrying it back to his sister he tore a rag from his shirt, rinsed it, and began to wash her.

He gasped. The stench was horrible. Some of her clothing had stiffened and stuck to the flesh where the filth had pooled most heavily. Her ribs showed against her side like slats on a basket. Several sores had grown where the dirt was worst. Kaehl sponged her as best he could, shushing her protests and pushing her fists away. When he finished he removed his outer shirt and laid it over her, letting her rest while he rinsed her clothes. Setting them aside to dry he sat beside her again.

She had water. She needed food. He carefully redrew in his mind what he had learned from Rec, going over locations of weakened households and hydroponics gardens. How far had they come? He hadn't been tracking it. He hoped the layout here was the same as what they had found below. He had to leave her to find food but she would be unprotected. Still, he had to find something she could eat, and soon.

The gardens. It was his only hope.

Giving her another sip of water, Kaehl bundled her more carefully in his shirt and wrapped her damp clothes on top. Kissing her forehead, he stood and moved to the door. He scanned the halls, satisfying himself that they were empty, then slipped out the door. He examined the entrance, reassuring himself that it still looked like the untouched wreck of a long deserted quad, and then disappeared down the hall.

One thing he knew: if layouts were consistent, mechanical systems and gardens were not on residential levels, they had their own separate areas. Kaehl returned to the ramps and glided down several floors. Moving silently he jogged through the halls, keeping to the brightest areas, running swiftly, pausing at intersections, listening. Down one floor, check it, down another. He kept careful track of his movements.

He slowed to a stop several minutes later, listening to a mechanical thumping echoing through the halls. Cautiously he edged forward, testing his steps.

He rounded the corner and stopped, staring at a mound of broken stones. He recognized this place. It was the same garden he had raided before. Two pack members had died here. He flattened against the wall, holding his breath. Mobs of vigilantes could be nearby. He had to be careful.

The broken wall where the Pack had entered was still unpatched, unguarded. The owners were either very sure of themselves or very stupid. Or maybe they were just busy.

Kaehl edged in and peered from behind the crates. Three or four tenders were moving among the planters, working with the vegetables. Kaehl carefully searched for others but could see no one. He settled among the crates to wait.

At length the tenders moved toward the far end of the room. Ages crept by. He took a breath and forced himself to wait.

As the workers reached the far end of the room Kaehl slunk forward, keeping low. He reached over the top of one planter and snatched a handful of carrots. He stuffed them into his pockets and moved forward.

Suddenly Kaehl froze. One of the tenders was moving in his direction. Kaehl squeezed under a nearby table, feeling naked and defenseless. The farmer walked up the aisle, a bucket swinging at his side. He moved past Kaehl then stopped and backed up, looking into the bin of carrots. Kaehl did not breathe. There was a moment of silence. The man muttered something about rats, moved to a pile of crates, and emptied his bucket into one of them. Then he turned and retraced his steps, whistling, swinging his bucket. He walked past Kaehl to the end of the room and began working again.

Quickly, Kaehl faded back behind the crates. He peered into one of them then dropped back quickly, his eyes wide. Beans! He slinked back to the wall. Prying open a loose slat in a nearby crate he reached inside. Celery! He moved from crate to crate, grabbing handfuls of bounty. Thinking quickly, he hefted a box of potatoes and staggered off with it. He would be back soon.

The box was heavy. By the time he reached the first ramp he was unable to continue. He set the box down and rested, munching a potato, grinning in triumph. After a few minutes he stood and hefted the box again.

Reaching his floor, Kaehl peered cautiously around the corner and stepped out. Grimacing, sweat trickling down his face, he staggered down the hall.

Suddenly he stopped. Noises. Indistinct. Shouting, laughing. Then the steady, echoing thunder of foot beats. The boy shifted his weight and hurried on.

A commuter crowd! Work time! A shift change, probably. He had lost track of time. In the endless hallways he couldn't be sure from which direction the sounds came.

His feet found new strength. The noises grew louder. Now they sounded like they were coming from behind. The boy staggered, crying. The box was so heavy! The hall seemed endless. He couldn't find a room, couldn't find the ramps. The crowd's noises crashed in waves against his ears.

They were close. One hall, maybe two, a bend in the corridor? His arms strained, his legs ached, his lungs screamed. Faster. The crowd was nearly there.

Suddenly the crowd broke into the hallway behind him. The boy screamed and strained ahead. He stumbled. The box fell and smashed open. Potatoes scattered everywhere. He stooped, grasping, desperate for the food. Then he saw the howling crowd. He grabbed at whatever was within reach, stuffed them in his pockets and took off. In the wild run, food fled from his pockets. Seconds later the crowd overran the broken crate.

Several in the crowd stumbled and fell. The rest stopped. "Food!" someone screamed. All else was chaos.

Wheezing, exhausted, Kaehl slipped inside the door to the deserted quad he had claimed and ran to the back. Sister was still there. He sagged against a wall, spent. The crowd. They had seen him. They knew he was near, knew he had raided their source of food. They would search, test every deserted home, every yielding door. They would search for him. Kaehl would have to leave.

He looked at his sister, sitting against the far wall. She was sitting up, smiling quietly, singing a simple song. Weak though she was, she looked much better than she had when he had left. He crossed quickly to her side and knelt. Pulling a few carrots out of his pocket he watched her greedily crunch them down. He broke a potato into several pieces and handed them to her, watching with satisfaction as she smiled up at him. She swiped at his hand as he brushed food from her lips. Carefully, he tipped a dish of water into her mouth and let her guzzle from it. She smiled and burped. His eyes crinkled into a smile: she looked positively radiant.

Turning, he picked up the leash and began fastening it around her neck. She made a face and batted at it. He pushed her hands away and stood her up. He felt himself grow dizzy but shook it off. Her clothes were still damp. He pulled at the leash. Shivering, whimpering, she rose and followed him to the door.

The boy put a finger to his lips. Sister stared solemnly at him. "Now

Sister," he said, "we have to leave. People will find us. We have to find a shelter. We're going to go up to where the rich are. Maybe they can help. I'm sorry I can't give you more food. We'll eat again later. We have to go now." She smiled. Kaehl gave her shoulder an affectionate shake then turned back to the door. He listened for a moment and peered out. Pausing, he listened again. Taking her by the leash, Kaehl sidled out. The two started down the hall at a slow trot.

A few moments later they reached a ramp and slipped inside. Kaehl looked ruefully at Sister. "It's gonna be a long walk," he said.

She smiled at him, her eyes like beacons.

Together they started up.

Gently, Kaehl laid her down and slumped against a wall. They had passed several floors, seeing no one, meeting no resistance. The air felt thicker and warmer than when he had begun. Now the two wheezed against the wall in another empty apartment, their legs trembling. His running with the Pack had given him muscle but he had been running constantly for days. Enough, he said. Even their slow pace had drained her body of its meager energy. How far to go? What would they find when they reached the Penthouse? Riot? Rooms? Kindness? Food? He ran a hand over her damp forehead. She had never worked this hard. Would she make it?

He looked tenderly at his sister. *Silly girl,* he thought, brushing hair from her face. *No—angel.* Untouched by the world, endlessly patient. And, he added, a lot of trouble. She sure slowed him down. *But,* he thought with a smile, i*t was a kind of trouble he loved.*

He grimaced as his belly growled. He rubbed it thoughtfully. The two could not go much farther without food. They had to have something.

Wearily, Kaehl stood up. His knees trembled beneath him. He held himself against the wall for a moment and then he turned and smiled at his sister. "Stay here. I'll be back. I'm going to get more food." She lay with her eyes closed, not moving.

He left the apartment and climbed the next flight. A humming sound filled the ramp, low but very pervasive. It made him edgy. He moved toward the ramp exit. The sound grew stronger, masking other sounds.

He edged to the door and peered into the hall. No one. Empty. Curious, he moved out of the ramp.

Kaehl tried to picture the makeup of the building. Rec claimed that he had climbed up to ten floors above and below the Pack's territory. He had reported that halls had all been alike, same width, same layout, although some were more damaged than others. The doorways seemed better kept the higher you went, the doors more solid. Rec had shied away from one area, not being able to identify a strange humming sound that filled the halls.

Maybe this was that area. Carefully, Kaehl sidled along the hall, keeping to the edges. The humming noise surrounded him, blocking out all other sounds.

He came to a door and tested it. Locked. Every door he tried was the same: Tight, well-secured, and strong.

The humming grew stronger. He saw an opening in the wall above his head. The sounds seemed strongest there. Leaping, he grabbed the edge and pulled himself in.

Kaehl found himself in a tight metal conduit that extended farther than he could see, with many branches and openings breaking off and disappearing in the glare. The humming pounded against him, echoing painfully off the walls. He edged forward, keeping to the largest tunnel.

The conduit ended at a large set of louvers. He hugged the floor and peered through. His eyes grew wide.

Beyond the grate was an immense room. Men labored in somewhat lesser light on vast machines that churned and clacked and screeched and hummed. Many were blackened and seemed broken; others stood silent, grayed with dust and laced with rust. Some looked like they hadn't been used in a long time. Some were in pieces, as if torn apart to feed others.

Kaehl stayed low, wary yet fascinated. Many men tended these huge chunks of metal. Were they like the machines Father worked on? They seemed to produce nothing. Why so much pointless effort?

With a tremendous roar one sprang to life. A freezing blast of air crashed over him, ripping the breath from his lungs. He scrambled back into the tunnel, hugging the floor. The blast howled around him.

The blast subsided, replaced by the humming of the machines. Air circulation. These machines moved fresh air though the building. Bending double in the shaft, Kaehl turned and scrambled back to the entrance.

He tumbled out of the ventilation hole, picked himself up, and limped back to the ramp.

After hours of fruitless searching he rejoined his sister. She was where he had left her, playing with a loose string frayed from her clothes. Kaehl sank wearily beside her. She turned to him and smiled.

Kaehl felt his gorge rise. The face that smiled so weakly at him was so unlike that of the sister he knew at home. Her teeth protruded like rotten corn, yellowed and malformed. The skin stretched tightly over her bones, the skeleton poking through. Her hair was dull and listless, clumps falling out.

Tears crawled from his eyes. “Oh Sister,” he groaned, pulling her to him. His hands went to his pocket. “If only I had something to feed you.” His hands closed around something. He gasped and pulled a hand out, laughing at the contents. He held the hand up to her and crushed her in a huge hug.

“Look, Sister, look! Carrots! Food! I still had some left! It’s not much, but it’s food!” She blinked and tried to focus. He shook his head. *Man, I must not be thinking clearly,* he thought. He quickly rubbed the dirt and lint away and broke them into smaller sections. Offering one to her, she took it and nibbled at it. He had six carrots that he had stuck in the loose pockets of his clothes during his last raid. He quickly chewed one for himself and passed another to her. She finished off the first then, with somewhat renewed vigor, ate another. They ate until the last one disappeared and then, in spite of the risks, fell asleep.

Work

BOOM.
BOOM.
BOOM.

A door cracked and began to open in front of him. Kaehl skidded to a stop and pressed into an empty alcove. Others began to open. Men peered out and moved through them into the hall, pulling them shut again. A crowd rumbled toward them. Commuters.

Kaehl sank farther into the alcove. He had left Selda in a remote apartment behind some broken crates and had gone scouting. Surely there would be more opportunities somewhere.

As he watched the crowd pass he weighed his options. Commuter crowds took people to a work site, perhaps, or a factory or a garden or something he couldn't imagine. If he followed them they might lead him to a food source. Setting his jaw, he took up an easy lope behind them.

The crowd moved through the halls, gathering people. They were slow, noisy, and undisciplined. If they had been a Pack, he thought, most of them would have been left behind.

At length the crowd left the halls and emptied into a large room. Kaehl slipped into an opening beside the door and peered out. His mouth dropped open.

He had never seen a room as large as this. It was three times higher and much longer than the garden he had raided. A mammoth man-made building dominated the center. Smaller buildings dotted the area in front of it. A tall wire fence separated them from the halls and a large open area. Several guards patrolled its length. Workers walked among the buildings behind them.

The commuters jogged into the open area and stopped in front of a set of heavy gates. Kaehl edged out of the doorway to get a better view.

Inside the fence he saw several starved-looking youth carrying boxes and barrels, scurrying aside as grownups strode past them. Two overweight adults appeared from a shack near the gate, waving papers and arguing together. They motioned to a pair of guards who pulled out a set of keys and unlocked the gates. One of the two pulled out a stylus and counted the people in the crowd. He nodded to his companion who returned his nod and shouted to the guards. One guard shouted something to the crowd, causing workers to dig into their pockets for papers. The big men pulled the gates aside and allowed the commuters to shuffle through. The officials counted each person, checking their papers as they passed by. As the last man moved through, the gates were pulled shut again and locked. The crowd shuffled into the large building. The overweight men disappeared into the shack, still arguing.

Kaehl backed away from the door and considered his options. Rec had described something like this. This was some sort of factory, maybe a farm, much bigger than a garden. That meant he could get supplies, food, water, clothing—anything, much more easily than by raiding apartments by himself. There was a lot of people inside, an untold number of guards, and a fence. He'd have to spy out the area before making a move.

He inched toward the corner and peered around it. He leaned forward, counting the guards.

Something touched his shoulder.

He jumped and whirled around, his fists balled.

"Ho, there. Sorry if I startled you." A tall, middle-aged man stood beside him, leaning back, his arms raised defensively, a smile on his face. Kaehl crushed into the wall, his chest heaving.

"Late for work, aren't you? Late or—hmm. Maybe you don't work here." He sniffed and wrinkled his nose. "Phew! You sure don't smell like you work here. When did you bathe last?"

Kaehl said nothing.

"You got a home?"

Kaehl hesitated, then nodded.

"Uh huh. Where is it?"

Kaehl pointed over his shoulder.

"Uh huh. Where's your parents?"

"Sick."

"Uh huh. You here for work?"

Kaehl lowered his eyes and nodded again.

"Well you're late. Let's go. Stragglers don't get paid."

Kaehl tried to hide his astonishment at his luck. The adult led Kaehl to the gate and motioned to a guard. The big man sauntered over and leaned against the fence.

"What ya got here, Lem?"

"Newcomer. Late. Wants work. Open up."

"Did the boss approve him?"

"He will."

The guard leaned close and sniffed. "No way, he smells like he died in a rat pit. Boss'd kill me if I put him on the line."

"Wash him, then."

The guard's face lit. "Wash him?" He rubbed his hands.

"Yes. Come on now or I won't get my finder's fee. Open up."

The guard produced a set of keys and opened the gate. Lem grabbed Kaehl by the collar. "You sure you got a home?" he hissed. Kaehl nodded vigorously. Lem pushed him through, nodded to the guard and hurried off. The guard closed the gate and smiled.

"Come on, Smelly. We'll get you fixed up. If you don't get going you'll miss breakfast." Kaehl's eyes focused. The guard lumbered off, Kaehl trailing behind, his eyes downcast and nervous.

They passed a few buildings and rounded a corner. Kaehl stopped. Three men stood in a small circle, holding buckets and brushes. A fourth man held a hose that snaked from a nearby tower. All wore eager, ugly smiles.

The guard pushed Kaehl forward. "Have at it, boys, but be quick. We have to feed him before he hits the line. I don't want him fainting in front of a supervisor. Looks like he hasn't eaten in two years."

Two of the guards grabbed Kaehl's arms and stretched him between them. Another turned a lever on the hose. Water gushed. They brandished their brushes.

Kaehl stood at the back of a crowd gathering in a low-ceilinged room larger than three quads put together. Boys streamed in through a series of doors at one end of the room. He gnawed at carrots and potato peels and dragged at bad-tasting water from an ancient flask. He winced as the brush marks on his chest stretched. Glancing down, he saw that the bleeding had mostly stopped. He pulled his wet clothes around him and tried to control the shivering.

A very fat man climbed onto a crate in front of the crowd. Several guards took up positions in front of him. Another official appeared and shouted to quiet the crowd.

"You get fed here, don't you?" the fat man said to the group. His voice wheezed like a broken teapot. "Do well and you'll get enough for yourself and others. Fail or be lazy and you're out. Steal or beg or get hurt or cause trouble in any way and you're out of here on a body bed or worse." He showed his crooked teeth to the other official, who smiled and nodded.

"You need this food. We need your help. We can work together, but if you don't work there are plenty just like you waiting to replace you. Understand?"

Heads nodded.

"No forgiveness. No excuses. No tolerance. You break it, you bought it. Am I clear?" Heads nodded again. "Then get to work."

The crew shuffled off toward the opposite doors. No one talked. Kaehl fingered the carrots and thin pancakes he had hidden in his shirt. He hoped the water in his clothes wouldn't ruin them.

"First days over here," a bored voice called out. "First days over here."

Several ragged young men moved toward the voice. Kaehl jostled toward them. He stopped at a loose crowd of boys and a pile of buckets. "Two buckets per boy. Walk the aisles, pick up trash, throw it into the compost heap, through those doors. Do it again. Keep it up. Break at lunch; listen for the call. No talking. Move."

Kaehl waded through the crowd and picked up a pair of buckets. "You and you," the bored voice said, nodding to Kaehl and a nearby boy. "Aisle six, over there. Move." Kaehl and the boy shuffled off toward the doors.

The two entered a large doorway and gaped. The room was just like the garden he had raided twice, only much bigger. Dozens of men and boys moved among boxes and trays of vegetables and greenery crowding huge tables extending the length of an enormous hall. Thousands of plants hung from the ceiling, water trickling down long tendrils. The walls were lined with baskets and barrels, all overgrown with green.

He watched the other boys. They moved down each aisle, picking trash off the floor. "Six?" the boy whispered at his elbow, wondering where to go. Kaehl nodded and pushed through the crowd. He found aisle six and began collecting trash.

It was dirty work, picking up dead leaves, weeds, rotten vegetables, crushed insect bodies and occasional dead rodents that the tenders had tossed to the ground. When his buckets were full he followed the others out a door at the back, emptying them onto heaps of trash. The stench of decay was overwhelming. Watching the others, he pulled up his shirt and tightened it over his nose. It made little difference. He hurried back to the aisles and did it again.

They paused for a meager meal at lunch and refilled their flasks. Hours later, dragging their buckets behind them, they formed exhausted lines and piled their buckets in a corner. After everything was counted twice they filed toward the exit, where they held their hands out to receive packets of discarded food. Then they joined departing teams and jogged out the gates toward their homes, munching leftovers, their steps lighter.

Kaehl slipped into the back of a group and followed them into the halls. Their heads were down, their eyes half closed, but they were smiling. No one noticed as he darted into a hallway and disappeared. A few minutes later he knelt at Sister's side, holding a radish under her nose. Her eyes opened. He set aside the radish and handed her a potato pancake. She nibbled at it. He dribbled some water from the flask into her mouth. She savored it with her tongue then grabbed the flask in both hands and emptied it in several long gulps. She coughed and gagged and looked up at him, her chin dripping, and laughed.

For several weeks Kaehl left his sister to go back to the gardens. He returned from work each evening, untied her leash and fed her from each day's packet and what he had could pocket, filling his flask from a tap at the back of the quad. He bathed her, washed her clothes and sang with her. For an hour or so he would play with her or teach her some new thing he had learned that day. She would listen, her gaze focused on him until her eyes grew heavy and then together they would fall asleep. Each morning he woke at one clock, gave her whatever food he had left, fastened her leash, and headed back to the factory.

Kaehl rejoiced in his job and the opportunities it provided him and Selda. His initial drive to bring her to the Top faded as her condition stabilized and slowly improved.

His greatest fear was for her safety. Without proper restraints she could slip the collar and wander away. She could become tangled in the cord or injure herself in some way and he would not be there to help.

Almost unspoken was his fear of the unknown. The Packs, for instance. Kaehl knew that Packs raided any time they needed to, not only at night as his mother had told him. Sister could be discovered by a Pack at any time and once again she would be helpless. Even if he was with her, Kaehl doubted that he could protect her from them.

And then there were the wanderers, stragglers who could chance upon their apartment as Kaehl had done. His mind would not picture what might happen should a stranger find her there, alone.

Added to these, he knew that he needed papers to work at the gardens. He had none. If management decided to run a security check and found that he had no papers they might do anything to him. Once again, Sister would be alone.

These fears kept him up late into the night. They added to his layers of guilt and quickened his steps home each evening. They had been able to escape detection so far but Kaehl knew they would have to leave eventually.

At work, more boys joined the workforce; others left. Kaehl was promoted to the water team. After breakfast his new team formed up behind a young male, picked up buckets loaded with food and scraps and headed out a rear door into a long hallway. At the end of the hall they stooped and entered a low door, passing several club-wielding guards.

The door opened into a wide, low-ceilinged chamber. The room's edges disappeared quickly in the intense light but their echoing footsteps gave an impression of immense space. The air was humid and thick and cold enough to raise goose bumps. It tasted different.

They traced a path worn into the sloping floor, keeping the wall to their right. As they traveled, something about the floor to his left caught his attention. He stared at it, trying not to stumble, mesmerized. It was fascinating, drawing his eyes irresistibly, light against the lightness with thin ripples of dark. And it moved.

He toed a small pebble into it, watching ripples spread and disappear. Water. From the little he could see, other than the thin edge along which they walked, the floor was entirely covered with water. It lapped quietly a few footfalls away, not in waves but with irregular patterns as if it was being pushed from within. It was silent and oily, reflecting the boys in lazy broken rings, distorting their forms as they moved ahead of him, disappearing as they faded into the distance.

"How did so much water get in here?" he whispered to the boy in front of him. His voice sounded muffled and choked. The boy, startled by the break in the silence, didn't answer.

The boys trooped around the edge of the water, feeling the air grow thick and rank. Kaehl's nose curled against the smell, a cross between decaying carcasses, pooled human waste, and rotting food.

They neared another wall, against which was camped a large knot of humans. They were bundled in rags, huddled on the shore. They looked up as the boys approached and got to their feet.

"Food?" one asked as they drew near, his voice thin and bubbling, fingers stretching toward Kaehl. "I have water. Clean, good. Much for a little food." His face was covered in a threadbare scrap of linen. Kaehl stared in horror at a hole in the middle of his face oozing some sort of yellow mash. Kaehl's stomach churned. He plugged his nose and moved away. Other creatures gathered around the line of boys, reaching, grasping, pleading. Bodies lay on the shore, some not moving, others raising their arms toward them, calling. Someone pulled at his arm. Boys began to shy away, others backed up. The line of boys wavered.

"Steady, boys. Faster," the leader called. The team jostled forward and moved after the voice, their buckets held close. Behind them, someone cracked a whip. A voice cried out. There were more sharp cracks, more shouts. Someone cursed. The voices grew louder as the boys approached a fence. The beggars converged, their voices desperate.

A large guard in front of the fence shouted and cracked a long whip. The boys stopped against the closed gate. He cracked the whip again and shouted, waving his other arm, moving toward the beggars who peeled away. The guard moved among them, snapping his whip over their heads. They cowered and staggered back. Other guards joined him, each brandishing a whip or club, and moved through the boys toward the mob. The crowd broke and fled.

The guards opened the gate and the boys jumbled through. They followed their leader through a loose collection of sagging tents. One of the flaps blew open as the team jogged past. Kaehl glimpsed a thatch of emaciated bodies crowded on dirty mats. He stopped, transfixed. One face looked up at him, dirty, skeletal. Kaehl's eyes bulged as he recognized the same vacant expression Selda sometimes wore. The team jostled past and the flap closed again. Kaehl stumbled after them.

The teen in charge stopped before a thin woman standing in front of a large tent. She stood, shaking her shoulder-length hair, wiping her hands. The boys gathered around, white-faced, looking over their shoulders.

"These my cleaning crew?" the woman asked the team leader.

The leader nodded. "Yes, Doctor Herstand. For today."

Kaehl caught his breath. "Doctor?" he whispered.

The leader brushed back his hair. "The mob was pretty thick today."

"They're not a mob, they are starving humans," answered Doctor Herstand.

"They got pretty close to my team."

She shrugged. "We'll send the guards out earlier next time. It'll be all right. They're harmless."

"Do you think you should move your camp?"

"Move it? Where? The people are here. We came to them. We're here for them. We aren't going to leave them. If we moved, think how many more would die!"

The leader shrugged. "You're the boss." He turned to the boys. "Okay. Put your food buckets on the ground outside that tent. See those carts? Pair up, grab one and follow Doctor Herstand. We're going to clean the aquifer today. Let's go."

The boys buddied up, picked out a cart, and hauled them to a shed. The lean-to was filled with picks, rakes, shovels, ropes, and hooks. Each boy took one and piled them into their carts. Following the woman they dragged the carts to the lake.

"Two by two. Stay with your buddy," the supervisor shouted. "We're here to clean the lake, not get lost. Stay inside the fence. Pick up anything that isn't water and throw it into the cart. Watch for sharp edges; I don't want any blood on my shift. Go out into the lake until the water covers your knees, no farther. You two, head off that way. You two over there—yeah, you—head that way. Yeah, over there. Follow the shore. The rest of you, follow them. I'll be checking on you. Okay? Go!"

Kaehl looked around, standing by his cart. His buddy had joined some friends.

"Odd?" asked a female voice behind him.

Kaehl whirled around. Doctor Herstand stood to one side, hands on her hips, looking at him. Kaehl dropped his gaze, confused.

"Yes, you," she said. "No partner, I see. You're the odd man out. Come on, let's go." She moved toward the lake. Kaehl looked at his supervisor who shrugged and moved off. Kaehl pulled the cart after her.

Kaehl and the doctor worked together the first part of the shift, pulling trash out of the water and dumping it into the cart. Runners emerged from the camp frequently to hand her messages. She read the notes, penciled a few responses, and sent the messengers away. Kaehl continued to work.

"Silent type, aren't you?" she asked as they sat beside each other during a break. Kaehl looked up at her, lowered his eyes and nodded.

"I'll bet. New here?"

Kaehl nodded again.

"You can talk, you know. You're a good worker, but talking's not a right you have to earn."

Kaehl smiled.

"You got a name? Mine's Herstand."

"Doctor," Kaehl corrected.

"Right. Doctor Herstand."

Kaehl blushed. "Kaehl," he muttered.

"What? You don't have to whisper."

He cleared his throat. "Kaehl."

"Ah. Your name is Kaehl? Nice to meet you, Kaehl."

Kaehl kept his gaze on the ground.

"A natural talker, I see."

Kaehl shrugged.

After the break they walked along the shore, Doctor Herstand spearing the trash with a hook and tossing it into the cart, Kaehl trundling it beside her.

"Where do you live, Kaehl?"

"Up the halls."

"Ah, an answer, even if it is evasive. Nice to know you have a voice."

Kaehl motioned back toward the camp. "Who are those people along the shore, the ones we met when we first came in?"

Doctor Herstand's head swiveled. "Did you say something?" She smiled broadly.

Kaehl's face burned. He cleared his throat. "Those people along the shore, outside the fence. Who are they?"

Doctor Herstand tossed a rock into the cart. "Those people? Some call them the poor, the hopeless, the homeless, the sick. Many people call them bums or beggars, people that live off the government. Some are patients. I call them guests. They have nothing to eat and no place to live so they come here. Here they can find clean water if nothing else. Quite a few of them had arrived by the time we found them. After we set up our hospital, more came. Maybe they think we can help them. Unlike the food processing facilities, we don't drive them away. We feed them."

"But there are big men here with whips."

"Yes there are. Our guests can get a bit aggressive. We have to control them sometimes, especially if we have visitors. Supply days are tough. If we don't control them there'll be trouble." She rubbed her shoulders and looked away. "It's happened before."

"Where do they come from?"

"I don't know. They don't say. All over, I guess. Does it matter?"

"How do they get in?"

"There are holes and entrances all over this aquifer."

"Aquifer?"

"It's a very big room with lots of water in it. People can get in from most sides. Some cross the water. They come for our food, you know, and for the waste, for our scrap. They eat it, take it back to their families and whoever else is back in their warrens. They'd do the same at the factories but those guards are too tough. We've been able to keep the poor under control and still help them. Maybe an occasional raid from a Pack or so, that's all we've had to worry about. Mostly." She looked into the distance. "I pray they never break through in force. A lot of people would suffer if they do. Maybe get sick. Starve. Fight. Be hurt. Lots of things."

"Yeah." Kaehl's voice was miserable as he relived his time in the Pack. There was a long moment of silence. "What do you do for a living?" Kaehl asked at last, his voice tentative.

She smiled, her eyes inquisitive. "I'm a doctor."

"Yes, I know. But you fix people, right? That's your job."

"We try. What else would I fix?"

"What was that camp back there, the one inside the fence?"

"Where we came from?"

"Yes."

"A hospital."

"Hospital? You said that before."

"Yes."

"They fix people there?"

"Yes."

"You work there?"

"Yes, Kaehl. That's where I'm a doctor. I'm the head doctor, actually. I lead the camp."

"Could you fix my sister?"

"Ah." She frowned, suddenly understanding. "That depends on what she's suffering from. We can try. What's the problem?"

"She looks a lot like those people in your camp, in your hospital."

"Very thin and sickly, can't talk very well?"

Kaehl nodded.

"How long has she been this way?"

"Forever."

"Was she born that way?"

"I guess."

She sighed. "Then I'm afraid there isn't a lot we can do for her. You can bring her in and let us take a look, but if she is like those you saw in my hospital, her chances are slim."

They walked in silence for several moments. "What does that mean, 'her chances are slim?'" asked Kaehl.

"It means that I don't know what we can do for her. We'd have to examine her first. If she's like the others, chances are we couldn't do much to help."

Kaehl watched her toss a broken pot into the cart. "Why are you picking up trash instead of being a doctor?"

"I am being a doctor. Caring for the water can help keep people from getting sick. If you look at it that way, keeping things clean makes my job a lot easier. Besides, it's my day off, and I want to be sure this job is done right."

"What's in the tents?"

She turned toward him and stared, her eyes assessing. Kaehl lowered his gaze. She shrugged and turned away. "Very sick people. We try to keep the worst cases isolated. Tents are cheap, quick, easy to move, easy to destroy if needed. Did you look inside?"

"Only a bit, as we moved past."

"What you saw in them wasn't very pretty, was it?"

Kaehl shook his head. "Will my sister get like that?"

She sighed. "I don't know, Kaehl. We'd have to examine her first. Nothing has worked for these people. If she's like them, there's nothing I can do. Nothing but be patient and comfort and care for her. Ease her passage." She lifted a broken door post from the mud and threw it into the cart, straightening to wipe her hands. "And pray."

Kaehl's eyes glowed. She fixed him with a glance and turned away, moving down the shore. He followed.

"Doctor," he said, helping her lift a broken piece of rusted metal. "How many people are sick like this?"

"Many. More all the time, it seems."

"As bad as my sister?"

She nodded. "From your description, yes."

"What do people do with them?"

"I told you. Care for them, one way or another. Some bring them here, or similar places. Others..." They heaved the metal into the pile and turned to look for more.

"There are other places like this?"

"Yes. I've been to a few."

"They don't have a cure either?"

She shook her head. "We'd fix it if we could, but we don't know what's causing it. It could be something they got from their parents. Maybe from their food. Maybe from the rats. Maybe from something in the walls." She fished out a sodden mass of decomposing clothing and tossed it on the heap. "Maybe from the water. That's why you're here. But more and more people are getting it. We need to find the cause and cure it."

"What's so important about this water?"

"It's our reservoir, Kaehl. It's where we get our water from. There are three reservoirs at different levels of the Tower. They are quite extensive. They are so big we call them aquifers or lakes. I think they are all connected."

Kaehl wrinkled his nose and surveyed the oily surface. "We drink this stuff?"

Doctor Herstand nodded. "And cook with it and clean and bathe."

"Eww."

She nodded. "So that's why we want to keep it clean. And not waste it."

"Yeah."

They worked together to pull a large mat from the water.

Kaehl turned to the Doctor, brushing the mud from his hands. "My sister… Are you sure there isn't anyone who can help her?"

She straightened, put her hands to her back and stretched. "At this level? No one. We don't have the supplies, the equipment, the expertise, or the help. Maybe at the Penthouse. I hear they have money and gear, even medicine. Doctors live well up there. Not like in a remote camp like this. Still, they caused this mess, they and their stupid policies. I doubt they would help someone sickened by it. But maybe…" She wiped her forehead. "I've never been there. They could fix her on the Outside, though."

Kaehl looked up sharply. She turned to him, smiled and bent to his ear. "There is an Outside, Kaehl," she whispered and straightened, smiling.

"You know that, yes?"

He backed away, his eyes wide. "Of course I do. Everyone does. But we're not supposed to talk about it."

"You can get there, you know."

"Who would want to?"

"You would, if it would help your sister. They might be able to. They have help you never dreamed of."

"How do you know that?"

Doctor Herstand didn't answer.

"But it's a wasteland," Kaehl said, "a desert, a terrible place. No one goes out there. They'd die. They all want to come in here, to get what we have. We're the lucky ones. They're starving."

She fixed him with a stern look. "Are they?"

Kaehl nodded vigorously. "Mother said."

"Your family helps with your sister?"

Kaehl's face colored. "Yes! Of course! Every day!"

"Your mother?"

"And father and sisters and brothers. Lots of uncles and aunts. And friends, of course. I have lots of those."

Doctor Herstand stood looking at him for a few moments. She turned and motioned to the other boys. The supervisor gave orders to gather the tools. She tossed hers into the cart. "Kaehl, do you have a family?"

"Yes!" His face was red, his hands clenched.

"And your home…" she asked gently.

"Right down the hall, two floors up. One corridor over."

"I see."

"An easy trip."

"That's good, because if you didn't have a home, the locals might be concerned. Around here, people without homes usually belong to Packs. If you were part of a Pack you might not get to work here anymore."

"I'M NOT!"

"Good, Kaehl. Of course. I'm glad to hear it. Lots of people without homes live here, you know. By the water. They don't belong to Packs and the residents don't bother them. You can tell any homeless people you see that there's food and shelter here, okay?"

"I will. Thanks!"

"You're welcome."

She winked at him and glanced around. The others were walking toward them. Kaehl's supervisor was watching him, his eyes suspicious.

Doctor Herstand bent near again. "Just remember, Kaehl. The Top. The Penthouse. Go there. You'll find your answers there. And don't forget the Outside. Or this lake. Come back tomorrow; we'll talk again."

Kaehl nodded solemnly. Doctor Herstand turned to the others as they gathered around. "That's enough for today. Let's head home."

Kaehl's supervisor nodded. "All right, gather your gear. Let's go. Quittin' time. Carts to the cesspit. Let's GO!" Doctor Herstand turned from Kaehl and walked away.

The boys piled their gear in the carts and trundled them toward the hospital. Not far behind it they found a large mat on the ground, heavily woven and reinforced. Following their supervisor's directions they wrestled the mat to one side, uncovering a huge, foul-smelling pit with no apparent bottom. They emptied the carts into it and replaced the cover.

"Okay, home," said the supervisor. "Light duty today, boys. More tomorrow." They trooped to the gate, picked up their empty buckets, and headed home. The beggars stayed in their tents.

That night, Kaehl slept little. Thoughts of Selda being healed by Doctor Herstand filled his head.

The next day Kaehl was first in line, his eyes eager. Another supervisor walked toward him along the line as he surveyed the boys. Kaehl avoided his eyes.

"You." The boy jerked a thumb under Kaehl's nose. Kaehl looked up. "Yes, you. Food line. Let's go."

"Food line? But…"

The supervisor loomed close. "Did you say something?"

"I was with Doctor Herstand. I thought…"

"You thought?"

Kaehl ducked his head and retreated. The supervisor followed him.

"Did I hear you say something?" he repeated. "I'm sure it was, 'Yes Sir, thank you Sir, right now Sir.' Because if that's not what you said you'd be out on your head right now. Or worse. Did I hear you say something? Did I?" His voice echoed in the room. The other boys tried not to look. Kaehl closed his eyes and shook his head.

"I didn't think so. Food line, let's go. And you, laughing boy. Yes, you. Think somethin's funny? You're with us. Let's go!"

Kaehl joined a line behind the supervisor. His world turned grey.

"New here?"

Kaehl looked up. A boy stood beside him, one he hadn't seen before. "Shut up," Kaehl hissed. "We're not supposed to talk."

Kaehl turned back to his job. He had spent the last several days sorting and pruning plants in trays cramming the cavernous garden room. Several boys were doing the same thing, plucking weeds and rot and insects and throwing them to the floor for others to pick up—his first job in the garden. When they found dead rodents in their traps they would empty the traps onto the floor and reset them. Sharp-eyed guards followed their moves closely. Kaehl was sore in several places where they had reminded him to be honest.

Kaehl's heart wasn't in it. He longed to talk with Doctor Herstand but hadn't been given a chance.

"It sure would be nice to get out of here, wouldn't it?" said the boy.

Kaehl nodded glumly.

"Ever hear of the outer world?"

Kaehl turned and stared at him, one eyebrow raised.

"The outer world," the boy repeated, trying to sound casual. "Ever hear of it?"

Kaehl nodded, returning to work. "Of course. Our preacher tells us about it every Sabbat. But most of us don't talk about it. We're not supposed to. It's an ugly place, dead."

The boy moved closer, his whisper strong. "No it's not. That's a myth, something they made up to keep you in their control. The outer world is beautiful!"

Kaehl turned back to his work. "You're the one who sounds controlled," he said. "You'd better get busy before an overseer walks by."

The boy looked at him furtively, absently turning potatoes over in his hand. He bent low and whispered, "I've been there."

Kaehl's hands froze. One of the overseers glanced at them. Kaehl forced his hands to move. "Get out of here," he said. "We've been warned about people like you." Kaehl moved down the row.

The boy eyed a guard and focused on his tasks. Casually, he picked up a bucket and carried it past Kaehl, emptying it into a cart. He came back with the empty bucket, sat it beside Kaehl and started sorting again.

"I've been watching you, you know," the boy whispered. "You seem smarter than the rest. I think you want to know."

Kaehl moved down the line. The boy followed. "What's the matter?" he whispered. "Are you scared, afraid of me, afraid to listen? It's true. I've been there. It's beautiful."

"I'm not afraid of anything except those guards. You're not supposed to talk. What are you, an idiot? Some kind of Outsider?"

The boy continued working, looking from side to side. "Yes; I'm an Outsider," he whispered.

Kaehl snorted. "Whatever you are, you're going to get us into trouble." He continued sorting potatoes. "If you're an Outsider, how did you get up here? I thought the entrances were blocked or guarded. Weren't you afraid of getting caught?"

"Afraid, yes," the boy answered, glancing over one shoulder. "But we still came. We wanted to; we had to. There are a lot of us down here. Not as many as we would like, of course..."

"Down here?" Kaehl smirked. "Did you come from the slums?"

The boy's eyes grew bright. "No. We came from Outside. For you, that would be down. For us, it would be up."

Kaehl shook his head. The overseers were moving near. His fingers flew. "You're crazy."

"No," the boy answered. He looked at Kaehl. "Have you ever thought about the Outside?"

"Sure, sometimes, I guess." Kaehl bit his lower lip. "Did Doctor Herstand send you?"

The boy smiled and nodded. "Been looking for you a while."

Kaehl's heartbeat tripled.

"You can get there," the boy said, his voice tight. "There's a way! I can show you. An empty shaft runs most of the way to the top, but it's sealed at the guard level. They don't even know about it. At the Penthouse the entrance sits at the bottom of the Shaft. There's a tower. I've been there... AHHH!" The boy cried out and crumpled, holding one shoulder. An overseer stood behind him, his eyes thin and brittle, his face flushed. A heavy club swung in his hands.

"Busy?" the overseer asked. Kaehl bent to his work, his fingers flying. The overseer gestured to two nearby boys. "You and you. Grab our friend here. Let's see what he has to say, what he had to say that was more important than work. Pick him up. Yes, grab him. Come on. Let's go!" The two sorters grabbed the boy under the arms and dragged him into a nearby room. They emerged again and the door closing behind them. Kaehl did not look up.

The overseer leaned close to Kaehl. Another walked over and stood beside him.

"What were you talking about?" His voice was slow and dead calm.

"Me? Nothing. Nothing!" Kaehl saw the supervisor tighten his grip on the club. "Honest! This guy came up to me. I've never seen him before. He said he'd been watching me. Talked like a crazy man about the Outside and stuff. I tried to move away but he followed." He finished pruning the plant but his hands kept moving. He did not look up. The supervisor snorted and turned to follow the Outsider. The second supervisor stood behind Kaehl for the rest of the shift. Kaehl ignored the screams that came from behind the door. He kept very busy.

"Selda," Kaehl said that night, "I've got to go. I can't stay at work much longer. What they did today! You could hear the boy all over the floor, even from the back room. I think they did it on purpose, just so we could hear. It was horrible. If this is what it was like for Father, or what he had to do..."

Kaehl washed down a bit of turnip. Selda squatted on the floor, holding her hands to her chest, rocking. "Only a few more days, three at most. I've fingered a good bit of food. It'll last us for a most of the trip, I think. No one seems to know how far the Penthouse is." Selda continued to rock. She looked better than when they arrived but was still thin as a breath. "Besides, I've got to get you to a doctor. I don't think we'll be able to get to Doctor Herstand anymore. We have to go to the Top. For real, this time; for real. She says we have to go."

Selda hummed a tuneless song.

The air outside the garden was charged with tension when Kaehl arrived the next morning. Workers paced back and forth in front of the gates, talking in low whispers. Small groups formed, casting nervous glances toward the entrance. Everyone had pulled out their papers.

Additional guards were stationed near the gate. They allowed one worker through at a time, each worker stopping on the other side to face a trio of supervisors. The supervisors spoke with each worker, checked their papers, consulted their own documents and then decided whether or not to let them through.

"What's going on?" Kaehl asked a nearby boy.

"ID check. They do this every so often, trying to match names to apartment numbers. They never tell us why they do this but we think they're looking for people they don't like—Outsiders, spies, Pack members, whatever." He looked over his shoulder. "Probably because of the boy they arrested in the garden." He shuddered. Kaehl's face paled. "Could happen to any one of us," the boy finished.

They turned as voices rose near the gate. Two guards were hauling a struggling worker toward a shack inside the fence. The youth was shouting something. They shoved him into the shack, slammed the door, and returned to the gate. The supervisors continued with their checking.

"Everyone gets checked?" Kaehl asked. Sweat beaded his brow.

"Yes. Really slows us down. Low production rate today, for sure."

Kaehl hung back as the crowd slowly thinned. Another youth was hauled into the shack. His screams echoed over the subdued crowd.

Only a few boys remained between Kaehl and the gate. The guards were considering someone a few places ahead of him, putting their heads together and consulting their papers. Kaehl lowered his gaze and steered back toward the halls, his gait deliberate but casual. A few heads swiveled in his direction.

"Hey," someone called.

Kaehl's pace quickened. People looked up. One guard started toward him. Another made a sweeping motion with his arm. Two others began to angle in his direction, running. Kaehl veered away.

"Stop!" Someone moved in from his left. The boys near him backed away, leaving him exposed. He turned to the right and darted away. Someone large stepped into his path.

"Hey, you no hear?" he said. He grabbed Kaehl's collar. "I got him!" he shouted.

The guards drew near. Kaehl wriggled out of his over shirt and broke free. "Hey!" the man cried, reaching for him. The guards sprinted forward. Kaehl skidded around a corner and knocked over a very surprised merchant, scattering crockery. Kaehl sprawled to the floor. Amid shouts and curses he scrambled to his feet and struggled toward the door. He fell once more as the merchant grabbed his feet. With a cry he kicked free and jumped up again. A figure loomed over him and stars exploded behind one ear. All was light.

A shock of cold water wrenched him awake. Groggy, gasping, pain lancing through his head, he tried to rub his eyes. His hands were tied behind him over the back of a chair.

Blinking, trying to clear his vision, he looked up. He sat inside a small room surrounded by six men. There were a few windows. Twisting around he could see a door. It was open. Beyond it he could see the factory gate, the almost empty entrance area, and the hall entrance.

One of the men sat an empty water pot onto a desk in front of him. Kaehl looked up. A fat, older man moved from behind the desk and sat on a corner next to him.

"Our fish is awake," he drawled. The other men chuckled. "Let's see what he's got to say." He bent closer. "Hello, boy, what's your name?"

Kaehl looked up with frightened eyes. The fat man smiled. He had no teeth. "Don't worry, boy, I'm the security overseer. I won't hurt cha. Got a name?"

Kaehl dropped his gaze. He heard the outer gate slide open. He flexed his arms. The knot at his wrists was strong but he could slide his hands up the back of the chair. He lowered them again. The gate closed. "C'mon, boy, speak. We ain' gonna hurt cha. We're nice enough guys." More laughter came from behind him. "Ya better say somethin'. Why didja run?" Kaehl shook his head.

One of the men grabbed Kaehl's hair, wrenching his head backward. Kaehl gasped, tears springing to his eyes. The older man leaned forward again.

"Hey, boy, you awake? Talk to me. Whatcha doin' here? Where'dja come from? Surveyor says you don't live where you say you live. Nobody does. Zat true?"

Kaehl said nothing. The older man nodded to someone behind him. Pain exploded in his side. Gasping, wheezing, Kaehl doubled toward the pain. His head was jerked upright again.

"Where'dja come from, I said. Can'cha talk?" Kaehl stared at him, terrified. The man nodded again.

The pain was exquisite. Gasping, gagging, he struggled against the restraints. The cords cut into his wrists. He heard the outer gate open again.

"Does it hurt?" the older man asked, sniggering. "I don' wanna hurt yeh, ya know. Not yet, anyway. Jus' tell me who you are, where ya come from an' we'll be all right." A smile slit the older man's face. "You're not from one o' them Packs, are yeh? A spy, checkin' out our stores maybe?" Kaehl shook his head.

"Let him go, Reecy." the older man said. Kaehl's head fell forward. The older man bent nearer. "Come on, boy, speak. I'll let cha go." Kaehl said nothing.

The overseer looked up. "Jep, go get the manager. He'll wanna talk to this one. We shouldn' rough him up too much 'til he comes." He smiled again. "Let 'im think for a bit. Then we can worry about whether to leave marks or not." More chuckles sounded behind him. One of the men left the room. After a moment he heard the outer gate open.

"Lem let this one in without checking," the older man said. "I warned 'im. Sloppy work; the boss won't be happy about it. Sloppy work, all right. Lem's gonna get burned." He chuckled and stood up, turning toward the desk. "I guess we'll..."

Kaehl slid his knotted wrists over the back of the chair and exploded upward with a thunderous yell. He kicked backwards, sending the chair crashing into the group. Their howls juiced his ears. He butted the overseer in the back, sending him sprawling headfirst into a wall. Turning, he leaped over the chair onto the back of one of the men who had been behind him, now bent and holding his knees, bellowing in pain. He planted a foot on his spine and pushed off. Something cracked. The man crashed into his henchmen. Airborne, Kaehl kicked at the ribs of one of the men near the door, heard a satisfactory crunch and then hit the ground and rolled. Thrown off-balance by the knots at his wrists, he staggered upright, bolted out the door and through the gate, which had just opened to let another boy through. The guards beside it looked up and stood immobile, dumbstruck. He sprinted down the hall as his captors boiled out of the shack. Behind him, he could hear boys shouting support.

He headed toward the halls, keeping away from the path that led to his apartment. Turning a corner, he risked a moment to twist at the rope around his wrists. He threw himself to the ground and inched his wrists beneath him, biting his lips at the pain. Angry voices grew near. Blood seeped into his mouth. Finally his arms swung forward. He tore savagely at the knots with his teeth. Levering himself upright he stumbled forward.

He could hear his pursuers approach. With a final tug he loosened the knots and tore the rope away. Throwing it to the ground he kicked at some boxes, sending them crashing into the hallway, and disappeared with a triumphant laugh.

Minutes later, gasping for breath and soaked with sweat, he leaped into the apartment and skidded to a halt next to his sister. Terrified, she screamed and backed away and flailed her fists.

"Shh-shh-shh. Sister, it's me. It's me!" He pulled her to him until she stopped. Taking her head in his hands he turned her face toward his.

"See? It's me!" he said again. He smiled, sweat trickling into his eyes. Her brows knit with concentration, then her whole face lit up.

“Gaaahh!” she cried.

“Shh-shh, Sister, yes, it’s me, it’s me. Okay. Oh, I’m so glad you’re safe!” They hugged each other. Kaehl felt waves of dizziness crowd over him. The pain at the back of his head roared.

Standing up, he leaned against a wall, waiting for the nausea to leave. He squeezed his eyes shut and wiped away tears. Sister looked up at him, questioning.

He shook his head and took her hand. “Sister, we have to go,” he urged. “People are coming. We have to go. Come on!”

Selda rose. He untied the leash, put a finger to his lips, kissed her forehead, ran a hand along her cheek, and smiled. Together they ran down the exit corridor and edged into the hallway, peering around the frame. All clear. Together they slipped out and ran to the ramps.

Top

Kaehl stopped and stood blinking, his eyes unfocused. He felt a shock of mild surprise. He had run into a wall. It stood there, mocking, hand spans from his face.

He backed away and stared. How long had he been wandering; how much time had elapsed since he had left the garden? Days? Months? Years? He had no idea. He was in a hall, standing alone. His head thundered with pain, his breath came in ragged gasps. Whoever had hit him in the head in the factory must have done a good job; it had hurt him more than he had thought. Dully, he remembered going up endless ramps.

He had been carrying something. What was it?

Kaehl looked over his shoulder. Ah—Sister! Wan, pale, very weak, she sagged against the wall where she had fallen or he had placed her. He couldn't remember which. That was what he had been carrying. Poor Sister. Their stayover hadn't strengthened her as much as he thought.

He remembered now. The enemy was behind him. He was alive. They had been traveling up the Tower to get away, to get help.

Darkness popped in front of his eyes. He shook his head and staggered, retching. Holding his head against the pain, his eyes streaming, he tried to focus.

His fists clenched. The food! In his rush to escape the factory he had entirely forgotten his cache of food. All their supplies were still at the apartment! The dull ache in his stomach roared.

Kaehl's mind whirled, feverish. He turned and tried to move forward. A tension at his wrist pulled at him, causing him to look down. The leash! He had tied one end to his wrist. He jerked at it. The other end circled Sister's neck. Selda's head snapped up. She groaned and struggled to her feet, her legs shaking and her face deathly white.

"Up," he ordered. He began clambering up the ramp, dragging her behind. One foot. Then another. One foot. Another.

The leash went taut again. Kaehl jerked at it. He heard a noise, a sucking, spasmodic gasping. Angrily he turned to his sister. She sagged against a wall, her face blank. She stayed there for a moment, her feet spread, trembling violently and then she dropped like a stone, her head bouncing off the floor. Her muscles cramped and locked, pulsing. Her breath came in stutters, her body bucked. Foam curdled from her mouth.

Horrified, Kaehl snapped awake and knelt, staring at the guttering figure. "Sister!" he gasped then screamed, "SISTER!" The gurgling, stuttering body kicked against him. He grabbed her by the shoulders, shaking her. Convulsions wracked her frame. He reached out and slapped her. "Sister!" he screamed again.

Selda slowed and relaxed, then sighed and sagged like an empty sack. She dropped into a heavy stupor, her eyes lidded. Kaehl cradled her in his arms, tears brimming his eyes.

Help! he cried in his thoughts, rocking the emptied girl. In his mind he searched the corridors, running from door to door, banging on them, seeking help. No one opened. No one would; he knew that. He had no one to turn to. Where could he go, what could he do? Nothing. There were no options. There was nowhere to go.

Help! he thought again. His mind reeled.

A feeling walked up from behind him and tapped him on the shoulder. Through his stupor he turned and inclined his head. The shape of a man stood beside him, smiling warmly. "The Top," the shape said. "The Penthouse. The Rich. The Doctors." The voice was clear, assuring.

"Yes," Kaehl murmured. "I remember." He had been going to the Top. Doctors lived at the Top. That was the one sure place in this empty, unfair tower where people lived who could help him, where someone could cure his sister. They would help her; they wanted to help her, they waited to help her. But it's so far…

The figure smiled.

"Help," he murmured again, his voice a ragged whisper. His hand reached out. Kaehl blinked and the figure disappeared.

"Help..." he cried.

No one answered. Carefully, slowly, he lifted the ragamuffin girl into his arms again and continued up.

Ages crept by as the boy and his sister dragged toward the top. The blank glare in the ramps left everything a meaningless void. He had no idea how far he had come or how much farther he had to go.

They slept in the halls or in the ramps, they didn't care. They hadn't seen anyone for ages so his fear of discovery had been dulled. Eventually the line between sleeping and waking blurred. They walked, they slept, they ate and drank when they could, they continued up.

In a daze, Kaehl topped one ramp and turned to go up another. He smacked his nose against a wall and fell backward, still holding Selda. He got to his knees, put out a hand and touched a wall. Despair closed over him: the ramp had ended; they'd have to find another way. Slowly, empty of feeling, he got to his feet, hoisted Selda, and entered the halls.

He heard noises. He seemed to be moving through a crowd. He

couldn't tell if he was dreaming or awake. The blurred masses saw him and parted, repulsed at the stumbling wraith, carrying his inert sister. The air was fouler, thicker, hotter. Sister hung in his arms like a rag doll. The two of them stank. Their pace was a crawl.

They fell.

Kaehl remembered sleeping, people stepping over them.

When he awoke, his bleary eyes blinking stupidly, he could not wake Selda. People stepped around them or turned away making ugly noises. He shook her, called her name, smacked her shoulder, slapped her face. She opened her eyes but they were blank, staring. They rolled in their sockets until they showed nothing but white. Her breath was shallow and quick, her body rigid, quivering. Trembling, Kaehl lifted her in his arms and staggered forward. "Help!" he croaked, his voice hoarse, high. "Help!"

He staggered down the corridor. He parted masses of people, tottering through them, gasping, trying to keep Selda from falling out of his arms. He bumped into something and reeled back. Someone screamed and backed away. Figures ran toward him, one with an arm raised, holding something thick and heavy. There was a noise and a flash and then there was nothing.

Kaehl dreamed of black stars shooting across an ivory sky, colliding with other stars and exploding in blinding black showers. The explosions burst inside his head, painful, blinding. The darkness faded and all was silence. The pain grew.

Kaehl opened his eyes.

He was in a blindingly lit room. The air was thick and still, humid and hot, tinged with some strong odor. *A pleasant scent,* he thought, his mind wandering.

He lay on some sort of luxurious cushioned platform, draped in sheets that were like his blanket at home yet very thin and much, much cleaner. They were wet where he lay, probably drenched with his sweat. Kaehl stretched cautiously and rubbed his eyes.

Where was he?

He felt underneath the sheets. Someone had taken his clothes.

Kaehl leaped off the platform. His feet tangled in the sheets and he fell to the ground. He rolled and sprang up, fists cocked. A wave of nausea washed over him. For a moment he swayed, battling to stay on his feet. Then he sagged against the platform. Well, if anyone was going to attack him they'd have done it by now. He could see no one else in the room.

He peered into the brilliance and felt a breeze. He needed clothes. He stood and moved away from the platform, his hands feeling in front of him. The floor was warm and soft, apparently covered with some sort of thick, soft blanket. It extended as far as he could feel.

Finding nothing with his hands he turned and moved in another direction. After several steps he found a wall.

The wall was like nothing he had ever felt before. Its texture was different from the cold, broken surfaces of home. It was smooth and warm and very bright. He felt along it until he found an adjoining surface extending from it at a sharp right angle—a corner. He continued along that wall until he found another corner, and then another. At last he returned to the platform. The size of the room astounded him. It was as broad as an entire quad but entirely empty except for the platform. Mystified, he started searching again.

Kaehl heard someone approaching on the other side of the wall with slow, heavy footsteps that clomped in the silence. He leaped onto the platform and pulled the sheet over him. The footsteps stopped. Kaehl struggled to still his breathing, his body coiled. He forced his eyes closed.

There was a clicking sound and a swish. He felt a breeze. The footsteps hesitated, then stepped onto the floor blanket and padded toward him. They stopped a short distance away. Kaehl went rigid.

"Good morning, sir," the figure intoned. "The Master hopes you slept well and asks you to join him in the breakfast room. Please take a few moments to freshen up. I have new clothing for you. Your old clothes will be returned later."

Kaehl heard the figure turn and move out of the room. There was a swish and a clicking sound and then the footsteps clomped away. Kaehl sprang up and leaped after the sound. With a thump he crashed into the wall. He ran his fingers over it and found a tiny crack, very smooth and regular, running toward the ceiling. Tracing it with his fingers he decided it was a door, an entranceway that fit so snugly into the wall that he had missed it during his previous search. It had little resemblance to the heavily barred wood and leather barriers that had protected his home. He bumped against a metal knob and turned it. The door opened.

The hallway was only a little less bright than his room. Someone stood across the hall from him.

"Good morning, sir. If you will please dress first, I will escort you to your meal."

Kaehl looked down, jerked back into the room and slammed the door. Pacing, his fists tight, he sized up his situation, sweating freely in the wet heat.

He searched the room again and found other closures like the door he had just opened. One led to a very small room with clothes hanging in it, another to a larger room with a stone floor and several metal and smooth stone objects along the walls. The air was particularly thick and sweet here. He found a low chair of some sort fixed to the floor with a lid over a large bowl. There was water inside. He was thirsty, but the water had a strong, unfamiliar smell. He closed the lid.

Next to the chair was a box with a hollowed top mounted by several metal objects. He returned to the seat, opened the lid and drank.

Behind a stiff, smooth curtain Kaehl discovered a tall, narrow enclosure that had been scooped out of the wall. One end held a small drain below more metal fixtures. He frowned. *Unnatural*, he thought. He leaned forward and aimed a stream at the opening. The drain was very small.

After finishing he returned to the platform and put on the clothing the man had left him. He marveled at its lightweight, smooth softness. He re-crossed the room and opened the door.

The man, still waiting across the hall, nodded and motioned to his left. "Breakfast awaits," he said. Kaehl followed him down a corridor past several closed doors, up two levels, and into a huge room that was larger than three quads combined. A large table was centered in the room around one end of which sat three men, hunched, silent, and still, empty plates and glasses in front of them. Kaehl followed his guide toward the table. The guide pulled back a chair and stood motionless. Kaehl glanced at him and then around the room. The man motioned toward the seat; suddenly aware, Kaehl sat on it. The man quietly retreated from the room.

The three silent men remained in their seats, eyes dull and fixed, heads nodding. They looked heavy and old, drained of color, their hair dull and wiry, their skin like paste.

The hall was stifling in its close, heated silence. Kaehl edged forward in his chair, fascinated by the luxurious surroundings. The table was old and heavy, constructed of wood with a surface polished like metal. The chairs reached over his head and around his back, engulfing him in plushness. The faraway walls appeared high, ponderous, and old. Cases and cabinets lined the walls, glittering dimly, almost lost in the bright lights.

Kaehl slouched in his chair, waiting. A round object on the wall made a regular tapping sound. It displayed numbers along its edge and had a thin wire tracing a slow arc through them. The men sat motionless. A heavy, fat fly murmured ponderously onto the table in front of him. Kaehl brushed at it. The pig-like monster squashed thickly against his hand. Surprised, Kaehl wiped it on his shirt.

Kaehl cleared his throat. "Hello?" he ventured. The men did not respond. He tried again. "Has anyone seen my sister?" The silence closed behind him. "She was with me at the ramp. I was wondering..." Kaehl looked from face to heavy face. Their eyes did not move.

At length a man dressed in black entered the room bearing a tray with a several covered bowls. He advanced slowly toward them, each foot set precisely in front of the other—plodding, deliberate, methodical. The slow-motion man reached the table, turned, and metered his steps toward the person at the far end. After an eternity or two he placed the tray on the table, wrapped his fingers around a bowl, lifted it from the tray, passed it in front of the seated figure, and set it down before him. He removed the cover from the bowl and set it in the tray. An aroma touched Kaehl's nose. He licked his lips.

The server placed both hands on the tray, lifted the tray from the table, straightened his back, took two steps backward, turned, trod toward the next person, and stepped around him. He placed the tray on the table and repeated his routine. Kaehl stared at the automaton, his mouth open. His stomach growled.

At last the man came toward him. As the hands set the bowl in front of him, Kaehl reached for a spoon. The hands froze in their glacial journey. Kaehl hesitated for a moment and then set the spoon down again. The servant reached for the tray, straightened, and backed away.

Kaehl looked into the bowl. The contents appeared nondescript and thin but smelled wonderful. His empty belly cramped. He looked at his hosts. Without moving their heads, three hands reached for their spoons. Kaehl snatched his spoon and dove into his broth, scalding his mouth. He drained it in one gulp. It tasted bland, almost ugly, like strained soap. He set the bowl down and wiped his mouth, expectant.

He looked toward his hosts. They were watching him. Kaehl coughed, his face reddening. They swiveled their heads back toward their bowls.

Calmly, carefully, they spooned one spoonful into their mouths, swirled it appraisingly, and swallowed. Another spoonful followed, slowly, deliberately, calmly. Each mouthful was tested, each swallow tested. One more and then another. The boy felt his gorge fight against the soup he had slurped. He looked around hopefully and licked his lips.

The men finished their broth and set their spoons beside their bowls. There was a pause for throat clearing and restrained dabbing of mouths. After a moment, one looked up at the boy.

"I," the old man began, his voice the texture of mud, "am Mr. Welswept. I am the head of this building. Mr. Jolley and Mr. Roeke," he paused, raising an arm and gesturing to the others, who nodded in acknowledgment, "are my able assistants. You," he added, one finger snaking at Kaehl, "are not from our levels. We find it good to be charitable. Accept our charity." Mr. Welswept braced his arms against the table and levered himself up. The other men followed.

The boy rose expectantly. "Uhh, thank you, sir. Sirs." The men began to file out of the room.

"Sir?"

The men stooped along, unhearing. Kaehl walked timidly to Mr. Welswept.

"Sir?"

The old man turned his pasty face toward him and smiled absently, like a parent to a nattering child. Then he turned again and continued. Kaehl stopped as the men entered a doorway and shuffled out. The door closed.

"Sir?"

Kaehl startled and whirled, his eyes alight. The voice had come from behind. A thin, dark man stood at his side, his face impassive, his eyes hooded.

"If you will follow me please, sir?" he said.

Kaehl followed him across the room. Kaehl shortened his gait to keep from passing him. Everything here seemed to happen at half speed. "Is there any more food?" he asked.

"There is always more food, sir."

Kaehl smiled and rubbed his belly. "I hope so. That was the smallest meal I've ever had. I'm starving."

The servant plodded on.

"Hey, yeah—have you seen my sister? She was with me when I blacked out. I haven't seen her since I woke up."

"I'm afraid I haven't, sir."

"Where am I?"

"The Penthouse, sir."

Kaehl stopped, thunderstruck. "The Penthouse?"

The figure nodded. Kaehl had made it! The rich, the doctors, the food…

"Uhh—how did I get here, anyway? I mean, the last thing I remember was being in a crowd, in the halls."

"I'm sure I have no idea, sir."

"How long have I been here?"

"Just follow me, sir."

"Where are we going?"

"Home, sir."

Kaehl stopped again. Home? Were they done with him already? Had they already healed Sister? Maybe they had! Look at what they had done for him—sleeping quarters, clothes, time with the Tower leaders, food—well, maybe not so much food, but still, maybe they had done the same with Selda! They could have done anything. After all, he had no idea how long he had been here.

Kaehl's eyes fairly glowed with joy. But then his enthusiasm dimmed as more questions arose. Had they found her? What happened if they hadn't? Did they even know about her? Where was she now? And when they said, "Home," what did they mean? How could they talk about taking him home when they didn't even know where he lived? Maybe they did; they probably had resources beyond anything he had seen.

Unsure, he followed the servant out another door and down a long corridor. They moved into a small room and down a ramp leading to a nondescript doorway in a smaller room. The servant lifted a parcel from a counter top and handed it to the boy.

"Here are your clothes," he said. "Thank you for coming." The servant turned and opened the door, motioning Kaehl through. Bewildered, Kaehl stepped forward and paused on the doorstep. He turned his head. "Is my sister out here?"

"She's dead, sir."

Shoved by a rough hand to his back Kaehl lurched through the door, stumbled into a small courtyard and hit his head against a wall, landing in a flurry of dust, garbage and cobwebs. There was an animal sound of disgust behind him and he turned to see the door slam shut.

Kaehl picked himself out of a pile of trash and looked around. Unbroken walls stretched down a corridor on either side of him. A hallway. He was alone. He had been thrown into an alley outside the Penthouse.

Furious, Kaehl rushed to the door and jerked the handle. It was locked.

"Hey!" he shouted, crashing a fist against the door. "Open up! Open the door. OPEN THE DOOR!" He listened for a moment. No response. "Sister! Where's my sister? Open UP!"

He kicked the door and pounded on it. No response. He smashed into it with his shoulder and stood back, rubbing the bruise. He kicked it again then returned to the garbage pile, brushing dirt and trash from his clothes. Tears rolled down his face.

He whirled back to the door and raised a fist. "SHE'S NOT DEAD, YOU HEAR ME?" He threw a brick at the door. It glanced off and landed in the dust.

Casting about, he found the package the servant had given him. He picked it up and unwrapped it. There, incongruously cleaned and pressed, lay his ragged street clothes. Thinking for a moment, he re-wrapped them and put them inside his shirt. With a vengeful glare over his shoulder he turned and trotted down the corridor.

The hallway branched to his right. He turned and followed it up a long, blank passage, slowing when he heard voices echoing near an intersection. At the crossway he stopped and peered around the corner, holding his breath.

Six large guards towered in front of what looked like an entrance to a large room, heavy clubs swinging loosely in their grips. Kaehl backed down the hallway and pressed himself against a wall. *Guards at the Penthouse?* he thought. *Insecurity.*

Thoughts tumbled through his brain. Sister, dead? No, not possible. The servant had lied. If they'd found Kaehl they would have found his sister, too; after all, they had been tied together with the leash. If they brought him inside and fed and clothed him then surely they would have saved her, too, or at least brought her inside. That meant that those in the Penthouse were holding her. They knew where she was, and they could help him find her. Kaehl was sure of that; the assurance burned through his bones. They weren't going to help him; that was sure. He would have to find her himself. But first he had to get back in. After that…well, whatever else happened would happen. He would find her, regardless.

Kaehl trotted back down the hall to the garbage pile and surveyed the area. The door was recessed into the wall, with a few empty storage drums and small trash bins cluttering the wall opposite. It looked like a service entrance, some place used for deliveries, like some doors at the factory. He shoved a drum aside and settled behind it, taking a position where he could watch both the door and the hall. Then he sat back and waited.

Centuries crawled by. Kaehl watched a line of ants attack a dark trail of something dripping from a box. Cockroaches and spiders made their way through the piles. An occasional rat emerged, its jeweled eyes watching him, its nose twitching and sniffing. Then it would disappear.

Kaehl's stomach ached. He considered trapping and eating one of the rats but didn't want to risk the noise. The stench dulled his enthusiasm for picking through the trash. He hunkered down to wait. He had no idea what he would do once he got inside but he knew he would find his sister. A few times he slept. His legs cramped, then his back. He stretched and continued waiting.

Something scraped behind the door. Kaehl froze, his eyes riveted. A bolt was thrown back, a lock turned, and the door groaned slightly on its hinges. Kaehl ducked behind the barrel, holding his breath. A man backed out, dressed in a stained white apron, carrying a heavy bag of greasy trash. He stumped toward the trash pile, whistling a mindless tune, letting the door shut behind him. He walked directly toward Kaehl's barrel. Stooping to lift the lid, he looked down. Kaehl looked up. The man stopped, color draining from his face. The bag dropped.

Kaehl stood, his eyes fixed on the servant. The servant began to back away.

"Wuddaya—wuddaya want?" he said, his mouth slack. He drooled. The garbage lid clattered to the floor.

"Nothing," Kaehl answered, his hands extended, trying to smile. He limped around the barrel. A thousand pins jabbed at his sleep-numbed legs. "Just let me into that apartment. Please."

"No. Don' touch me. No money. Lossa food, give ya wacha want don' hurt me. Ain' gonna be no trubble. won' tell no one. No pain. Please..." The man babbled, his eyes fixed on Kaehl, backing toward the door. He stumbled and almost fell. He backed against the entrance.

Kaehl stopped. The man felt behind him for the handle. "Listen," Kaehl called, "No problem, no pain, of course. I only want to talk with Mr. Welswept. No problem. I won't hurt you. Just let me in."

"No-no-no, can't do it. They'd kill me. Go. Please!"

"Please," Kaehl said, taking a step forward. "I promise..."

"No!" the fat man shouted. He turned and grabbed at the handle.

Kaehl sprang at him. The two collided against the door and bounced back into the trash. The man was blubbering, shouting. He smashed Kaehl's face with his fist.

Kaehl moaned, cradling his face. "Why did you do that?" he said. He got to his knees and scrambled toward the door. The servant grabbed his legs and jerked him back into the trash. The man was screaming, now, calling for help.

Kaehl kicked backward and rolled free. "No pain!" Kaehl yelled. "I don't want to hurt you! Shut up! Shut up! You're going to bring the guards!" He knocked the man's hands away and grabbed at his mouth.

The two rolled in the garbage, the servant struggling to throw him off. Kaehl was hitting him now, his fists clenched, eyes wild.

"Shut up! Shut up! Shut up!" Kaehl cried, smashing the rolling flesh. The man and the boy were panting, covered with filth. The servant was mewling, gurgling, tears in his eyes, blood on his cheeks. "Guards, guards! Help!"

The servant covered his head with his arms then heaved sideways and lifted upward, knocking Kaehl against a barrel. The lid fell and crashed onto his head. Kaehl picked it up and scrambled toward the man, who was on his knees, scuttling toward the door.

"Shut up!" Kaehl screamed, bringing the lid down heavily. "No pain! No pain!" He brought the lid down again. "I promise!" He struck again and again. The figure below him collapsed and went still.

Kaehl stopped, his chest heaving. The lid fell from his hands. "I promise."

The servant lay on his belly, his face buried in the trash. Blood covered the back of his head. Kaehl bent down. The man was still breathing.

Kaehl heard footsteps pounding toward him. He sat against the man's back, paralyzed, gasping for breath. Their fight must have only taken a few seconds. The sounds drew closer.

Three men walked around the corner toward him, carrying boxes of produce. They saw Kaehl and stopped. Kaehl leaped up. Considering for a moment, he sprang for the door.

The men dropped their boxes, turned and ran back the way they had come and were immediately bowled over by sprinting guards. Clutching the door handle, Kaehl wrenched the door open and swung inside. The door crashed shut. He slammed the bolt home. He smiled in triumph as the guards pounded on the outside.

He turned. A maid stood frozen before him, her eyes wide, a hand over her mouth.

Kaehl stepped forward. "Please..." he began.

The maid screamed and turned, flying down the hall. Kaehl leaped toward her but stopped, thinking. Looking around him, he crouched and ran down another hall.

The maid was still running through the apartment as Kaehl came upon the glassed-in door of a large kitchen. Food! A group of cooks and maids were gathered in a knot opposite him, their backs toward him, looking out a door. The maid ran past them, screaming.

Kaehl's eyes fastened on a carving knife on a counter. His look hardened. Creeping forward, he lifted it and advanced on the group. They were still staring out the door, muttering to themselves, craning to get a better look at the woman. Easing up to them, Kaehl leaned forward, his teeth clenched, and raised the knife.

He lowered it. He couldn't kill these people; they were innocent. Twisting the weapon in his hands a moment, his face split with a twisted grin. He leaned toward them and pursed his lips.

"Boo!" he said.

Screams and shouts echoed as the servants shot through the door and down the hall. A faraway door slammed and all was quiet.

Kaehl smiled grimly. He returned to the kitchen and wolfed down meat and bread and vegetables. He took a long drink of water and vomited. Pale, he stood up, forced more down, and stuffed his pockets. Meat cleaver in his hand, he moved out of the room.

He searched the hallway. Rooms followed rooms, hallways led into closed and locked doors. The Penthouse was big but not that big. The servants would be bringing the guards soon, he knew. He had to find his sister quickly.

He opened a door. A narrow ramp led up. As he examined it the lamps flared, flooding the hall with absolute white, blinding him. Sweat trickled over his brow. He wiped a hand across his face. The heat was oppressive. Stepping in he gripped the knife, closed the door, and padded up.

Kaehl reached the top of the ramp, stopped and peered around. He could see nothing. All was silent. The blindness was complete. He moved one step forward, then another, feeling with his feet. He passed an entranceway. There was no door. He moved forward. The ramp leveled off. He edged forward again.

Kaehl's hand touched a wall. Carefully, sliding his hand along, he felt his way forward.

Kaehl edged along the hallway for what seemed an eternity. There were no sounds. The knife grew slippery in his palm. Moisture trickled down his forehead.

Kaehl collided with a wooden stand. An object on it rattled, rolled and fell, crashing explosively in the quiet. Kaehl gripped the stand and froze, his heart smashing against his ribs.

There was no reaction. Gently he released the stand. Another object on it wobbled and fell over. He listened again. No response. He edged forward, feeling with his hands.

The heavy air thickened with the smell of alcohol. "Potato beer," he grunted to himself. The odor brought to mind unpleasant memories. With an effort he pushed them away.

His hand came across something soft. Gingerly, he outlined it with his fingers. It was a hand.

A startled grunt erupted. The hand jerked away. Something blunt smashed into him. Without thinking, Kaehl swung the cleaver. The knife bit deep into something soft. There was a gasp. Kaehl wrenched it out and reached back to swing again.

Stars exploded as something smashed into his arm. His fingers went numb. He brought the cleaver forward again, felt it sink into something, and crumpled against the wall. Something heavy fell against him, the weight wrenching the knife out of his hand. Frantically he shoved the mass away and scrambled back. Holding his injured arm he rocked silently against the wall, tears squeezing down his face.

Gritting his teeth, Kaehl stretched his arm and flexed his fingers. The pain lessened. He stooped to feel for the knife. A red haze blossomed behind his eyes and he staggered. He shook it away.

He came upon an arm lying on the floor. It did not move. A bunch of keys lay beside it; Kaehl picked them up. He felt along the arm until he reached a chest. There was a sucking sound. Something was gurgling from it. He felt farther and discovered his knife buried halfway into a belly. He pulled it out and levered himself upright, bracing himself against the wall.

He felt sick.

Feeling his way with his good hand he fumbled upon the edges of a closed door. He found the handle and twisted it. It would not open. He looked over his shoulder then tried the keys until he found one that fit. The door opened.

Truth

Kaehl stumbled into a lushly carpeted room lit by dim lamps. The room was lined with bookshelves and thick cases. A heavy desk stood against the far wall behind which sat a large figure, cloaked in shadows.

"Ah, Mr. Charity," said the figure. "You're back. Please come in."

Kaehl glanced around the room. He startled as the door clicked shut behind him.

"It does that," the figure chuckled. "Locks. Security feature. Did you say hello to my guard? Or was he off drinking someplace? From the looks of your knife I'd say the two of you must have met. And you have his keys, too. Well done."

Kaehl held up the knife. It was dripping. He scanned his surroundings. Seeing no one else in the room he moved forward, extending the cleaver. His hand shook. He brought up the other hand to steady it, flinging away the keys. The figure grew clearer as he approached the desk.

"You're one of the people from breakfast this morning," Kaehl stated.

"Yes, very good," the man responded. "I'm Mr. Jolley."

"Yes, Jolley, yes." He gripped the knife tighter. "I need to find Mr. Welswept. Where is he?"

"Not here. Not anywhere you are going," he said. "By the way, you're dripping on my carpet." He stretched his mouth in an ugly smile, the lips thin and crooked.

Kaehl tightened his grip on the knife. "Where's my sister?"

"Your sister? Sister? Ah, you mean that tiny slip of a girl my guards brought to me when you were dragged in? She's your sister, eh? Is that what you're here for?" He picked up a huge cigar, lit it, and regarded him. "She's dead."

The knife dropped to the floor. Kaehl stooped to pick it up but his knees buckled and gave way. He shook his head and levered himself back to his feet, swaying. He brought his eyes up to focus on Jolley, who was watching him with steely, slightly amused eyes.

"Yes, dead," Jolley intoned. "So you don't need to worry about her any more. Relax."

Kaehl dropped into a nearby chair. "How do you know?" he rasped.

"One of our guards brought her to a doctor. She was barely alive then; I don't think she made it much farther. She's in one of our morgues."

"Morgue?"

"Yes. A place where they store dead people. Or experiment on them. Or whatever."

Kaehl gasped and sobbed. "I was trying to save her, to heal her. That's why I brought her here. Selda..."

"That was her name, Selda?" Jolley pulled another puff of smoke from the cigar. His jowls rolled as he chewed on it. "Too bad." He gestured toward Kaehl. "You going to get rid of the knife? You don't need it, now."

The weapon drooped in Kaehl's limp hand. He looked down at it, then up at Jolley, his eyes vacant.

"Here, I'll take care of it for you." Jolley stood and moved toward the boy, his hands outstretched. Kaehl blinked and pulled the knife away.

"Let go, son, let go. There's nothing you can do for her. Give me the knife."

Kaehl frowned and tried to stand, moving away. Jolley shoved him backward into the chair and grabbed for the knife. Kaehl rebounded and darted beneath his arms. He leaped to the desk and whirled to face the older man, fiercely gripping the knife. Jolley, his eyes dark, turned and glared at him, his cigar smoldering. He tapped ashes from it and returned to his seat.

"What do you want?" he asked, his voice thick. Kaehl thought that he seemed to be breathing faster. A drop of sweat trickled down his forehead.

"My sister."

"You want her body? She's dead. Forget her. What else?"

"Forget her?"

"Look, son, I'm busy. I'm being very patient. You want answers? Give me the knife. Otherwise, get out of my office."

"But..."

"Do it now."

Kaehl felt his grip loosen again. He searched Jolley's face looking for hope, for comfort, for anything. He saw the sweat bead across the fat man's brow. One of Jolley's eyes twitched.

Kaehl brought the knife up. "No," he said.

"Then leave. You're filthy, you stink, and I've got things to do."

"Show me my sister."

Jolley sprang up and slammed his hands on the desk. Kaehl jumped back. "You'll do what I tell you. Now leave. Now!"

Tears edged Kaehl's eyes. "But my sister..."

"'My sister'," Jolley mocked, settling back into his chair. "'My sister.' Pitiful. You assault my staff, break into my house and threaten me and now you mew like a newborn rat. 'My sister.' You disgust me."

Kaehl's hands lowered again. "But you were going to save her."

"I was? News to me. We don't go around saving alley rats."

"She wasn't a rat! You were supposed to be these powerful, good leaders, the ones we looked up to and envied, the ones with the power and money and doctors. You were supposed to have all the answers. Why don't you help?"

"Wow. All of that, eh?" Jolley thought for a moment then his eyes flicked to the knife. "I don't bargain with criminals."

The knife fell to Kaehl's side.

"Now sit."

Kaehl moved back to the chair and sat. Jolley leaned back and twirled his cigar. "You need my help, eh?"

Kaehl nodded.

"Everyone does. Why should I help you?"

Kaehl's eyes widened. "Because you're a Framer, or one of their children, aren't you?"

"Twentieth great-grandchild or more."

"So you take care of us."

Jolley snorted. "Do I?"

Kaehl nodded again, a little less sure this time.

"Okay, I will. First give me the knife."

Kaehl stared at it then back at Jolley. "I won't hurt you."

"Prove it. I can't help if you're a threat."

Kaehl shifted his grip on the knife and held it out, handle first. Jolley's eyes widened imperceptibly.

Kaehl pulled it back. "You'll give me what I want?"

"Whatever you need."

"You'll show me my sister?"

"Of course."

"You won't hurt her if she's alive?"

Jolley scowled. "The knife."

Kaehl stared at the blade. It was still wet, crimsoning his hand where he touched it. Jolley held his hand out. His fingers were thick, broad and drenched in gold. Sweat beaded his palm. Kaehl looked closer. The hand shook, ever so slightly.

Jolley snapped his fingers and roared. "NOW!"

Kaehl jumped as if shot. The knife nearly flew out of his hand. He gaped at the fat man, his arm trembling. "I know you," Kaehl said slowly, as if waking from a dream. "I know your kind. You're using me, aren't you, trying to control me. I can see you clearly now. You won't help me. You won't help anyone. You're in this for yourself—for money or power or control or anything but other people, aren't you?" His voice strengthened. "You're just like the Packs, aren't you? You are in charge but you cause more problems than you solve. You don't fix things; you destroy them. You created the dying people at Doctor Herstand's lake, didn't you, you and your policies? You're in charge so—you created the Packs, too, or created the circumstances that bred them. You'll kill them like you'll kill Selda. Maybe like you killed her already." He reversed his grip on the knife. "Like you plan to kill me."

Jolly put both hands on the desk. "You live in a fantasy world, son."

"No, I don't."

"You're dead anyway. Give me the knife and I might help your sister. Keep it and…" His voice trailed away.

"No. I had hope. I had hoped that you would heal Sister. But you won't, will you? There's no hope here."

Jolley sat back. "What do you care?" he said. "I scrape dirt like you from my fingernails every day. There are thousands of people like you in this sewer, none of whom will ever know your name. When you die you will be gone and that will be the end of you and your idiot sister."

"No! You couldn't live without people like me. We make your little world possible."

"My world? You know it so well? Yes, I need dirt like you, but I can flick you aside and not even notice it. I can change your world with a word. There are thousands like you, all whining the same thing: 'Come help me,

Mr. Jolley.' 'Fix things, Mr. Jolley.' 'Feed us, Mr. Jolley.' It sickens me. You think you have value but to me you are nothing, less than nothing. GIVE ME THE KNIFE!"

"No!"

"GUARDS!"

Footsteps sounded outside the door. Kaehl threw a glance over his shoulder and sprang toward the desk. He stopped inches from it, his knife quivering as he raised it.

Jolley ducked. His pasty face went white. "GUARDS!" he screamed. Fists pounded on the door. The cigar rolled to the floor. Kaehl twisted the blade.

"Don't!" Jolley stammered, scraping away from him in his chair. "The guards are right outside. You'll never get out. Touch me and you're dead!"

Kaehl stood over the desk. The cleaver rose high. "Look," Jolley quavered, "I'll pay you..."

Kaehl brought the cleaver down heavily onto the desk. The blade sank deep.

"Mr. Jolley!" shouted someone.

"HEEEERRRE!" he screeched. He pulled open a drawer and plunged a hand in, pulling out a small knife.

Kaehl yanked his knife out, dove across the desk and landed on Jolley. The two tottered backward for a moment. The knife flew out of Jolley's hand.

"HELP MEEEE!" he squealed, trying to push Kaehl off. The door crashed open, pieces flying. The guards poured in.

Kaehl blunted Jolley heavily across the cheek with the back of the knife and dropped behind him. Grabbing his hair and yanking back, he held the knife to Jolley's flabby neck. Kaehl sank down behind the chair and pressed in the blade. Blood trickled.

"Stop!" Kaehl commanded. His eyes were wild, his hair flying. The guards pulled up in front of the desk. Kaehl shook Jolley's head.

The fat man's eyes bulged. He sucked in a huge gasp of air and tried to rise. The blade bit deeper. He crashed back onto the chair.

"Do that again and die," Kaehl hissed. Jolley did not move. Kaehl bent closer.

"Order your men away," he said. Jolley hesitated. Kaehl yanked his hair.

"Yes, yes, away!" he squealed. Tears flooded his cheeks. "Oh the Framers, for the love of..." The guards backed out of the room.

"My sister," Kaehl demanded. "Where is she?"

"Dead!" Jolley squealed, eyes rolling back. "Oh, dead, dead..."

"SHUT UP!" Kaehl screamed, standing up. The troops bolted back in. Clubs whirled toward him. He ducked. They whistled past his head and smashed into the wall behind him. He dropped behind Jolley again.

"Stop!" he commanded, his knife at Jolley's throat. The guards halted, clubs ready.

"When did she die?" he demanded.

Jolley blinked stupidly for a moment. "I don't know; I wasn't there. Doctor diagnosed it. See them all the time; miserable, rotting poor. Don't last a day down here."

Kaehl brought the knife in closer. "Where is she?"

"Dead!" Jolley replied. "I told you! Garbage pit, maybe the doctor's office, the morgue—I don't know. Dead! Forget her!"

Kaehl thought for a moment and then shifted the blade away from Jolley's throat. "Stand up," he said, pulling on Jolley's arm. "Slowly. And order your guards away."

"Where are we going?" whimpered Jolley.

"The morgue."

Hesitant, trembling, Jolley arose. The guards moved back, gripping their clubs tightly. Knife at Jolley's throat, Kaehl pushed him toward the door.

"Order your guards away," Kaehl repeated.

"Go!" Jolley shouted. The guards backed away. Slowly, Kaehl pushed Jolley toward the entrance. Kaehl kicked at the door. Silence.

"Back away from the entrance!" he shouted. Guards shuffled out from behind the door, fixing Kaehl with murderous glares. Kaehl and Jolley stepped into the hall. The room was ringed with guards, faces eager for blood. Standing with his back to the door, Kaehl motioned to the biggest guard.

"You! Tiny!" he called. The muscled giant glanced at him. "You're gonna walk in front of us. I want to make sure there won't be any surprises. Tell your buddies to back off, out of sight. The old man can't take too much of this and neither can I. You'll get him back once I get my sister. Now move."

The guard motioned to the others in the room. They faded back down the halls and into rooms.

"That's real good. Keep it up. Now, listen to the fat man and we'll be off." He jerked at Jolley's arm. "Tell him."

"Lenny. Doctor Heppner. Take us there. No tricks."

"Yeah," Kaehl said. "No tricks. Let's go."

The trio started off. Many eyes shadowed them as they moved out of the apartment and into a main corridor but no one moved. Lenny turned at a ramp and started down.

"Down the ramps?" Kaehl asked.

"Up the ramps, you cretin. Yes, of course," Jolley answered. "Heppner's just a doctor. He doesn't live in the Penthouse."

"Penthouse," Kaehl spat.

"The Penthouse, yes."

"The top of the Tower," said Kaehl "Where the rich live. Paradise. Rot."

The trio descended five levels and then moved along a circular corridor. Jolley, wheezing and panting, staggered and nearly fell. "Please, no more!" he gasped.

"Almost there, right?" Kaehl responded. "You'll make it."

They moved down the corridor a hundred paces. The halls were squared off and decorated, covered with garish colors. Lenny stopped at the doorway.

"This is it," Jolley squalled. "Let me go now." He moved to break away.

"Not yet," Kaehl said, jerking him back. Kaehl motioned to Lenny. "Any of your friends in there, clear them out. Now!"

Lenny ducked inside. Troops began to file out. Eventually Lenny reappeared and Kaehl shoved Jolley forward. Together they edged inside.

The entrance opened into a large waiting room. Kaehl slammed and bolted the hallway door. Easing forward, he walked carefully through the room searching for hidden guards.

"Tiny, stop." Hauling Jolley with him, Kaehl backed up to a door. Pulling the door open he glanced quickly inside. The small room was vacant, some kind of storage area. He moved forward again.

"Okay, Tiny; in." Kaehl motioned into the room.

Equably, Lenny walked into the room. Seeing no chairs he quietly moved to the center and stood waiting. Kaehl slammed the door. He found a doorstop and wedged it under the door. He jerked on the handle a few times. The door didn't move.

With a huge sigh he thrust Jolley from him and began checking doors. "Okay, fatso, where's my sister?"

Drooping his shoulders, Jolley shook his head and turned. "I told you, you crazy Downer, your sister's dead. She must be by now. She..."

Kaehl opened a door. It led into a large room that stank of powerful chemicals and disease. A putrid, rotting smell saturated his nose.

Tables were spaced regularly along the walls. Upon each table lay a body covered in a white sheet. Some had their faces covered, some did not. None moved.

"Sister?" he breathed. He pointed to Jolley with the knife and motioned toward the room, his face white. "In."

"It stinks."

"So do you. In."

The two moved into the room. Kaehl shoved Jolley against a wall and closed the door. He moved among the tables, scrutinizing each face.

Suddenly he stopped. "Sister!" The yell exploded from him. Her head lay exposed on one of the tables, her body covered. She lay on her back, her eyes closed. Her face was deathly white.

"Oh, Sister!" He knelt at the foot of the table, not daring to touch the emaciated body.

Jolley approached, wiping blood from his neck.

"That's her, eh? I told you she was dead."

Kaehl rose and faced him, his face volcanic. Jolley backed away. "What did you do to her?" Kaehl demanded.

"Do? The doctor said he didn't do anything. Poked, prodded, listened a bit. There wasn't much to do. The girl was mostly gone already."

"But I had hoped you could help her! That's why I came here, so you could heal her. And you let her die!"

"Help her? You dragged her all the way down here for that? Look at her! There wasn't anything we could have done for her!" He leaned over her, shook his head, and moved away. "She should have been killed long ago."

Kaehl stopped breathing. His teeth ground together. The cleaver felt alive in his hand. Slowly he moved around the table.

Jolley stopped and turned around. He backed away, his hands up, eyes wide. "I-I-I mean, look at her! A walking skeleton. What hope did she have? Even if we could have helped her, she could barely speak. No one could understand her. The doctor said she was an idiot! What could you do? There's not enough food in the Tower for cripples..."

"You heard her? You had a chance to talk with her?"

With a great yell Kaehl dashed forward, his knife held high. Jolley backed against one of the tables and screamed. He whirled and yanked the table between him and his attacker. Kaehl circled, trying to get close.

As Kaehl gathered himself to leap, the two froze. A weak, wheezing gasp came from the table behind them. The figure on it moved.

"Sister!" Kaehl breathed.

He whirled back toward the table. Jolley backed away. Gently, anxiously, Kaehl cupped her face, caressing her tenderly. "Sister, Sister..." he groaned.

He held the inert figure for a long time. Gently he put his ear to her chest then to her mouth, listening. He massaged her arms and shoulders. "Sister!" he pleaded. Tears grew in his eyes.

She coughed. A ragged sigh escaped her again. Her eyelids fluttered.

"Sister! Bless the Framers; Sister!" Kaehl clasped the girl to him, tears washing over them both. Jolley, who had been watching, backed toward the door.

Kaehl noted the movement. "Hold it, fat man," he warned. "I still need you."

Jolley grew pale. "Need me? She's alive; okay, so I was wrong. I'm sorry. But what are you going to do now? A dead boy holding a nearly dead girl. You have no chance of getting out of here. And you certainly can't take her with you!"

Kaehl stiffened. Jolley was right. The guards surrounded them, waiting for him to come out. They might bust in any moment. Where would he go? He had made it to the top but it had proved a sham. No family, no friends—he had nowhere left to go. He had left them all behind, had run from them to save himself and his sister. He had let them die.

Now what?

He looked down at Selda again, who had closed her eyes. She looked so peaceful in sleep, her features relaxed. But so pale, so thin, so near death…

No! he thought.

Kaehl picked up the knife again. His hands trembled violently; sweat glistened on his palms. He held them before his face wonderingly. His heart raced, his mouth felt caked with dust.

He had left his family behind but he had returned. It was by accident, yes, but he had found Selda and tried to save her, climbed the whole tower to save her and then fought Jolley's men. No, he was not his father. Yes, he had killed but it hadn't been out of hate. He had done it to save himself and someone he loved. He had done it for his family. He was not his father. He had won.

He looked at his trembling hand. But something was happening to him, something coming over him like a blanket. Something powerful, crippling. What was it?

He recognized it with a shock: Fear. He was afraid. It wasn't the fear he had felt at home. It wasn't fear of becoming his father; he had proved that. And he wasn't afraid for himself; he wasn't afraid of what might happen to him. It was a different kind of fear. He was afraid for his sister. Running the halls with the Pack and again in the Penthouse he had acted out of despair and self-hate and a desire for revenge; his life hadn't mattered. Now he had his sister again and his reasons for living had returned. At home he had sheltered and protected her. In the halls those feelings had only gotten stronger and now he had a powerful need to live. He needed to live to protect her.

And so he was afraid—afraid for her and for her life. He feared to fail her, to finally let her die. He was terrified of dying and leaving her alone one more time, a final, absolute failure. He could not do that. His actions had put her life in danger several times. He would not do it again. Now that he was close to being a dead man himself he desperately needed to live.

All of this flashed through his mind in an instant as he confronted Jolley.

He squared his shoulders, drying his palms on his shirt. He had found his sister again. They were together. That was all he needed. He had something to live for, something to fight for. He pushed the fear away. They would live.

Kaehl brushed past Jolley and headed into the waiting room. He went to the closet, kicked away the doorstop and inched the door open, his foot wedged behind it. Lenny stood in the same spot. He looked at Kaehl and blinked slowly.

"Tiny. We're moving. I want you to carry something."

Kaehl moved back to Jolley. "I don't want to hurt you, old man, but I don't want to die. I have to leave and I'm taking my sister and you're coming with me." He backed Jolley into a corner. "You can come peacefully or I can hurt you more. You have many body parts to lose. Your choice." He grabbed the fat man by the shoulder and whirled him around. His knife fitted near his throat again. Jolley whimpered.

Kaehl turned. Tiny stood placidly, awaiting commands. The boy motioned him to the table in the next room. "There is a girl over there on that table. Pick her up then come back out here. You will walk in front of us, carrying her."

Lenny moved to the table, indifferently hefted the inert girl and carried her into the front room. Kaehl opened the hallway door.

"Listen out there," he shouted down the hall. "I'm bringing out your boss. Stay back and he'll live." He jabbed Jolley in the side. "Agree with me," he hissed.

"Yes, yes, agree with him, agree with him! Stay back!"

Kaehl tried to smile through the sweat. He motioned Lenny forward, then he and Jolley moved out.

A crowd of huge guards stood silently along the walls, watching the four balefully. "Keep your distance, lovelies," Kaehl murmured. He inched along the gauntlet toward Lenny who had reached the end of the hall. The heat nearly gagged him. Jolley smelled like a cesspit. He sniffed. He probably didn't smell all that good either. Sweat rolled off Kaehl's forehead and trickled into his eyes. He shook his head to clear them.

The silent wall of guards loomed all around him, suffocating. He glanced backward quickly, carefully. They were closing in. The wall of clubs and arms seemed sewn to him.

Kaehl bent closer to Jolley's head. "Convince them," he hissed. The blade drew blood again.

"Oh my world—stop, stop, get back! The idiot is murdering me!" Jolley began choking.

Kaehl propelled the fat man before him, breaking through the line of guards. As they moved off he cast another glance behind him. The guards remained motionless.

"You go first, Tiny," he ordered. Obediently, Lenny turned and started walking.

"Where are the ramps?" Kaehl asked Jolley.

"To the left."

"Go, Tiny."

The group climbed a few flights of ramps. A waft of cold air rushed over them through an exit. On a whim Kaehl motioned for them to break out of the ramp and trace the draft. "At least you can breathe out here," he murmured.

Several minutes of silence followed. The draft had picked up and died several times. Now they lost it entirely.

"Any idea where we are?" Kaehl asked.

"You don't know?" Jolley shouted. His laughter filled the corridor until the knife brought it up short.

"I thought you were headed home," he whimpered. "Of course I don't know where we are. I don't come up to these levels."

Kaehl ordered everyone to halt. "Where are we going?" Jolley asked timidly.

"We're going to rest," Kaehl said, releasing the old man. "I think it's safe for now. No one's going to come close while I have this knife. Right, guys?" He shouted this last over his shoulder. "Tiny, stay there. We'll be leaving soon." The three figures sat down gratefully against the wall, Kaehl across from Jolley. Lenny lowered the girl to the floor. She lay still and deathlike. Kaehl had to steel himself to keep from going to her. "Is she alive?" he asked. Lenny nodded indifferently.

Jolley wiped at the blood on his neck. "You monster," he said. "I treated you like royalty, brought you into our home and cleaned you, clothed you, and fed you. You were just a charity case! And look what you did to me!" He held out his bloody hand.

Kaehl glanced at him grimly.

"You came to us for help. I helped you and you assaulted me!"

"Look, old man," Kaehl muttered leaning forward. "Your thugs knocked me out and kidnapped me into your fortress. I came to you seeking help for my sister and you peeled her from me like an old shirt and told me she was dead. Then you treated me like dirt and when you were done you swept me into your trash pile. I am not dirt. I came here seeking answers but you wouldn't even let me ask the questions."

"What did you expect?" Jolley retorted. "You are from the gutter, a Downer. We get your kind here all the time. People want food, people want money, people want jobs, people want homes. They come to us constantly, trying to suck off us. We pick who we want, use them and then toss them back outside—the survivors, that is. We never hear from them again." He wiped his brow. "You were just another pebble in a rock slide."

"Use them?"

Jolley nodded. "Yeah. We were going to use you but Welswept argued against it. Said we couldn't harm you, had to release you unharmed. Idiot. We should have killed you."

"If you weren't going to use me then why did you knock me out, carry me inside, and feed me? If I am just a pebble why did you coddle me? You knew I'd want to talk, to try and use you, to tell my problems to someone in charge. Everyone would."

Jolley laughed harshly. "Not everyone. You'd be surprised at the number of mice out there. No one raises their head above the crowd, no one raises his hand. Except for a few, like you."

He continued. "No one gets an audience with the Tower leadership unless we bring them in. We needed someone for our annual feast, someone that we could treat nicely so that you could go back and tell your fellows that, yes indeedy, charity exists among the leaders; we have your best interests at heart. Bread for the masses; it was a public relations gimmick. The people are growing discontented so we toss them a crumb. You were that crumb, our very first attempt at this. You were convenient so we brought you in. Gave you a bed, a bath, breakfast, a tribute. Real luxury, right?"

Kaehl's mouth hung open.

"And then we were supposed to sweep you away. That's how we did it in the tests that we ran; there were no problems. Afterward we could tell the masses about it and they would be quiet for another year. But you came back. Somehow you got in again and threw it all back in our faces. No one gets as far as you did, no one gets into our own homes, right through the middle of our guards. How did you get in, anyway? I was told you were taken care of. What happened?"

"My sister," Kaehl said, his brows tight.

"Ah, yes, your sister," Jolley grunted. "You were separated. Motivation. We didn't know who she was or what your connection was. Our bad luck. We'll have to think about that more clearly next time." He spat on the floor. "It was Welswept's idea."

"You boys don't get along too well, do you?"

He spat again. "Welswept is an incompetent sack of cement. He claims power, claims authority. But behind him and before him and beside him stands me. I decide, I lead. Welswept claims power from the people, but he never enforces it, never uses that power. I ensure that our laws are followed. I give them what they want whether they want it or not. I don't claim power from the people, I take it. I lead, I enforce. I stand alone, the others—fall."

"You're crazy."

"No. I get things done. You'd be surprised how effective I can be."

A cold breeze passed over them again sending Jolley into a fit of shivering. Kaehl looked away from Jolley and lay back, enjoying the respite from the oppressive heat.

"Someone must've left a window open someplace," Kaehl mused.

Jolley looked at Kaehl askance for a moment, his jaw slack. Then he gave in to a fit of coughing, laughing hysterics. Kaehl, at first amused, then annoyed, stood up.

"What's so funny?" he asked.

Jolley quickly stifled his laughter. Tears squeezed out of his eyes. "Windows," he replied. "Windows. Someone must've left a window open." He held his sides trying to contain the laughter.

Kaehl stabbed him with a foot. Jolley dried up like a sponge.

"You're serious, aren't you?" Jolley asked, wiping a tear. "You really think someone may have left a window open."

"What's wrong with that?" Kaehl returned hotly. "I've never seen a window that opened to the outside but I've heard of them. If it wasn't for the poisonous mists outside, people could leave them open and let the breeze through all day."

"Ah, boy, you are a Lower, that's for sure. I haven't laughed that much in a long time. Do you know where we are?"

"Of course. A few levels below the top of the Tower."

Jolley blinked and shook his head. "I can't believe it. We'll really have to bring you Lowers to our penthouse more often. You actually believe it." He pointed to the ceiling. "Mr. Charity, how tall is this building?"

"Over a thousand floors I hear. Maybe more."

"Not counting the test wells we've dug and all the expansions—883 stories. You've lived here all your life?"

"Yes."

"You've never seen the outside of this building or an outside window, have you?"

Kaehl sat down again. "No. I've never been to an apartment on the outer ring. I've been all over several floors but I never broke into the outer ring. Too well protected, too strong. Some people have, though. I've heard about them."

"The fables they tell you Lowers! I'll bet you believe in the Framers, don't you?"

Kaehl stared at him, uncomprehending. "You use their name…"

Jolley howled with laughter. "I swear at them all the time, that's for sure; but they're not gods. Boy, the reason you've never seen the outside or an outside window or anything like it is because there aren't any! As far as you can go up or down, there is no 'Outside'; it's all rock, just like the rock your apartment is made of, like the rock in your hallways. You can go up forever and never see anything but rock. You're underground, boy, do you get it? Underground! This isn't a tower, it's a mine."

Kaehl blinked, his mouth open.

"There's nothing below us," Jolley continued, "nothing livable I mean. Those test wells I mentioned? They extend far below us, down there." He pointed to his feet. "The farther from the surface, the hotter it gets. You think it's hot here? Try going into those little tunnels. I have. Things get really hot. And it's all rock, very hot rock. No one could survive down there. In fact, the only fresh air we get comes from the central shaft and what we can pump in from above. So there's nothing below us, no sky, no air, no place to go. Except for the emptiness beyond the opening at the very top of the tower—up there—" he jabbed a finger toward the ceiling, "there is nothing but solid rock, all around us, forever."

"Nonsense."

"It's true!"

"Nonsense. Rock forever. What kind of world is that, where there is only rock above us and below us is nothing? Mother said that our building stands on a solid foundation—the Earth—and extends miles into the sky."

"You're mixing your terms, boy, up and down, just like we taught you to. We're underground. What you've heard are legends and myths, twisted stories that we made up and taught you, over and over. And a little bit of imagination. I must say, they came up with a pretty good system for this to keep going so long."

"Impossible."

"This is so delicious," Jolley exulted. "To see someone who bought it all. I'd heard that our marketing people were good, but I never got to actually see the results. And now to see you, the results of hundreds of years of effort..." He leaned back. "It's too good to be true." His voice grew dreamy. "Tasty. I was right; Welswept was a fool. You would have been great back there in the Penthouse, all tied up and gagged."

Kaehl looked flustered. Jolley looked at Kaehl through half-lowered eyelids and smiled. "It's false, you know."

Kaehl, uncomprehending, raised his eyebrows. "What is?"

"The whole thing. Every bit. There were no wars, there were no Framers, just a bunch of architects and engineers. There was a threat of war—but then, when was there not? This 'tower', as you call it? It was built not to save us from war but to preserve the Founder's obsessions. The Founder and his followers were rather eccentric, you know, rather extreme. They thought the end of the world was coming, preached about it, built this pit and dived in."

Kaehl blinked, not understanding. Jolley stared at him, his eyes wide. Then his lips curled, his head tilted back and waves of laughter crashed out.

He gurgled, coughed, and sat forward, wiping his eyes. "Oh, you have no idea, do you? I'm going to have to give our teachers a raise. No, we couldn't afford that. Maybe a pat on the back." He chuckled and leaned toward Kaehl, stabbing a finger at him.

"There is no tower. Never was. This isn't a tower; it's a pit, a mine, a hole in the earth, a well. The Founder hollowed out a depleted mine shaft, built some apartments into it, sealed the top, and called it his Tower. Then he spent a lot of time and effort convincing his followers they were being saved. And his followers bought into it." He pointed at Kaehl's chest. "Every. Single. Word."

Kaehl shook his head. Jolley straightened and laughed again. "Oh, you'll have to visit more often. This is too delicious. I never knew we were that effective. I need to get out more. Would you like to know something else?"

Kaehl shifted uncomfortably. "What are you talking about?"

Jolley grunted. "Listen. I'll use small words so you can understand. This religious fanatic, the Founder, the guy who headed those people you call the Framers, he gathered followers. There were wars, pollution and hate so that made getting converts easier. But he embellished the truth a lot. He preached about the end of days and the evils of the world and convinced them to join him in this cave."

"Oh, he fixed it up, of course. A lot. He was no idiot. Rather a genius, actually. And rich...! He had lots of money, although his followers didn't after he was done with them. He spent years planning, digging, building and refining, making this mine into an organizational and technological marvel. Self-sustaining, powered by the Sun, room for hundreds, plenty of water, self-regulating—he'd thought of it all. And then, when the time was right, he pulled his people inside, capped the top, and abandoned the world."

"The end never came for those Outside, of course. Not like he predicted. No poisons, no evil beasts. But he didn't tell his followers that. He harangued them and preached his religion and kept them busy talking about how bad it was outside, all the time continuing to organize, finish, and keep building. He limited births, mandated deaths, developed technologies to feed the expanding population, controlled information. And he used fanaticism as his glue. And it worked quite well."

"But he was nuts. Not at first, of course, but when he died years later he died stark, raving, foaming-at-the-mouth crazy. His followers never knew but in his last years he couldn't even control his own bowels much less the Tower."

"His son, however, was another matter. Cool, quiet, and deadly smart, he took over for his father and made everything happen. As his father faded, his son rose. By the time they locked dad away in the crazy room the son was in complete command."

"The son knew the followers would get restive, that they would want to go back outside. He knew the fanatic grip his father had on their hearts would slip once the old man died. So quietly, years before the Founder passed away, the son began to change the rules. He began to educate the people, to tell stories. He made up legends and myths, trained educators, and set up ministers to teach them. And he would trot out his father and get him to nod and wave at the right times so people believed him."

Kaehl shook his head.

"Guess what, young man. This tower is a pit, like I told you. But that's not the best part. Well-Tower, get it? The name doesn't mean 'the good tower' or anything like it; it means a tower that is actually a well. It's a contradiction, a hint of the truth behind the lies, and it's also a clue to the son's massive arrogance. That name was a risky choice for someone who was trying to brainwash his people but it worked and ended up as a monument to his own ego. Delicious!"

"Throughout the building they ran cables filled with power from the solar concentrators on the outside but after a while there began to be problems. Things started to go bad. People would try to fix things in massive expansion efforts called "Installations" but their efforts ran short. The power cables were shorting out and they couldn't fix them. They had to conserve energy so they hit on the idea of getting people to prefer the dark. Tough to do, eh? But they did it. They preached that light was bad and dark was good. They gave rewards to people who conserved the most power, who lived in the dark the most—extra food and such, you see? After a while they reversed their definitions so that light became bad and dark become good. And where light still represented goodness they changed the meaning of the word to say that it represented darkness. After that, darkness represented good and light represented evil. You see? Light was dark and dark was light, but where light still represented goodness we called it darkness.

"The son made slogans, put up posters. You've heard them before, right? 'The best light is dark.' 'Dark is good.' 'Do you really need that light?' My favorite was, 'Dark: The new light.' Your mother taught them to you, right? Remember the jingle, 'Need that light? Need that dark! Kill that light before you kill us stark.' Catchy, eh? It worked. Some over-anxious zealot even ran a crusade, smashing globes in the hallways, trying to do away with all light. Fried himself, I think; hit one too many globes."

Kaehl nodded, confused. He had heard these slogans since childhood, had seen them on the walls and heard them preached over the pulpit. He had hummed that tune and many others like it. He had never questioned them. Living in the light—the dark, if what Jolley said was true—was patriotic. It was survival. The more light, the better.

"It was all propaganda," Jolley continued, "all advertising played over and over again in your schools and churches and along the walls and wherever he could place them until they became true, the only truth. Anyone who wouldn't listen to him got ridiculed and reviled and even locked up. And the people, lacking any other information, accepted his ideas completely. Brainwashing at its best. The mindless masses. Do you see?"

Kaehl nodded slowly. "Why?"

Jolley's eyes glittered. "Because truth is power, but truth is in the eye of the beholder. Truth changes. We changed the truth and that gave us power."

Kaehl shook his head.

Jolley frowned at him. "This Welltower—what's it filled with? Why can't you see very well?"

"Because there's too much light, of course."

"No, no, you've got it all wrong. Brilliant! You can't see because there is so very little light. It is almost cave black in here. You can't see, not because there's too much light but because there's not enough. Do you see? We reversed the terms!" He let loose another peal of laughter.

"And guess what?" Jolley continued. "Up is down and down is up. We changed those terms, too. Do you think we wanted people to get out? We wanted them to go deeper, to hide away from the Outside. Easy to do if you make them believe that the Outside is a toxic wasteland. So we strengthened that by telling them that up was down. And they believed it. It took a few generations but it worked. Incredible."

Kaehl wiped his brow. The heat and heaviness in the room was stifling, clouding his thoughts. What was it the juggler had said?

"What's the point of reversing the terms?" Kaehl asked. "Isn't the meaning the same no matter what you call them?"

"Ooo, the boy with the knife has a brain. Excellent question. Words have meaning beyond the words themselves. Up means freedom, independence, growth, escape; it means Outside. It has value. If we reverse the direction so that up actually points down then those who want to go up to escape are actually going down, deeper into the mine. They'll never get out. Eventually they'll despair and give up. Light means hope and understanding and peace. If by seeking light they are actually seeking the dark, we have them trapped."

"People aren't dumb. They'd figure it out."

"Would they? Have they?" Jolley shrugged. "Some have. Most don't. Most are mice and don't care. Those who do are worn down through social pressure, embarrassment, continual picking at their dignity. We bombard them with propaganda constantly; bury them with criticism if they disagree. We reverse the argument and make them think they are out of the norm, portraying ourselves as the victims. They are the ones who are hurting but we are the ones crying for help. Wonderful! Or we hijack the conversation by crying about how they frighten or offend us—my favorite tactic, by the way. We shame them from the pulpit, in the news, in the schools. We legislate against their beliefs and cover our own. We say our rights are being abused then decimate theirs. Even the hint of disagreement must be crushed. You've never been bullied until you've been bullied by us. But we never admit that. 'They're the bullies,' we say, pointing at the doubters, those who held to the old standards. We have to keep the pressure on, constantly. Those who still protest... well, we erect barriers. We get rough. We educate them." His eyes grew wide and darkened. "After all, we have a professional force."

Kaehl leveled the knife at Jolley. "Murderer."

Jolley shrugged. "Sometimes. Or we use fines, or prison. Yes, I know," he said with a sigh. "Cost of doing business. Keeps us alive, doesn't it? Keeps the Tower population at bay. Saves the many by inconveniencing a few. It works, wonderfully."

Kaehl shifted the knife again. "That's not why you did it. It was never about saving anyone. It was about power, about greed. This tower or pit or whatever you call it, it wasn't built to save us or keep us free. It was built to advance your ideas, to give you power, to twist people into doing what you wanted. Even after you had browbeaten the protesters into silence, their silence still galled you. Everyone had to fully and actively support your cause or you attacked them. You wanted total commitment; you wanted them actively on your side. You knew you were wrong, you knew you were corrupt, you knew you were trying to change human nature. But you wanted it your way, you wanted power, you knew how to get it and you did whatever it took to seize it, no matter the right or wrong. Slick, serpent-like, evil. Even if all you could do was shame most people into silence, you counted that as progress. If you kept up the pressure you believed they would eventually cave in. But they never will, you know. Not completely, not always. You can't change all of us forever. There are powers greater than you, people who will never give in. Try all you want but eventually we will win."

Jolley laughed. "Well, well, an idealist. A dreamer. You are a very perceptive young man." His eyes glittered. "People may win over time, perhaps. But we can try, can't we? It's worked so far."

"Never."

Jolley reached into a pocket for a cigar and came up empty. "Do you doubt scientific proof? I know your story is false. Mine is true. Factual evidence is irrefutable. Can you deny the inevitability of scientific fact?"

"I thought you made up the facts."

Jolley grimaced. "We can influence conclusions but facts are facts. I can prove what I said."

Kaehl looked skeptical.

"Pick up that rock."

Warily, Kaehl picked up a small stone.

"Now toss it in the air."

"Why?"

"Just do it."

Kaehl shrugged and tossed the rock a few inches into the air. It landed in his palm.

"Now, which way did it fall?"

"Which way, when I tossed it or when I caught it?"

"Fall, bright boy. Up, down. Which way did it fall?"

"I tossed it up and caught it coming down."

"So this direction is up and this direction is down, right?" he said, pointing first to the floor and then to the ceiling.

"Yes."

"When you walked to the top of the Tower, which way did you climb?"

"Up, of course."

"Did you?"

Kaehl looked puzzled. "Of course! I threw the rock down; it came back up. But—well, that doesn't make sense. I threw it up and it came back down—but wait. That only works for throwing things, I think. I've never thought about it. When you are using the ramps, you walk up or down them. Maybe the direction is wrong. Yeah, it has to be." His face screwed up in confusion.

"Why?"

"I don't know. Because you are walking, I guess. Walking up and down ramps and tossing rocks are two different things."

"Are they? The directions are the same. You walk up ramps, you toss pebbles up. You walk down ramps; the pebbles fall down. The same directions."

"They're the same directions but we call them differently."

"Why?"

"Because we have. We always have."

"Yes you have. But why? Is it right?"

"Well sure, I guess."

"No, it's not right. It is wrong. Everything that goes in this direction," he pointed to the ceiling, "is going up. Everything that goes in this direction," he pointed to the floor, "is going down. That's the facts. Your facts are screwed up. We influenced you. You are living a lie."

Jolley gestured with his fingers, mimicking walking down and up his arm. "You say you're walking up ramps but you're actually walking down ramps. You say you're walking down ramps but you're really walking up them. If it's the same direction as the rock then it should have the same name."

Kaehl's face was a mask of confusion. "I don't understand. It doesn't make sense. You did all of this just so you could have power?"

"We did all of this so we could have control. Control is power. The best control is willful, unquestioning obedience. And we achieved that by influencing conclusions; in effect, changing the facts." He tilted his head back and laughed again.

Kaehl stood up, his brow wrinkled. "Stand up," he commanded. Jolley stopped laughing. "We have rested too much. I will not hold the knife at your throat. You seem smart enough to know it will be at your back every second. We will go and…I'll think about your words."

Jolley swallowed and stood. "Go? Go where?"

"Go!" Kaehl shouted. Jolley lurched forward. Kaehl motioned to Lenny to stand up. Lenny arose, picking up Selda.

So close to death... Kaehl thought, looking at his sister. He squared his shoulders. "Let's go. That way."

The group set off, tracing a path toward the source of the wind. Kaehl's pace was slow, weighed down by Jolley's words.

As the wind grew stronger Jolley slowed. He began to stagger. His breath became strained and hoarse, his lungs heaving. Jolley turned and grabbed Kaehl's arm, pleading.

"Please, no more," he rasped, staggering, his face red and swollen. "Something evil is in the air here. I can't breathe!"

Kaehl looked back at Lenny, who seemed untroubled. He shook the fat man off.

"You live in your prison too much," he said, and pushed the old man forward. "The air here is better than in your Penthouse." They climbed two more ramps, emerging into a wide hallway.

"Look up ahead—the light, the light!" Jolley gurgled after a few more steps. "The darkness—it's too bright! I can't stand the light!" With Kaehl's insistent shove Jolley staggered on. The light did seem to be disappearing but the wind was blowing steadily from the same area. The air was noxious, fetid. It was growing worse but he pushed them to advance. He looked back at Tiny. Even the imperturbable guard seemed slowed by it.

The darkness seemed to thicken and grow intense, overcoming the light. Kaehl found that he could see much more clearly. Jolley, however, stopped, shielding his eyes, whimpering in fear and pain. Kaehl kicked him and then grabbed his arm and pulled him forward.

"Please, no more, no more," Jolley pleaded. "The dark—it hurts my eyes—I can't see!"

Kaehl grabbed his collar. "Darkness, or light?" he shouted in his ear. Jolley moaned.

Kaehl hauled Jolley around another corner. The hallway opened into a huge doorway through which flooded a burning darkness—or light. The air was full of the smells and sounds of decay. The wind blew strong and cold out of the opening. Unidentifiable things crawled through the darkness around them. The air swarmed with flies.

Kaehl turned to Jolley. The old man had fallen to his knees, sobbing and gasping. Kaehl wrenched Jolley's head up and forced him to look. "There. That door. Through there. What is that?"

Jolley stared. "The end, the end, this is the end of our world, the bounds to the outer world. The darkness that burns, the cold that kills. We have to get away from here, get away! The Outside! We'll die here!" Jolley began struggling.

Kaehl shook him. "Stop talking nonsense, man. You're not scaring me."

Jolley pointed upward with one hand, keeping an arm crooked over his eyes. "Up there, where the light is, the real light; that's the Outside. That is the source of light, the Sun. Its rays can burn and blind you." He made a wide, all-encompassing gesture. "This big opening is the Shaft, the central access way of Welltower. You can fall all the way from the top to the bottom, more than two miles. The air in here—it comes straight from the Outside. It's open and moving and alive. People can die from that! We live in the earth where it's dark. It's hot under the earth, hot and dark and still. Out there it's too bright. We have to get away." He jerked Kaehl's hand from his collar. Kaehl grabbed him again.

"No," shouted Kaehl. "Go forward, you idiot. There is no danger outside, remember? Isn't that what you told me? Or were you lying then, too?" Kaehl tried to pull Jolley's hands from his face. "If they're anything like you, your guards will never follow us into the Shaft. We're going in. Come on!" Kaehl wrenched and pulled at the struggling man, dragging him toward the opening.

Suddenly Kaehl looked up. Lenny stood in front of him, towering, his eyes flaming. He had raised one arm high above his head, his fist huge. Sister lay in his other arm, her head lolling.

Kaehl released Jolley and swung his blade. The handle of the weapon crashed into the big man's knee. Lenny gasped and went down, dropping the girl. Kaehl swung again and hit his head. Lenny crumpled.

Kaehl looked back. Jolley had gotten to his feet and was mewling down the hallway, stumbling blindly, out of reach. He reached a doorway and leaned against it, screaming and gesturing wildly toward Kaehl. Guards flooded in from the corridors and leaped forward. Kaehl whirled, picked up his sister, and sprinted for the opening. Curses filled the hall.

Kaehl cleared the door. The darkness was thick, the wind intense. He ran through a scattering of insects and mud and trash and tripped and fell headlong into a pile of wet garbage. Scrambling, heaving, he picked himself up and leaped higher onto the pile. The guards were yelling, clamoring, running, closing, picking their way through the trash toward him. Something thudded into the pile beside him. Other things flew overhead.

Scrabbling and clawing, throwing his sister over his shoulder, the boy reached a level point in the pile. He got to his feet and scrambled forward, trying to keep his balance. He slipped on something, landed on his back, and together they slid down a hill.

The curses behind him faded. Nearly blinded by the dark and the trash-filled wind, gagging in the fetid air, the boy picked himself up and surged ahead, carrying his sister.

At length he collapsed, gasping, sweating, his sides heaving. Sister lay beside him, face down. She tried to vomit. He pulled her face out of the garbage, brushed the trash from her hair and held her, rocking.

At last his breathing stilled. He lowered his sister into the trash and crawled to the top of the hill, his ear cocked. Nothing. No signs of pursuit, no lurkers. He couldn't see much but at least the darkness wasn't lethal. He prayed that it would keep the guards at bay. Breathing heavily, Kaehl crawled back into the pile and lay beside his sister.

The breeze raised bumps along his flesh. After the heat of the Penthouse they were both thoroughly chilled. Kaehl rolled over and sat up. He brushed a few pieces of garbage aside. Selda was shivering uncontrollably. He put his hand to her forehead: feverishly hot. Casting about for something to cover her with, his hand brushed against the bundle in his shirt. Quickly, he pulled his old clothes out, unwrapped them, and pulled them over his sister's hospital wrap. He pulled pieces of packing and garbage over them and sat with her in the dark, their arms about each other, rocking slowly, in the cold, alone.

Miserably, Kaehl reviewed his situation. Little food, no place to go. His family had rejected him and now they were gone, probably dead. The Pack was a brawling bunch of young criminals; he had a death sentence among them. He had no hope of seeing Doctor Herstand and no hope of survival in the Penthouse. Wherever he went, he was a wanted man. Rejection had hit him between the eyes. His journey to the Top for answers and help was the worst disaster of them all.

And his sister...gentle, mindless Sister. Trying to save her life had probably doomed her. Maybe the Pack would have let her live. He snorted. Maybe. After they had tortured her and left her to die. Still, that kind of death might have been kinder.

Now his sister lay next to him, shivering, burning with fever, starving, dying. And there was no other place to go. No doctors, no family, no friends, no anything. Alone in the dark, in the cold, in the center of a garbage pile, surrounded by bloodthirsty enemies, running for his life, trapped.

There was no place left to go.

Kaehl's eyes began to glaze. His head sagged. That nonsense spouted by that toad Jolley. If his words were true, they would turn his world inside out, everything he had been taught. But endless rock over his head and emptiness at his feet? Or was it the other way around? The man was insane.

Dully, idly, Kaehl picked up a broken pebble and tossed it in the air. Emptiness below, where you could fall forever. Who would build a tower on that?

Sister coughed weakly. Kaehl turned and bent over her. She was so weak... Her eyes had sunk into their sockets, leaving a shadow deepening around them. The cheekbones stood out like planks; her lips hadn't the flesh to cover her teeth. He brushed a stringy lock of hair from her forehead.

The deep-set eyes fluttered and then opened. She blinked a few times and tried to focus. Looking at him, she lifted the corners of her mouth in an attempt to smile.

Tears came to Kaehl's eyes. "Here, silly girl," he said, taking her hand. "No—Angel." He opened her skeletal fingers and placed the stone in the center. He gently bounced the hand, flipping the stone in rhythm.

One a finger, two a finger, three a finger, four
Jump a stone 'till there ain't no more
If you raise it high then it drops so low
One a finger two 'till there ain't no more.

Kaehl stopped. The stone fell to the ground. He picked it up. He bobbled it in his hand then let it drop again. He scrabbled through the debris, searching for it again. He found it and tossed it into the air, bouncing it high. Catching it again he threw it over his head. He reached out and caught it.

Kaehl pondered. Each time he tossed the pebble up, it came down. And yet he was not tossing it up, he was tossing it down—or was he? He picked up another stone and tossed it down, toward the earth, but it returned up, toward the Penthouse. Letting it roll and fall out of his hand it fell up, toward the Penthouse, toward the day, toward up. Or did it? Impossible. It was the same direction every time; he just had different names for it. He'd lived with this contradiction his whole life and had never recognized it. Up was down and yet down was not necessarily up. It was too much to take.

He remembered sitting on the edge of his apartment, watching the vapor descend the Shaft. And yet objects thrown from the apartment descended, they did not follow the vapor. They went the other way; up? Why? Because up was down? He had never thought about it.

The craziness of it all struck him. Jolley had jabbered about the top of the building being encased in rock and the base of it opening into nothingness where one could fall forever. Was it possible? Was it all a lie? What about what he had he seen so far? What was true?

He looked up, shielding his eyes from the glare. Jolley had cried about the dark devouring the light. Was this false, too? Certainly the dark could overpower the light, but what if the dark was not dark, what if dark was light? A light globe was supposed to dispel the light, but didn't it provide the light, making it easier to see in the dark? And how do you provide light? Was the light really dark? What if it was not just a light globe, but a real lamp?

Kaehl's head whirled with the possibilities. It was so crazy and yet it seemed to fit. Was that what the juggler was trying to tell him at the market so long ago? What about the boy in the food line? Doctor Herstand? What about his mother? Did she know or suspect? Was she keeping the truth from him as well?

And what of scientific fact? Was it fact, or was it just guesses based on observation? Who made the observations and who drew the conclusions? Obviously, people did, people just as fallible as him. And their prejudices and follies made all the conclusions questionable. How much of reality did they really know? All he had been taught—what of it was true, and what was a deliberate lie? What had been made up by people clawing for power?

Kaehl's eyes had adjusted to the glare. Most of the Shaft was illuminated by a soft glow ascending—or descending—from the opening over his head, far, far away. It dawned on him—this was the Shaft. He had looked down—or up—at that same opening as he sat on the ledge outside his apartment. The mouth of the Shaft seemed covered with light punctuated with burning holes but it shimmered and twinkled and seemed alive. Somewhere, on one of the many dark ledges leading into the apartments in the Shaft, he imagined another young boy looking up at the same wonderful sight tossing stones into the dark. One day, if he had any power, Kaehl would meet him.

"Framers..." he pleaded. But he didn't know what to say.

Kaehl rose. Sister was sleeping, her mouth gaping, only the slightest sounds coming out. She needed the rest. They both did.

He scanned the area. The refuge Kaehl and his sister had found was roughly circular and very wide, the floor covered by a huge collection of decaying trash thrown or dropped or spilled from above, apparently accumulated throughout the life of the Tower. Scavengers probably picked through it for anything of value, just like at Doctor Herstand's lake.

Immense fans lined the walls, sucking air into the hallways. He grimaced. Now he knew where the breezes came from. Halls branched off from this core, access ways for maintenance workers and anyone else. Right now the place seemed empty. Maybe the guards had gone. Maybe they stayed away when the light was too intense. He would have to be prepared for them when the darkness thinned and they came hunting.

Kaehl noticed a large metal tank squatting in middle of the trash. Pipes and tubes ran through the garbage, snaking away from it on all sides. Curious, he picked his way toward it.

Finding a ladder on one side of the tank he climbed to the bottom—the top. A heavy grating covered most of one side of it. Something dripped inside. He ducked under the roof and peered into the shadows. Water! This big tank was a water catcher! When rain fell through the Shaft it would drizzle down the roof and sift through the grates, to be used for storage or distribution or whatever. Maybe it supplemented the aquifer system used by most of the Tower. Kaehl shook his head and smiled. That is, if rain fell. Or did it rise?

Looking around, he spied an unbroken jug in the trash. He leaped down and pulled it out. Climbing back up he squeezed into the tank, washed the jug and filled it with water.

He leaped off again and slipped, landing on his back. Shaking his head he retrieved the jug and rolled to his knees. A rat poked its head out of the rubbish beneath the tower, sniffing at him. Kneeling closer, Kaehl saw the huge brute's eyes glint and then blink and disappear. Kaehl scrabbled after it, a hand shooting out. He dug into the trash until his hand broke through into emptiness. Curious, he pulled aside the garbage.

The rat had disappeared into some sort of ragged pit covered by a grate. Water dripped into it, echoing against a pool not far below. A smile spread over his lips, his eyes lighting. A drainage system, large enough to hold a boy. With enough luck he and his sister could squeeze through.

And then he remembered the boy in the factory. He had talked about the Outside and an opening, a way to get there. He said it was somewhere near the Penthouse. Kaehl looked up at the water tank. A tower? He nodded his head.

Kaehl returned to Selda. Gently he raised her to a sitting position and wet her lips with water from the jug. Her jaw convulsed spasmodically and she coughed. The sound was ragged and painful. She gulped greedily. Kaehl poured small amounts into her mouth, tilting her chin and massaging her throat to help her swallow. He continued dribbling small amounts of water down her throat until she pushed his hands away. He fished a crushed lump of bread from his pocket and fed it to her. At least they had gotten something from the Penthouse. She tasted it, coughed, and chewed.

Kaehl arranged the trash around her, trying to make her comfortable.

As he did so he pulled out a flat, palm-sized stone. It had been split in two. The rock looked familiar, like the stones he had written on in his apartment. He dug through the trash to find its mate. After a few moments he found it, the other half having a rag tied over it. His heart quickened. He put the two halves together and examined them. Wiping away the dirt, he read: "FIND ME." It was his rock; the last one he had thrown from his apartment. It had probably broken upon landing.

He pocketed the pieces and searched for more. Scattered somewhere around the bottom of this Shaft was his complete message split among several stones: "Kaehl/Level 321/Community Center/Every Sabbat/Searching for Truth/Find me." He found no more stones.

Kaehl looked over his head, upward, toward the light. Help was not here. Help was at the Top, at the bottom of the Tower, at the real top. Wherever it was, it was up there, toward the light—or darkness. He cursed. Jolley had inverted Kaehl's brain; how could he sort it out?

Whatever Jolley had said, Kaehl had definitely been going the wrong way. The whole Tower was. He lifted his head again and looked toward the light. It was all a lie, everything he had been taught, a determined attempt to keep him scrabbling like a rat toward the bottom, like everyone else, away from the light, staying under the Penthouse's thumb.

Sister groaned. He fed her again and gave her more water. He pulled a bit of meat from his pocket and squeezed the juice into her mouth. He ate a morsel—delicious stuff!—and then chewed a bit more, placing the softened delicacy in her mouth. Soon, before the light disappeared, they would slip into the water system and he would carry her to the Top.

Light

Kaehl was desperate. He had pulled his sister through the drainage system, evaded the guards at the bottom, climbed seemingly endless ramps for seemingly endless days, threaded through hallways, and evaded Packs and howling crowds. He had passed gardens, factories, manufacturing centers, and apartment levels. He had avoided them all, living off what he had stolen from the Penthouse. By his count he had traveled most of the length of the Shaft. The Top—or the base or whatever it was called—was near. He could feel it.

The higher he went, the less developed the hallway structure became. There were fewer people in the halls and those he met seemed more backwards, more fearful, and more violent. He avoided them whenever he could.

Eventually the ramps had ended. He searched for days, climbing up and down the ramps, traveling the corridors, trying other routes up. All led to dead ends—solid rock walls; ancient doors, hopelessly barred and impassible; and collapsed entrances. His frustration grew. Their supply of food diminished and rotted. Selda was peaceful now but deathly pale and thin. Her eyes were unnaturally bright and her breathing shallow. Still, her smile was strong and she didn't complain. He considered going down a few levels and trying other routes.

Another broken door appeared before him. Kaehl sat Selda inside the entrance and searched the apartment. Feeling with his hands he came upon a fissure in the back wall, a crack barely wide enough to admit him. Squeezing through he saw a shaft leading up, lit by ancient light globes. A light breeze lifted his hair.

His heart leaped, his chest compressed. Squeezing back out he ran and knelt next to Selda. "Sister, I think we found it."

He carried and pulled his inert sister into the passage. They traveled several steps into the hole before it opened up, allowing them to stand with ease. He carried Selda a few more steps before stopping, his mouth agape. The passage ended at a jumbled pile of stones. It had been filled by a landslide a long time ago. The way was totally blocked.

Tears of frustration and rage rolled down his cheeks. He smashed his fists against the stone. The air was fresher, the temperature cooler, the light in the Shaft clearer, but it was just as blocked as everywhere else. The Top of the Tower was there, just on the other side. He knew it, he could feel it. His goal was very near. But he couldn't get there.

Exhausted, he sank to the ground, defeated. He could only dimly see his sister. Her eyes were open. She looked up at him. She smiled.

Kaehl stroked her forehead and leaned back. A cool breeze sighed past him. Holy Framers, full of mercy, never changing Spirit. Praise the…

No, that wasn't right. It didn't feel good; that memorized supplication did not apply to what he needed. It wouldn't help him at all. But it was the only one he had learned. *I need something different,* he thought, *something personal.* He needed his own prayer. He needed to talk to God.

He closed his eyes. "Holy Framers," he said, his voice rough, "or whatever you are: Our journey to the Penthouse was not a journey up, it was a journey down. Instead of finding the top we found the bottom. We learned some things and turned our steps once we learned the truth. But now that we are here, closer to our goal than we have ever been before, we are stuck. We can't get through. We're starving, Framers, we are dying. If there is a god and if you are it—or them, or whatever—I'm sorry I don't talk to you folks enough. But please, can't you help us? Has our whole journey been a waste? Are you going to let us die so near to the top? Please, we have nowhere else to go. Have pity on us. Help me save my sister."

Another breeze blew over him. *The air up here smells so good,* he thought. So different, so fresh.

So fresh! A breeze! With a cry he leaped up and began feeling for an opening. He traced the breeze to the edge of a huge boulder. He examined it. The stone had been juried into place with broken timbers and spars. It was as if someone was trying to keep it here.

He clicked his fingers. This wasn't a landslide; it was a barrier. It was intentional. Someone had blocked the entrance. Someone wanted to keep people out—or in.

He would unblock it.

He tore at the barrier, kicking and slashing. The timbers began to groan. He stopped for a moment, his heart pounding. What if everything broke loose and caused a real rock slide? What if he got hurt? What about Sister?

He turned and picked her up. Backing out of the fissure he found an empty room and placed her inside, covering her with a few pieces of furniture. Then he hurried back to the barrier.

He stood to one side and kicked at the main support a few more times. With a roar the timbers broke loose. The cavern filled with noise and dust and fury. And then came silence.

Kaehl had been knocked to the floor. He coughed and pushed rocks off his chest. He got to his knees, sneezed several times, and stood up, swaying. A swirling storm of rock and dust filled the passage, coating him in white. He staggered into the passageway, gagging, brushing at his clothes and hair. Stones broke free and crashed onto the passageway around him. He rubbed his eyes and looked up. Darkness flooded the cavern—no, it was light.

An entire section of the passage had broken away. Boulders had crashed through the cleft, smashing through the wall and plunging into the Shaft. He gazed in awe at the huge opening, looking through the settling dust into the Shaft. He turned and looked into the tunnel. The opening was now filled with blinding light. Stones broke loose as he leaned against the wall.

"Sister!" he breathed, his eyes suddenly wide. He turned back down the tunnel. "Sister!" He began to run, leaping over the wreckage.

He found her where he had left her, protected from the blast and dust, huddled against the wall, her hands over her ears, a thin stream of tears trailing down her cheeks. She cracked open her eyes and gave a tiny wail as he reached for her. He crushed her to him. "It's okay, Sister, it's okay. We're almost there." Tears flowed down his cheeks, not tears of frustration or pain or rage but tears of real anticipation. He lifted her carefully and kissed her fevered forehead. Cradling her like a handful of mist he started back toward the cleft.

There were doors beyond the barrier, heavy and thick, once protected with chains and massive locks. But they had broken long ago and stood open, their hinges rusting. From here the passageway stood open. He picked his way around boulders and fallen beams and trash. The darkness in the passageway lightened as he moved forward. Sister's confused whimpers quieted as she struggled to adjust to the glare. She put an arm over her face and shivered.

Together they rounded a massive boulder and emerged from the passage. Struggling to keep his footing, he kicked at an old beam and straightened up.

They stood, alone and exposed, not surrounded by rock but on an open plain. They had broken free of the Tower.

The light was dazzling. They stood with their mouths gaping, their eyelids closed, trying to adjust to the glare.

Eventually he could open his eyes into slits. Blocking the glare with his hand as best he could, Kaehl stared open-mouthed at the endless expanse of color and light that spread before him. As far as he could see there was openness, emptiness and unbroken expanse. Tears filled his eyes. He put Selda down and wiped his cheeks.

Not far from where he had emerged Kaehl could see a small building not much larger that the common room in his apartment. Behind it lay enormous fields of reflective blue expanse surrounded by a fence. Stupendous green plants and man-made structures dotted the landscape, towering over top of each other into the distance, ending with gargantuan upwellings of rock in an unfathomable faraway, topped with white.

Above them was space. He didn't know what to call it—emptiness, openness, expanse, a vast abyss of endlessness that extended over his head without end, beyond understanding. Hundreds, thousands, millions of Shafts from the Tower could have fit under that openness and still never have touched its nearest point. He dropped to his knees. He felt humbled, mote-like, alone, insignificant. He felt vulnerable. But he also felt something building inside of him, something that filled him to bursting, pushing behind his teeth and eyes and threatening to explode, an overwhelming, wild, volcanic flood of heart-hammering emotion.

Joy! They had found it! They had made it to the Top! It was all true—they had made it to the Top!

Tears flooded from him. He rocked back and forth, over and over, his head in his hands, sobbing. They had made it.

The air was alive with sound and motion and fragrances that made him dizzy. A breeze fluttered over them, chilling him after the lifelong closeness of the Tower. But it was very pleasant. It made his skin and his lungs tingle. The breeze felt natural, not pumped-in and filtered. It invigorated him, filling him with freshness and energy.

Kaehl tingled all over, goose bumps rising from his skin, energy rushing through his pores, around his spine, into his belly and out again. He didn't know whether to dance or clap or sing or fall into a trance. He simply knelt there, awestruck.

The ground was covered in a carpet so deep you could sink your hands into it. Its long green fibers were far softer than any rug or blanket he had seen before, except perhaps in the Penthouse. Some came apart in his fingers as he ran his hands over them. Startled, he tried to put them back.

Kaehl looked at his sister. A wafting, winged chaos of color had fluttered to her shoulder and landed, stretching its wings. Selda raised a frail hand to touch it. The creature lifted its wings and twitched but did not fly away. Selda smiled.

Kaehl bowed his head. He thanked the Framers for their mercy in opening the way for them. He thanked Doctor Herstand and his parents and the factory boy and Jolley and everyone who had led them here. He thanked them all and then he opened his eyes and looked up at the sky. And he was grateful again.

He rose and walked to an immense hole in the ground, the edges of which were weed-grown and unkempt. Rocks and plants cluttered its side. A gargantuan metal disk lay to one side, battered and ancient, anchored with some massive, rusting machinery. He walked to the edge and peered over.

The opening was black and filled with thick vapors. *So this is the Shaft,* he thought, the opening to the tower he had just come from—Welltower. It really was a mine. He could not see into its depths. It stank. Kaehl smiled thinly—it smelled like home.

Movement caught his eye. He turned and saw a figure, a female dressed in white hurrying toward him from the small building. The edges of her clothes lifted slightly in the breeze. He shielded his eyes and focused. The brightness was dazzling. She appeared to be made of light.

A smile tugged at his lips. He glanced at his sister and turned back toward the well—the Tower. Digging with his toe in the dirt he unearthed a small stone. Bending down, he palmed it and stood up, tossing it absently into the air. He heard a sound behind him and turned. Selda was humming the finger song, her eyes focused on the stone. The butterfly stood on her fingers.

Tears filled his eyes and he finished with her: "...Till there ain't no more." He turned and peered into the Shaft one more time. With a shout of triumph he threw the stone over the edge and watched it disappear into the darkness. He didn't hear it land.

Appendix: Light in Tower Literature and the Arts

There is no space where there is no light.

—Saleen Vreckhusen, philosopher, 3rd Installation

Above, below
inside, out,
Light is what
life's all about.

—Government slogan

Dark is the new light.

—Government slogan

Light is great
light is good,
Please dear Framers
bless this light.
Amen.

—Child's prayer

"If you take away my light, where will I be?"

—Reminiscences of the Arken 7:23

"Please—the light—don't leave me!"

—Ratmer, Ellis Dreams, scene 4 line 37

Everywhere the light went,
the light went,
the light went—
Everywhere the light went
we were sure to go.

—Childrens' rhyme

"More, please."

—Alif Skaderhaand, when first shown the Outer Reaches

Bright Light
Little Sun
Come and make
my workday done.

—Workers' Chant

Light is here and light is there,
Living light is everywhere
Sacred light above the stars,
Give us light to heal our scars.
—Children's primer, Tower year 93

Gillies: *"So you see, this is the deeper value of light, not what it is but what it carries with it: meaning and power."*

Radner: *"I see no light. Light cannot be seen. There are only gradations of darkness."*

Gillies: *"That is where your theories fail."*

Moderator: *"Gentlemen, please."*

—33rd annual Oxram Debate, Day 2 Session 6

I have seen the light and it is beautiful.
It warms my insides;
my pores sip its gentle fire.
—Brana Ta, Tower year 283

"The real question, of course, is the meaning behind the words. It took several generations for Welltower's leaders to change the meaning of those essential concepts, so whenever you read something that came from the Tower you have to determine what they meant when they wrote it. Words like 'up', 'down', 'light', and 'dark'—when did they say them? What was their frame of reference? What did they mean? Even their own governmental communications are inconsistent. It is all inversion and inversion of inversions, intentional or not. It is a mess."

—Alizon Historical Society, *"The Problem with Welltower Historicity"*, page 42.

Award-winning illustrator and author of *Remember the Child*, Lester Yocum lives in Maryland with his very patient and supportive wife. Besides his day job and his responsibilities within his family, religion, and community, Lester enjoys creating works that uplift and inspire.

For more information see his website at lesteryocum.com

Made in the USA
Middletown, DE
21 May 2022

66029744R10136